LOST GEMS

RHYS CUTTS

This is a work of fiction. Names, characters, places, and incidents either are the product of the author's imagination or are used fictitiously. Any resemblance to actual persons, living or dead, events, or locales is entirely coincidental.

Copyright © 2024 by Rhys Cutts

All rights reserved. No part of this book may be reproduced or used in any manner without written permission of the copyright owner except for the use of quotations in a book review. For more information, address: Rhysamondo@gmail.com.

First published by Rogue Sonobe April 2024

Book design by Rhys Cutts

ISBN 978-1-7635317-4-1

Chapter 1

Tomorrow was the day that my future would be decided. I would either fail miserably and be sent back down to Earth to join the peace-keeping corps, or I would succeed and get to fly through space defending our solar system from……well……from whatever might come our way. It didn't really matter what we were supposedly protecting ourselves from, the existence of the 'Hypernova Inter-terrestrial Navy of Earth' or 'HITNE,' was more of an excuse for the superpowers of Earth to have the largest military presence in the solar system. Colloquially it was often referred to as 'Hit-Me' on account of its eagerness to fight some aliens, but moral obligation not to attack anyone unprovoked. The problem, however, was that no human had found any aliens yet. We had explored our whole backyard from Mercury to Pluto and no living aliens were to be found. We knew they were out there though as we had found remnants of different species scattered across the solar system, from footprints on Mars, to a frozen limb of sorts on Enceladus, one of Saturn's moons. It was because of this that Saturn had become the hub for scientific research into extraterrestrial biology and technology. Research stations orbited many of its moons, and larger starships circled the planet itself, including ours, as this was to be the location of our final test tomorrow to join HITNE. It would be a grand battle between hundreds of new recruits in what was essentially a dogfight, although they refused to call it that, weaving in and around Saturn's rings, dodging micro-meteoroids and electromagnetic (EM) blasts alike.

"You'll do fine tomorrow Ender, it's just nerves. Before you know it you'll be piloting one of those big fancy ships from one end of the universe to the other," My sister, Hailey, spouted confidently over video-chat in a way that made me unsure whether she was using hyperbole, or was oblivious to our current inability to leave the solar system and reach even the closest galaxy. At least not before everyone onboard died of old age.

"Yeah, well, I'm not so sure. It's not like I'm top of the class or anything like that."

"Oh that can't be true. You're probably in the top ten and don't even know it!"

I wasn't. I was ranked two-hundred and fifty-third out of five hundred recruits.

"Yeah, maybe." I replied, ignoring Hailey's attempt to try and cheer me up. I had always been extraordinarily average. I had thought that coming up here might be my calling, that this could be the thing I finally excelled at. At least that's what I told my parents and sometimes myself. In reality, my oppressive mediocrity was never good enough for my parents and this was simply the easiest way to get the furthest from them.

I exchanged farewells and good-lucks with Hailey and hung up the call, got up from the little desk in the cramped privacy booth, and left the lower-decks communication hub. If I made officer one day, I would get my own quarters with a desk and communications access to Earth. Then again, I only had my sister to call. No one else on Earth really wanted to talk to me, or me to them.

On the night before the exam, I tried to get some sleep amongst the rows of bunks housing the new recruits—those who would be my comrades or targets in the sky tomorrow, but there was too much weighing on me for sleep. In the morning I would fight for my future and either have to go back to Earth and face my family, or I would stay out here floating through the void between planets for the foreseeable future. I wasn't sure which I dreaded more.

That night, I had strange dreams, but as I tried to recall them the next morning, they slipped away as dreams often do, leaving me with a fleeting sense of loneliness. As the day's reality and its impending events creeped on me, the stress took over, and my dreams were forgotten altogether. I heard the voice of my commanding officer somewhere in the room and immediately sat upright and mechanically swung my legs out of the bunk and began to pull on the light-grey jumpsuit with a single patch on the shoulder, of the HITNE logo, that was the required uniform for all recruits aboard the U.E.S Cronus. Cronus was the largest ship in HITNE and one of only a few ships ever built with an extra engine room designed based on current theoretical working knowledge of warp-drive technology. Of course, no one had any kind of Faster-Than-Light travel yet, but we were due to figure it out soon, and we were ready, especially those few ships just waiting for a breakthrough.

I laced up my boots, hearing my commanding officer shout again, much closer now. I finished lacing my boots and quickly lined up at the foot of the bed. Colonel Amir Summanus wasn't a particularly aggressive man, but one could see the fierceness and intelligence behind his eyes. He was slightly taller than I and had a thick, dark-brown moustache, which was an unusual style in modern times on Earth or in space.

Colonel Summanus strode down the gangway between the recruits with his arms behind his back, impeccable posture, and a cruel smirk on his face, knowing what was in store for us all today.

"Listen up recruits. You all know what happens today." He paused, scanning the faces around the room. He appeared to draw satisfaction from our nerves. What a dick.

"After breakfast you will all report to hangar bay three."

He scanned the room again as he strode slowly back towards the entryway. He turned around again to stare us down, all of us looking straight ahead, watching him only in the periphery.

"Dismissed."

And just like that we all broke rank, Colonel Summanus disappeared around the corner and we all made our way to the dining hall, voicing our worries only in whispers. As I turned towards the door, someone behind me nudged me with an elbow. I looked back and saw Erwin, who locked eyes with me as he launched into his usual nervous rambling.

"Oh man today is gonna be brutal. I know the EM blasters on the fighters are supposed to be relatively safe, but there are always a few ships that blow up for one reason or another. They always blame it on meteoroids but I reckon that's way less common than fried circuitry causing an explosion. It's just impossible to predict things like that when there are so many variables, especially when it comes to spacecraft and…"

"Erwin. Your ship is not going to blow up today. I mean your chances are like, what? One in three hundred or thereabouts? That's pretty good odds. Plus, if you just avoid getting shot you won't have to worry about exploding at all."

He scoffed, then mumbled back, "Easier said than done."

We continued in silence, each lost in our own thoughts, as we made our way down the final stretch of the hallway before the dining hall. The smell of breakfast and the thought of food soon overpowered any other thoughts that had been consuming us.

Breakfast was devoured as quickly and quietly as usual. The end of breakfast was strange. It was like no one wanted to be the first to leave, the first to arrive in the hangar that would decide our futures. A few of the cockier recruits stood up, and raised a few eyebrows at the crowd seated in the dining room, like they didn't understand why everyone was so on edge. Before long more from their table followed suit and soon the crowd was moving, filing through the hallways towards hangar bay three. This walk was mostly in silence, but a few recruits were speculating the details of the battle that was about to commence, and the rest of the crowd seemed to listen silently, including myself. As we entered hangar bay three, I saw recruits streaming through entryways on all sides of the hangar, all of us filing into formation in front of Colonel Summanus who stood in front of a line of fighter ships in the centre of the room. The fighter ships took up the entire hangar—two hundred and fifty ships aligned in rows along the floor of the hangar, and columns on the rows of platforms above. The remaining ships must have been in one of the adjacent hangars.

Once everyone was in formation, the statue of Colonel Summanus came to life, his voice thundering through the hangar.

"Recruits! Today your future will be decided. Today some of you will return to Earth, unfit for the brutal conditions of war among the stars, to join the peace-corps. A noble pursuit, but we all know the real dangers lie out there somewhere on the edge of space, and those of you who succeed today will become proper HITNE soldiers, and have the chance to protect the peace in our solar system, and defend it from any and all intruders, within or without." He paused, presumably for dramatic effect. "Today you will all be divided into teams of a hundred pilots. You will all decide internally the structure of your squadrons and your chain of command. You will be graded on this as well as how you fight, fly, co-operate, lead, and improvise. You will have one hour to do this, after which you will be expected to be at the designated rally point for your team, which has been programmed into each of your ships. The goal and targets for this exercise have been programmed into your ships as well, so use this next hour wisely to strategise your approach. Your teams will now be sent to your epicodes. Dismissed."

As he finished saying this, an alert notification appeared on my epicode, starting up the system. Epicode was the name used for the device E.P.I.C.O.D, which stood for Electro-Physical Intra-Cranial Optic Display, and was a cranial implant attached to the optic nerve capable of many things, including showing me my team number, along with a list of the names of those in my team. Once I selected 'Team View' using eye-movement-based commands, my team became much easier to spot in the crowd, as they were shaded slightly bluer. The other teams were also shaded in their respective colours, along with their assigned ships. Additionally, visual directions to your ship were provided in the form of holographic arrows painted on the ground.

I looked back over to my right at Erwin after spotting my ship on the fourth row above the main floor. He was slightly yellow, which made me instinctually think he was about to vomit but then realised that it was just his team colour. After a moment, he broke his stare, presumably at something on his epicode, and looked at me with a disappointed frown.

"I guess we're at odds today," He sighed and walked off, switching into soldier mode as he always did, heading towards hangar four where the yellow team's ships must have been hiding. There were none in this hangar, only blue, green, and half of the red team's ships.

A shout rang out in my direction which took me a moment to register was directed at me.

"Oi, Herman, get your ass over here."

I swivelled to the left to find a large group of recruits huddled together and shaded slightly blue. Great, less than a minute in and I was already a straggler. I hurried over to the rest of the team, as fast as proper conduct would allow. For my benefit, the recruit who had called me over, Conrad, briefly explained the structure and chain of command which had apparently already decided.

"So, for simplicity's sake we have divided up the chain of command based on the current rankings, with myself in command, as I am currently ranked second—"

I already didn't like this guy, but I could see through the epicode how he had achieved second position, and I had to admit that his reflexes and improvisational skills in the heat of battle were impressive.

"—Below myself is Adelaide, who has the power to take control of half of the hundred of us if the need arises, whether that is through strategy, incapacitation, or loss of communication. The squad leaders of each group of ten ships will also report to us and they will each have a second in command with the same ability to take command of half of their squad if the need arises."

He turned to look at Adelaide who gave him a quick nod, which he responded to by turning back and continuing.

"We have just finished dividing you all into squadrons and are sending you all you need to know now. Please get acquainted with your squadron and make your way over to the rally point. I will expect everyone there twenty minutes from now for strategy."

And with that he turned back to Adelaide and went straight into strategy discussions while recruits started to join their growing circle. My squadron was ranked sixth in the team, and I was just a regular pilot. I wasn't expecting to have any power given my ranking but second in command of even the tenth squadron might've been nice. I would have to try and excel at everything else since I wouldn't have the opportunity to showcase my leadership skills—not that I really had any.

That hour went by all too quickly. Our squad had come together and decided on some basic formations before heading to our ships. I said virtually nothing. Once we had reached the rally point, we sat there in silence for nearly five minutes while we waited for the other squads to show up. We spent that time going through the mission objectives that had been programmed into our ships. It looked like for our team to win we had to first find and disable a particular ship within each team's fleet containing the frequency data of that team's turret. Doing so would mean that we would be able to tune our EM blasters to that frequency and take out their turret. We would also have a designated turret onboard Cronus as well as a designated pilot to operate that turret, and one to carry the frequency data. To win we must be the last team remaining with a turret and more than fifty percent of our ships left. This description of winning was intentionally vague, as there could be significantly fewer or more than fifty ships per team when the last turret was destroyed. However, this final test was meant to be qualitative, and we would not necessarily be judged on victory itself, but on our performances in striving to achieve it. The turrets and ship counts were merely useful metrics for determining when the battle should be considered over. No matter what happened I just wanted to be one of those surviving ships, I just needed to survive, to fight. I didn't need to be the hero. I couldn't be the hero, but I could be a soldier, and I could be a survivor. If for no other reason than the battle could be long and floating around in a disabled ship for hours sounded boring as all hell. The last squad arrived and a team-wide call rang out through our epicodes. When I accepted the call, Conrad's face popped up in the centre of my vision, startling me'slightly. Next to his face was a smaller one—Adelaide's. As I noticed her, I also saw a flood of faces filling up the sides of my vision as the rest of the team joined the call. They began discussing strategy and tactics and choosing who would hold the turret frequency data and such. I just sat and listened, as did most of the fleet, who sat in silence, our tiny faces almost invisible at the edge of the epicode call, just ghosts in the periphery, while the squad leaders and a select few tacticians cemented their faces in the centre, taking turns being the focus of a hundred sets of eyes. I realised when the call switched to audio only of our squad, that I had zoned out for the last bit of the call. I had listened to all the strategy discussions but the bit I missed seemed to be the bit where I found out exactly what my squad was supposed to do. What *I* was supposed to do. Luckily our squad leader was a think-out-loud kind of person and started to ramble on about our goal and potential attack scenarios.

Apparently, our squad was tasked with finding the ship carrying the frequency data for the yellow team's turret. When found, we would contact squadron two to help us obtain the data, or squadron three if two was already engaged. After learning that for the second time, I relaxed a little too much and my mind drifted to Erwin, knowing that he was on the yellow team and I might end up having to attack him directly. He was already worried about a malfunction, or an EM blast causing his ship to explode. I would hate it if I was the one to cause such an explosion. Then again, the blasters were safe, much safer than real weapons, and the chances of anyone dying out here, at least only from ship fire, was highly unlikely. A timer silently popped up in the corner of my vision. It was counting down from five minutes.

The final test, the entrance exam into the ranks of Earth's greatest Inter-terrestrial Navy, was about to begin, and I was too busy worrying about the unlikely event of me killing my best friend by accident. I shook my head and stared out the cockpit window at the big yellow ball ahead, trying to focus on the events about to unfold. I closed my eyes and pictured the fight, ships whizzing by me, some giving chase, others drifting sideways through the dark. The clock kept ticking; a minute left to go. I opened my eyes and looked around at the ships I could see above me. Our squadrons were grouped close, each squad pointing their ships at a different angle, towards their respective targets. Our squad was pointed towards what we predicted the trajectory of one of the yellow team's squadrons would be. It was the squad that was pointed more or less directly at us and could be scanned the fastest for the frequency data. The clock continued to tick. My nerves fluctuated between fearful and relaxed, unsure how to feel, unsure how to prepare. The timer reached three seconds and I was ready to plunge the throttle forward, launching myself right into the storm, into a cluster of hostile ships, one of which could be my best friend trying to shoot me down just as much as I was him. Two. The switches were all primed and I was locked onto one of the fighter ships with both my ship sensors and my epicode, ready to be scanned once I was close enough. One. My wrist was almost spasming under the tension I was inadvertently putting it under. Zero. My hand shot forward, my vision narrowed, and my whole body crushed itself into the seat. Once my vision started to widen again and I could suck down a deep breath, there was no time for relief, just triggers ready to be pulled. Both our squadron and the yellow squadron started firing simultaneously, both of us flying straight on towards each other, knowing that we were locked into this game of chicken. We had no choice but to keep straight and fly through the gaps between the enemy ships. Any attempt to veer away would most definitely end in a head-on collision and a resulting explosion that could destroy the entirety of both squadrons in an instant. Why was this our plan? This was a terrible idea.

Both sides shot at each other until we were too close and any blast that made contact would turn a ship into an obstacle that none of us would be able to dodge. We silently zipped by each other, each of us scanning one another. Two seconds after passing the yellow squad I heard the second in command of our squadron yell, "We got him!" and flagged the ship so that our whole fleet knew who had the frequency data. We all looped back around to chase them, in a formation we had practised a bajillion times, and gave chase to the yellow team, who had also looped back around, almost mirroring us in our wider formation, with the key difference being the one ship that continued to speed further away, knowing it had been flagged. Now this was the hard part. We knew if we broke through their formation we'd be shot from behind and immediately disabled, so we broke formation, swirling through the air, blasting everything we had at the defensive ships. In return they shot back at us, desperately trying to simultaneously block us from their escaping ship as well as keep themselves alive.

Two of each of our squad ships took each other out, giving neither of us an advantage, except for the one escaping ship. As we drew closer and each one of our manoeuvres became more acrobatic and harder to track, I noticed a window. A chance. My chance to shine, to do more than be a soldier, to be the soldier that succeeded, that made a difference. I took it without looking back. I noticed that after we had taken out two of their ships as they had two of ours, we had all locked onto an opponent. Each ship was paired off, engaging in one-on-one combat, but I found myself without a partner to dance with. I was the odd one out, the one whose partner would have been the ship speeding away if they had stayed, so I shot through the window as the rest of the squad circled back once more. I veered off course, unexpectedly breaking formation, and sped towards the escaping ship. My squad was too busy to notice as they were locked into their deadly dances, not seeing me disappear into the dark just as quickly as the yellow ship. I was starting to gain on the yellow ship now, which could only mean that they were slowing down. I was directly behind them, getting closer, almost within blasting range. I pre-emptively re-calibrated the blasters to shoot further above me, predicting that the ship would loop back around on the vertical, but I was wrong. Just as I came within range, they banked left at forty-five degrees before looping hard, the g-forces of which would surely have made them lose their sight for a moment, but that didn't matter in these ships, not when we had epicodes which could see even when you couldn't. My blaster fire missed and before I could re-adjust, they had completed their loop and were flying above me just slightly off to my right and so close that I could see them through the cockpit. They were so close to my ship by the time they straightened up and could fire their blasters at me that I froze, shocked at their manoeuvre, but even more shocked that I was now locking eyes with Erwin through the cockpit window as he shot me with an EM blast at so close a range that all my systems lit up as I was hit. Most of them were completely dead the next instant, the same instant that Erwin was gone from my field of vision, presumably speeding away back towards the fight. I couldn't confirm it though as I couldn't use any of the cameras or sensors anymore. I only had the cockpit window left, and an uncomfortable heat seeping through my seat. Before I could turn around to investigate the source of the heat, my head was slammed back into the headrest and the wind knocked out of me. I don't know how long I was unconscious, but it couldn't have been too long as I could still feel the extra heat leaving my seat and my epicode had come back online for long enough for Colonel Summanus to find me and start yelling in my ear, "Recruit! I am aware your ship has been disabled, but you are headed for restricted space. Get your ass out of there by any means necessary. Recruit! Respond!"

My head was still spinning but I was conscious enough to respond to the Colonel. I quickly discovered, however, that along with my neck, my epicode's microphone had also cracked in the explosion and the Colonel wasn't hearing anything I tried to say.

"Recruit! R…ond! You a…..fo….restricted s…."

I was now too far from the Cronus to be able to communicate via epicode. My distress signal was active but I otherwise could do nothing but sit here and wait. I couldn't use any of the sensors so all I could do was sit here and look up at Saturn through the cockpit. Judging by the speed the rocks of Saturn's rings whizzed by me, I'd say I was going pretty damn fast, and right through restricted space apparently. I wasn't too worried about that though. Everyone in space always seemed to claim a massive volume around their ships or structures for no reason. I would probably pass in and out of the restricted area without ever seeing anything or being seen by anyone, especially with my ship in this state.

I watched the rings of Saturn outside the window, and I realised I had forgotten all about the consequences of what had just happened, on what would probably mean my re-assignment back to Earth. I had tried to be a hero and failed. Instead, I ended up as a piece of space junk floating off into the ether. There was nothing left to worry about now. My fate was sealed. I continued to stare at Saturn, starting to look past its edges for one of its many moons. I thought I saw one, somewhere in the vicinity of where I was heading. As it got closer though I saw its shape and it was not a moon at all but a space station, probably a classified military space station given the restricted space warning from the colonel. I couldn't tell from this angle if I was going to hit the station or not, but it would be at least close enough for me to get a good look. What was strange though was that they hadn't tried to contact me. I was in a HITNE fighter ship and even though it was disabled, I was close enough now that I could be seen with the naked eye and yet no one had tried to contact me, or made any attempt to shoot me down for some reason. I peered closer, trying to make out details, looking for clues as to why one no-one seemed to notice me. As I drifted closer, I noticed a smaller ship disengage and start flying away, then another, then another. They were all personal ships, some large and some smaller. The larger ones would've been big enough to live on and wouldn't need to be disconnected from the space station at all. I activated the digital zoom on my epicode and ran my enhanced gaze over the station until I found a logo painted on one of the exterior walls. The station was part of the scientific research division of HITNE. Then it hit me. This had to be a warp-drive research facility. Everyone knew that's what today's modern space race was all about and there wouldn't be any other kind of research that would warrant such a large facility. But why were so many people trying to leave? Did something go wrong?

Oh no. I wasn't sure at first, but I was sure now. Some parts of the space station were changing colour at such a slow pace I had almost missed it. But they were definitely changing. Some were becoming brighter, not changing colour per-se but giving off more light, becoming glossy even. Other parts had paint that wasn't prepared for whatever was happening inside and so it peeled away, turning into a blotchy mixture of cobalt and copper. I watched as the station started to give off even more light, the departing ships doing so more and more frantically, causing some of them to crash into each other, not fatally so, but they didn't even stop, they just kept going. Whatever it was they thought was about to happen, they were expecting a decent blast radius. I was stuck here floating right by it unable to do anything about it.

There were no more ships departing now, but I could see small somethings being jettisoned out the side. Escape pods. Before I had the chance to zoom in on the escape pods, a big gold crack ruptured the station, slashing it from one end to the other, ripping it into halves to reveal a mirror, in which I was close enough to be able to see my tiny little ship, not much bigger than an escape pod, floating though the darkness. The edge of the gold rip fluctuated, like they weren't ripping through the space station, but through the space it occupied. The gold whipped out and around like a solar storm from an angry sun until the mirrored sky warped like a giant cosmic eye refocusing, inverting its edges like the inside-out version of a black hole. The hole grew, the gold tendrils getting longer, threatening to snatch escaping ships out of the sky like a celestial kraken. There was no more space station. There was not even any debris, just a big gaping hole in the universe and I was heading right for it. The initial explosion caused by the destruction of the space station was enough to re-direct me ever so slightly, enough to give me a sliver of hope that I could zip right by this disaster just as fast as I had approached it.

I gripped the straps that were pinning me back in my seat until my knuckles went white. My breathing was shallow and quick and I wanted to squeeze my eyes shut as hard as I could until it was all over but despite it all, I couldn't look away. Despite its destructiveness, the tangle of golden tendrils weaving themselves around a fragmented reflection of the stars was kind of beautiful. If not beautiful then at least mesmerizing, like it was a glimpse into another universe, one inhabited by sentient suns and flaming kraken. I was whizzing by, but I was close enough now that I knew I wasn't going to pass it by, I was heading straight for it, into my own warped reflection. Before I crashed into some version of myself, the tentacles of the sun kraken went taught and started to wrap around itself, making the whole thing look more like a knotted ball shape than the flailing mess it was before. As this happened, it started condensing, the golden arms strangling the mirror universe. It wasn't fast enough. The tendrils whizzed by just nearly missing my ship as they layered back in on themselves, and the edges of the plane of warped reality ahead of me was moving, it was getting closer and smaller simultaneously, the edge moving frighteningly fast. But would it be fast enough to stop me from crashing into my own reflection? Would it even be a crash or just instant vaporization? There was no way to know and nothing to be done, so I let the straps cut into my hands and held my breath as I raced towards the plane which ran out just as the edge reached my ship, causing me to hit the very edge of the mirror, right between the darkness and the sparkling coronal edge where a wave of strange heat washed over me. My hands released their death grip, and I passed out surrounded by a burning light that felt inexplicably upside-down.

Chapter 2

I woke, head throbbing and hands burning. I opened my eyes slowly and found that they took an excruciatingly long time to focus on the sky. The sky, even through the shattered cockpit window, looked strange—like it was the wrong shade of blue—and it seemed to be moving. I sat upright all too fast, immediately regretting it as I clutched my ribs, wincing. I looked down at the rest of me, surprised that there wasn't more blood given the amount of shattered glass scattered around me. My palms were sliced open, spilling the most amount of blood, but it wasn't the glass that had cut through them, but the death grip I had had on the straps. My bleeding hands shook and my breath trembled. I looked back up at the sky, realising that I was breathing the atmosphere of a strange planet that didn't look like any in the solar system. None of them, aside from Earth, certainly weren't breathable.

I watched the sky ripple, near-invisible ribbons hiding in a sky that was just barely the wrong colour. Now that I was sitting up, I could see the clouds, but they weren't clouds at all. They looked more like patches of sky, painted with watercolours, in pastel shades of pink, yellow, green and even one the colour of rust, all stitched together to paint the sky like a patchwork canvas. A canvas that kept rippling.

My gaze drifted towards the horizon, where visible heat distortions rose up from the colourful sand dunes surrounding my crashed ship. These dunes, in all kinds of earthy shades—silvers, reds, browns, and yellows—were mysteriously separated by colour, seemingly unwilling to blend. It was harder to see, but aside from the lines drawn in the desert by the edges of different coloured sands, the shapes of the dunes themselves sat at strange angles, as if not formed by natural winds like on Earth, but by something else entirely. Some dunes even had soft but distinct ninety-degree angles bent into them. Wherever this planet was it was far away from Saturn, or Earth, and wholly alien. Even the air itself seemed to vibrate or… was it the air? Now that I could feel all my limbs properly again, including the numerous bruises and potentially broken ribs, I noticed my jaw chattering, but it wasn't cold. It was quite hot. I could have just been still trembling, but this felt different.

A figure emerged on top of the dune ahead of me wearing pretty much exactly what you'd expect someone emerging from over a sand dune to be wearing, except for the large tan-coloured combat boots with overly thick rubber soles. They were moving in my direction down from the ridge they had emerged over holding a long stick with a disc on the end. A metal detector most likely. They were pointing it directly at me when they looked up and noticed me. I was still in my ship, sitting around and marvelling at the sky. The figure shouldered the metal detector, striding towards me now with

24

long steps as they half-slid down the sand dune. At that moment, my military instincts kicked in. I jumped up and grabbed the seat straps, severing the ends on the jagged edge of the broken windscreen. I leapt out of the cockpit, holding the severed strap ends, let the buckle fall to the end of the strap, and froze. The man also froze, close enough now to examine me and my ship properly, and I him. At least I would have been able to if my eyes hadn't started to water when I jumped up, the straps digging into the cuts on my palms and my ribs, which were most definitely broken, causing me to gasp sharply like a dying fish.

We both stood there, my temporarily blurred vision locked on the man as he looked between me and my ship.

He spoke first, "I can help you." He paused, studying me, "If you let me look around your ship, show me where the motherboard is even, I'll take you to the city."

When I didn't respond he added, "You're in bad shape, the city has healers, and water, and shade." He looked down at my feet. "And you won't turn to sand there."
He eyed me knowing I didn't have a choice. I looked at my feet, then to his clunky rubber-soled boots. I didn't know what was up with this weird desert, but it was pretty clear I would die soon one way or another if I stayed here much longer. I sighed and lowered my makeshift weapon, still clutching it, as blood from my palm started to trickle down the strap. I held my ribs with my other hand.

"Ok." I rasped before swallowing the dryness in my throat, "The motherboard is behind the panel under the console."

He circled the crashed ship slowly, searching it with his eyes, before stepping into the remains of the cockpit and reaching under the console. He broke off the panel with no tools somehow and carefully pulled out the motherboard along with some adjacent components and as much wiring as he could pull free. His grin widened the more wiring he managed to pull out. Once he reached the end of the cable and shoved all the components and wiring into a satchel, he stood up and threw me a small flask. I caught it, still clutching the strap, and looked it over briefly before looking absently back at him.

"It's water. Good water." His eyes flicked down to the strap-weapon in my hand and the blood trickling down it. "Rub some on your hand too. It'll…fix it."

Fix it? Fix what, my hand? I frowned at him before looking back at the flask. I dropped the strap, both of us knowing I didn't have the energy to use it anyway. I poured a fraction of the contents of the flask onto my palm, not because he told me to, but because I wanted to check if it really was water. The clear liquid pooled in my palm, briefly swirling with pricks of red from the blood already on my hand before reverting to its original clarity. It was so clear that it was magnifying the cut in my palm which was getting paler now too, the stripes of red turning pink and the clear liquid draining from my palm. Before long the liquid was gone and my palm had stopped bleeding. It had more than stopped bleeding. It had almost fully healed. I stood there staring at my palm, not believing it. I raised my other hand to compare the difference. One was still bleeding, with a nasty gash containing small grey fibres pulled from the strap that had cut into it. The other cut was a dark pink, like the flesh of wild tuna. It was still cut-shaped and tender, like a fresh tendon with no skin. I poured some more so-called 'water' into my healed palm but it didn't do much except turn the cut a shade of pink lighter, closer to my skin colour. My hand didn't absorb the liquid fully this time, so I stuck the flask between my teeth and slapped my hands together, rubbing the healing water into both of my hands. I coughed, almost dropping the flask, my throat hoarser than before and my lungs grating with every breath. I flung my head back with the flask still between my teeth and downed the rest of the liquid. It was warm, my throat tingling and relaxing as it worked its way down through my insides. I could breathe normally now, my lungs no longer grating against the air. I pressed my hand to my ribs hoping somehow that they had magically healed too, but I withdrew it once I felt the sharp pain indicating that something there was still broken. The man saw this and piped up as he strode over to me.

"If anything's broken it won't be able to heal right away. It'll take a few days and at least another dose."

He was standing in front of me now staring blankly, almost bored looking.

"I…what is this stuff? It certainly isn't water but it's amazing."

I found myself staring at my palms again, one healed cut slightly darker than the other.

"Well of course it's water. It's just got a little bit of magic in it is all." He responded matter-of-factly. "Now are you coming? That cloud of iron there is headed right for us and I'd like to not be here when it arrives."

He pointed to the rust-coloured patch of sky.

"That's a cloud? Then why does it look so… I'm not actually sure."

Despite my scepticism, the rusty patch of sky was noticeably larger than before. He sighed, clearly getting irritated.

"It's not really a cloud but more like a pocket of atmosphere that's full of iron rather than oxygen, meaning we can't breathe it or we'll die. Now can we go?"

He held out his arm in the direction he had come and I begrudgingly started up the dune.

"Oh, here's your flask back."

I turned around and handed him the flask, sliding a little down the dune and pushing sand over his boots. He took the flask and continued walking. I followed. From the top of the dune I could see more of the desert, with its patchwork of colours and strange repeating patterns. The desert itself formed a sprawling maze, turning at odd angles between the sands, with angular tendrils reaching right up to the edge of the city. The city itself was a mass of sand-coloured buildings forming their own ridges and converging at a cluster of towers surrounded by a circular wall.

"So that's the city?"

"Obviously."

We slid down the next dune, through a patch of brown sand which felt less like sand and more like fine dirt.

"So if the sky has elemental patches, is it the same with the colours in the sand?"

"Yes and no. The patches in the sand are also different elements, like dirt, silver and stone. The patches of sky are mostly gaseous elements, with a few exceptions like the rust-cloud, but for the most part they stay separated through magnetic repulsion."

"Oh, okay sure." I pondered this as we made our way up and over the next dune. "But why does it all separate? Why are they all in patches and not one big homogenous sky or desert?"

"I don't know, that's just how it is. Ships and rocks and whatever crash into the planet all the time, some explode in the atmosphere, becoming part of the sky, or they crash into the dunes and become a puddle of sand in a few days."

"Wait what? My ships going to melt into a puddle of sand!?"

"Sure will. I'll be back in a day or two to scavenge its rare metals if you want to join me. We can carry more back that way too."

"But how? What could possibly turn a chunk of steel and glass into sand that quickly?"

The man stopped at the bottom of the dune and looked at me, puzzled, like I should have figured it out already.

"Can't you feel the vibrations?"

The vibrations. Of course. The vibrations eroded everything here until they were sand, which also explained the strange shapes of the dunes; Chladni patterns. But the city…must have been built on standing waves, where the frequencies vibrating the planet's surface cancelled each other out. Weirdly this planet made a bit of sense now. It was still crazy that I was on another planet, in another solar system, and there was magic here? That part was still a mystery to me, as well as why the planet was vibrating to start with, but at least some things made sense. At least in an alien kind of way.

We were almost to the city now. As we reached the top of the last dune before sliding down to the edge of the sandstone pavers, I felt my jaw start to relax, the vibrations fading. A strange wave of stillness hit me as I stepped into the city, like it was only now that there were no vibrations that I could feel just how shaky it was in the dunes.

"Come on, this way."

I followed the man through the maze of small, sandstone-brick buildings, no more than two stories high in this part of the city. We had only crossed two streets when we emerged on the other side of the sliver of city to find a small river running alongside the edge of the buildings. The other side of the river was endless calico dunes. We continued following the river towards the centre of the city for a little while before ducking into a small shop along the riverbank in which the shopkeeper immediately recognised the man and struck up a conversion.

"Achan! Back so soon? Did you use up all my water already?"

The woman behind the counter was broad and wore a string of large pearls around her neck, along with two large pearl earrings. Both accessories looked out of place given the apron and rain boots she wore, which were adorned with the occasional mud stain.

"This kid used it all up is why. He crashed his ship right in front of me while I was out in the dunes."

Achan jabbed his thumb at me over his shoulder as he said this. The woman with the pearls looked at me almost like she was impressed.

"You're lucky y'know. There are rarely any survivors when ships crash here. And even when there are they usually waste away in the dunes. That's if that crazy Priestess doesn't get to them first." The woman shook her head and grabbed a small flask, identical to the one Achan had, from the wall behind the counter. "You're lucky Achan was there to find you, and even luckier he had this."

She held up the flask before giving it to Achan in exchange for his identical empty one.

"What is it." I piped in, "How can water heal like that? Are there nanobots in it? Or some sort of rapid healing enzyme or something."

Achan frowned, "I told you it was magic remember?"

I ignored him and kept my gaze on the woman.

"He's right, it's my magic. I just take some water from the river there, infuse it with my magic and pop it into these little flasks. That's all there is to it."

They both looked at me for a moment, but when I didn't say anything, Achan turned back to the woman and handed her four copper coins before exiting the shop.

"Thanks Marnie. I'll see you later."

Achan left the shop and turned left along the river. I followed, but something caught my eye, making me stop and look to the right first, catching the stare of someone, a young woman, who quickly disappeared back into the maze of buildings. She disappeared so quickly that I couldn't even recall her outline—only those sharp green eyes, staring into me for an instant. I was frozen for a second, unsure of what just happened, before I turned around to find that Achan hadn't broken his stride and I would have to jog to catch back up with him. Before I reached him however, he pivoted, and disappeared back into the streets, forcing me into a run to catch up with him before I lost him in the maze. When I turned back into the street, I did a sweep, finding him walking up the street towards the city. As I caught up to him, he must've heard me panting because he turned his head with a smirk and his eyebrows raised to ask me,

"What happened to you? Something catch your eye?"

"No," I lied, because I knew I couldn't explain what, or who, exactly *had* caught my eye. Achan gave me a look before breaking away from the main street, making a few zig-zagging turns through smaller streets. The city seemed to be wider here, with taller buildings, some even reaching four stories tall. There was also a wider variation of colours in the brickwork. Some structures utilised darker brown bricks, while others incorporated a mix of different colours, creating an earthy patchwork that resembled the dunes themselves. We approached a three-story house at the end of the street predominantly made from sandstone bricks, except for the lowest story which had dark-brown bricks that seemed to twinkle as we got closer. Achan informed me that the bottom story was his workshop, and as he was a blacksmith, it got pretty hot in there, requiring more heat-resistant bricks. The twinkling was the steel aggregate in the bricks. He was also proud to point out the darker-coloured bricks around the door and windows which were instead laced with copper for decoration and that he had made these bricks himself. The entrance to the workshop was marked by two wide, reinforced wooden doors. Achan swung one open and disappeared inside, telling me to wait there. He came back without his satchel and having removed some of the head and arm wrappings he was using as sun protection, revealing a deep tan and a collection of bracelets. Each one was a string of black beads cut through by veins of brown gold, all carefully strung together. Achan noticed me looking at them curiously and held his arm up.

"They're black moonstones. Not the fanciest things around but I think they suit me."

We both admired them for a moment before he dropped his arm and invited me inside. We went through the front door and up to the first floor where we entered the kitchen.

"Welcome, this is my daughter, Ava, and my wife, Kalona."

Kalona gave me a smile and a brief wave. Ava was intensely focused on some sort of strategy game that was laid out on the table and didn't seem to notice me at all. As Kalona turned away, the sun glinted off a large, tear-shaped, pale-yellow gemstone hanging from a chain around her neck. It was then that I noticed the subtle adornment of the same gemstone stitched into her clothes, and decorating her shoes. Ava instead wore dark, ovular stones, similar to her father's black moonstones, but hers were a deep purple and contained flecks of silver and rainbow that sparkled, making them all look like tiny universes trapped in stone. The one around her neck was slightly different, with clouds of orange throughout, making it look more like a tiny nebula. Kalona frowned at her husband, giving him a stare that he couldn't discern the reason for, before she turned to me with a softer expression, "And what's your name dear?"

"Oh me? I'm Ender."

The lightbulb went off in Achan's head as he realised why his wife had given him a death stare earlier.

"Ah, right. Sorry about that." He stepped forward and pivoted to face me, standing next to Kalona. "My name is Achan Gehazi." He bowed apologetically, with a smirk on his face indicating that it was only for his wife's benefit. Kalona smacked him on the arm, astonished.

"You brought him all the way back from the dunes and didn't tell him your name!?" She shook her head and turned back to me, "I'll make you all some lunch, you must be starving."

And with that, she disappeared into the pantry. Ava chose that moment to groan frustratedly and slapped a few of the game pieces off the table.

"Perfect timing Ava. Why don't you take Ender here to the museum. I'm sure he's got a ton of questions about our little city here."

"Do I have to?"

"Yes."

Ava sighed, looking grumpy and stood up, still without looking at me.

"Oh and Ava, grab him a necklace from my workshop. It'll be too suspicious if you walk that far into town without a gem."
Ava rolled her eyes and walked over to a door next to the pantry.

"Come on then."

I followed her awkwardly through the door, down to the workshop, my confusion about the constant wearing of a single kind of gem finally getting to me. Ava sounded reluctant to answer any sort of question, or talk to me at all, but I had to know.

"So…about these gems. Why do I need to wear one? And why is everyone wearing a different one, and only that one?"

"Whoa, hold your horses buddy."

She turned around at the bottom of the stairs, looking at me for the first time since I entered the house. She sighed again, looking me up and down for a moment. She turned around and strode through the workshop, starting to talk, "The gems are a reflection of one's natural resonance. Everyone has a frequency with which they are in perfect harmony, as do gemstones, and so we use those particular gems as a way of telling others."

"Okay but why?"

"Why what?"

"Why do you need to show people what your 'natural resonance' is?"

"Ah, well that's a harder question to answer." Ava paused for a moment, trying to decide how to phrase it. "Well, because it makes it easier to find your soulmate. You see finding your soulmate is considered a great accomplishment here, and your soulmate can only be someone with the same natural resonance as you. This pursuit of soulmates is how it started anyway. Then the Fovan Church got involved going on about truth and putting your true self on display through the wearing of your gem. Then it became a social status issue, where all the 'lesser gems'"—she motioned air quotes—"live out here in the limbs, while all the diamonds, sapphires, and whoever else frolic around the inner city, doing who knows what."

She finished, finding a necklace on the rows of shelves, before handing it to me. "Here. It's kyanite."

I put the cloudy blue gem around my neck, my gaze then finding again the tiny nebula around Ava's neck. She looked down, following my gaze.

"It's a bloodshot iolite sunstone. My dad found it out in the dunes in a meteoroid. The rest are all just regular iolite sunstone though. She held up her wrists for a moment, to indicate her bracelets, but quickly pivoted and walked out the door, grabbing a long coat off a hook and throwing it at me, reminding me that I was still wearing my shredded flight suit.

"To the museum then. You can ask the rest of your questions to the people there instead."

I pulled the coat over my undershirt, discarding the top half of my flight suit, and caught up to her, following her out of the house and through the endless winding streets of the city. After we had taken enough twists and turns that I was officially lost and couldn't tell which way we had come or which way we were going, we emerged from between the four-story buildings into a large plaza, probably a hundred meters wide on either side. At the other end of the plaza was a large building with suspiciously classical architecture, portico and all, with a few additions such as the gold creatures clawing their way up a few of the columns, and the ornate stones embedded in the windows. As we approached the entrance, my gaze was drawn to the gold creatures. Their claws dug into the stone columns and their faces, shaped like a large cat, sported stubby horns or tusks protruding backward from their cheekbones. Despite their outlines, these creatures were not feline. They had a distinctly reptilian appearance up close, covered in scales. Their tails, however, were entirely alien, resembling some kind of deadly ancient weapon.

"They're called Chryacal. Creatures that lived here thousands of years ago. Rumour has it that the High Priestess carries around one of their tails as a staff, but I think it's just made to look like one."

"Wouldn't something like that, y'know, decay over a thousand years, or turn to sand even?"

36

"Chryacal don't decay like humans, they petrify. Turning into rather sturdy crystalized fossils. That's how we have such detailed replicas of them."

"Huh, cool."

Ava swung the door open and we entered the museum. The inside was one big room, the walls all lined with books and the occasional doorway to private offices or bathrooms. The middle of the room was populated with endless displays, from cool crystal formations to entire spaceships, not much bigger than my own, but of entirely alien designs. One of the ships looked like a black sphere, cut in half to show the interior, which looked super high-tech, but I couldn't make sense of the design at all.

"Okay, we're at the museum now. No more questions. Go ask one of the people or something, I'll be over there looking at proelium strategy books when you're done."

And with that she was gone, leaving me alone between the alien spacecraft and fossilised Chryacal claws. I wandered past the small, single-pilot ships, wondering if there were any other human ships or if I was the first to crash into this planet. My eyes lit up for a second then, and a glimmer of hope ignited as I realised that there were plenty of alien ships, but no alien skeletons. If their ships survived then many of them probably did too. But there were no aliens around here, just the very human-looking tan people. At least so far as I had seen. But nevertheless, if the aliens weren't here then they must be somewhere. They might've even found a way home. If ships were always making their way here, it couldn't be too hard to make their way back, right? I had been trying not to think about how I would get home until this moment. I had been suppressing it, knowing that I didn't have any obvious way to get back, and trying to focus on what was right in front of me until I did find a way, which was easy to do given all the strangeness I had encountered so far.

I continued wandering through the wreckages when I noticed a long metal arm reaching towards the ceiling, towering over the rest of the ships. I followed the arm to its base, ducking around displays to see what it was part of. At the base of the pole was a satellite dish. The very same satellite dish that belonged to Voyager One, the first spacecraft to leave our solar system, which we eventually lost contact with nearly three decades ago. Most of the rest of Voyager One was here too, if not quite assembled the right way. What piqued my interest, however, was the next display; a gold disk covered in diagrams and scribbles. It was the golden record placed on Voyager One, in the hope that alien species might one day find it and learn about humans and what life was like on Earth. It would be way outdated now but it made me curious to know if anyone had discovered how to play it, and learnt all about us.

"Hello!"

A woman had appeared next to me, with curly dark red hair and small crimson gemstones sprinkled orderly all over her clothes.

"Ah, interested in the golden record are you? Yes it's an interesting one indeed, unlike most of the ships that crash here, this one," she pointed to Voyager, not missing a beat, "Seems it was sent to us instead, to teach us all about humans, that's what the gold record is you see. It's a storage device containing tons of information about a species from another planet, the humans. Crazy to think about isn't it?"

She stopped talking, but I didn't say anything, sure she would jump right back into explaining something else if I flinched.

"I'm Cybele, by the way. Head curator of the museum."

"I'm Ender."

"Nice to meet you, Ender."

She looked me up and down, and squinted slightly, trying to be subtle about observing me.

"Say, Ender, what brings you to the museum today?"

Shit. Could I tell her the truth? I was supposedly wearing this necklace to avoid suspicion, but who exactly was I supposed to be hiding from? Everyone? Or just certain people? Perhaps half-truths were the way to go here. Besides, Cybele didn't seem dangerous. She was just a chatty nerd as far as I could tell. Whatever gems she was wearing though were pretty impressive. They were such a vibrant red. You'd almost think they were glowing.

"Oh, y'know, I'm new to the area so I thought I'd see the sights, check out the museum and whatnot."

"New to the area? Right…ok."

She gave me a slightly suspicious look as if my answer didn't quite make sense, but she tried to mask her doubt.

"That's a pretty gemstone you've got there. May I ask what it is?"

Shit. Ava never told me what it was called. She just handed it to me and off we went. Cybele knew something was up—I just couldn't gauge how much she suspected.

"You're the head curator of a big rock collection. Surely you can figure it out."

She squinted at me a little before her eyes flicked to the golden record and back to me, a slight but noticeable smirk creeping into her expression.

"Well, there are certainly other ways to find out."

Before I could frown at this comment, she had already pulled out a handheld device from her jacket, pointing it at me and firing it. At first, I thought it was a weapon and flinched away, ducking. But when she activated it, it only seemed to affect my epicode, making me blind in one eye, temporarily filling half my vision with static. I stared back at her, confused, but she was preoccupied, staring at the device as she whispered, "Inconclusive?" under her breath. When she looked up at me again, I knew I had to run. She shouted out behind me, "Wait!" but I didn't, and kept my pace running for the exit, remembering my broken ribs as they grated against my heavier breaths.

Ava had clearly noticed the commotion and had arrived at the entrance seconds before I did, looking confused but not particularly surprised. She ducked out of the museum ahead of me, telling me to follow her. I did, but not before I caught the gaze of a lone pair of bright green eyes at the other end of the plaza. It was only after I had turned to follow Ava that I registered seeing them. I glanced back once more before disappearing into the maze of the city, but they were already gone.

Chapter 3

Back at the Gehazi household, Kalona had made sandwiches. It was nice to know that some things were universal, even if the meat was a strange colour and tasted like pickles. After living in space aboard Cronus for the last few months, I was glad of some real food. Achan and Ava were sitting at the table, listening intently to my version of what had happened at the museum.

"So, I was making my way past some of the crashed ships when I found another ship from Earth. Well, more of a probe really. Anyway, I was standing there in front of it and the museum's head curator approached me and just started talking. I think her name was Cybele. I think she might've recognised me as human, from the golden record. It wouldn't have helped that I said I was new to the area."

Achan and Ava looked at each other and back to me before Achan responded, "The only way to get to the city is to crash here. There is nowhere else you could have come from."

"Oh."

I had given myself away before I had even realised it.

"I thought she had figured it out when I wouldn't tell her what gemstone this was." I held up the necklace. Ava frowned.

"And why didn't you just tell her?" I frowned back at her.

"Because I didn't know. You didn't tell me."

She dropped her head to her palm, now propping her head up, mumbling at the table.

"Yes I did. It's kyanite." She lifted her head back up, looking sheepish, "Never mind that then. What made you run?"

"Well, she whipped out some sort of device and pointed it at me, I don't think it was a weapon or anything but it…well you see, I've got this little device in my head, connected to my eye that lets me do all sorts of stuff, and whatever the device was that she pulled out interfered with it, making me go blind temporarily. That's what made me run."

Ava was quick to figure it out.

"She must have been scanning you, trying to figure out your gem type. Did she figure it out?"

"No, I heard her say inconclusive before I ran off."

Achan was quiet, seemingly lost in thought. Ava looked at her father as if about to ask something, but stopped, seeing his concentrated expression.

"Dad?" He looked up at us and started, "This device in your head. What exactly can it do?"

He leaned closer over the table as he asked this. I listed some of its functions, not including communications which weren't really applicable here, which primarily left me with some scanners and optical zoom.

"Interesting."

Achan sat back, pondering its usefulness.

"I'm going to get the resonance scanner from the workshop."

Ava announced before heading downstairs.

"Great idea. I find myself suddenly curious as to what kind of gem you could be, Ender."

Achan said with a wry smile, more than mere curiosity on his mind. Ava appeared from downstairs with a device similar to the one Cybele had had but slightly larger and clunkier. Ava placed it on the table in front of me and sat down opposite.

"Ready?"

"Yeah."

Ava switched the resonance scanner on and my vision was once again filled with static. I tried to adjust the input frequency range to exclude that of the scanner, but quickly gave up, turning the epicode off all together. My vision immediately returned and my fresh headache ebbed away. Ava frowned at the scanner, leading me to assume the results were inconclusive once again. Still frowning, she looked up at Achan and me and asked, "What's alexandrite?"

Achan shrugged and looked at me. I had no idea either. Achan peered over Ava's shoulder to look at the results, his eyebrows slowly rising higher on his forehead. He looked back at me.

"Whatever it is, I think it must belong with the upper gems."

"What makes you say that?" I asked.

"Well, the information here is limited, but alexandrite is mighty hard and extremely rare. That's about all I can tell you."

"How do you know how rare it is?"

He smirked, "It must be if I've never heard of it."

Ava sighed, thinking hard for a moment, before jumping up ready to go.

"Well it sounds like there's only one way to find out. We have to go the inner city and ask around."

"But Ava, you can't. You know what can happen when lower gems go prancing around higher gem hot spots, especially in the city centre."

He gave her a stern look, concerned.

"No it's okay I have a perfect cover story. I'll pretend to be Ender's servant, and they'll have to believe him because of his gem's rank." Ava proposed.

"But how will they know that? It's not like we have alexandrite just laying around?"

"Exactly. No one does. Probably. We can say that it's so rare we haven't be able to find any yet, and that we're out on a stroll shopping for some. It's a perfect cover for not having any, as well as to ask around about it."

Ava was proud of her plan, and despite Achan's concern, he could see the value in the excursion, and the genius in Ava's scheming. He smiled reluctantly.

"Alright." He shot Ava a serious look. "Make it worth it."

She nodded, and his expression reverted to normal as he held out his hand to me. I took the Kyanite from around my neck and handed it to him.

"I'll be in my workshop."

And with that he disappeared downstairs, leaving Ava and I to plan our trip to the inner city. We left that afternoon, Ava having shown me a map prior, mapping our way through the city so that it wouldn't look like I was following a servant around. I was already feeling tired before we left, wondering how long it had been since I was on a ship orbiting Saturn. I guessed it to be no more than eight hours, considering the time of day. However, Ava informed me that the day/night cycle here was twenty-seven hours, with only seven of those hours being dark. This meant that it could easily have been closer to sixteen hours. No wonder I was tired. We were making our way towards the inner city, purposefully avoiding the museum on the way. I was also wearing nicer clothes, pulled from Achan's closet. No one would believe I was an upper gem in the torn flight suit and borrowed coat I was wearing prior. Even *with* a resonance scan. It was nice to wear something fresh though; flight suits weren't exactly designed for breathability.

We were past the museum now, Ava indicating for me to take the lead as we approached a large archway, signalling the entrance to some sort of inner district. There were guards on either side of the archway, eyeing those that passed through, but not stopping or disrupting anyone. I strode through the archway with Ava in tow, pretending that I felt important. The street on the other side was noticeably cleaner and wider, transitioning quickly from the between-building streets to structures with open lobbies and shop stalls, and arcades that wound through rows of buildings. After my initial wide-eyed gaze upward at the collection of towers that populated the inner city, I remembered to keep my cool and hide my intrigue, restricting my gaze to street level. Ava had suggested we start by strolling through the arcades, as that was where she guessed more bespoke items might be found. That and they were away from the crowds; some of which were eyeing us already, unsure what looked wrong about us. I casually strolled over to the entrance of one of the arcades and entered through another, smaller archway that displayed a list of shop names outlined in gold trim. The inside of the arcade was elaborately adorned, with soft brown walls, covered in carvings and gold trim that reminded me of timber but had no wood grain. There were countless windows winding their way through the passageway, offering glimpses into small shops selling a range of things, from ornate sculptures of strange creatures to exotic foods, some of which smelled like oranges and mint.

We made our way down the arcade, noticing the sections between buildings often had skylights full of stained glass, all depicting scenes presumably of historical significance. Ava whispered harshly trying to grab my attention.

"Ender."

I spun around too abruptly, startling Ava as she pointed to a shop two doors down on the right. It was a small store, set into the wall but extending a fair distance along it, showcasing collections of rubies, emeralds, and sapphires in the arcade halls rather than in a separate shop. I approached the long table and bent down to look at a collection of rubies. There was a large ring with maybe twenty tiny rubies embedded in it, and a string of ovular rubies laid out on a stand shaped like a neck, next to a smaller string held aloft by a fake wrist. I was only pretending to be interested in them of course, as I had no money, and had merely come looking for information. The shopkeeper wandered down from the middle of the stall.

"Ah, looking for rubies are we?" She looked me up and down, noticing my severe lack of adornment. "You look like you're in need of a fresh set."

She squinted slightly, not sure what to think of me. She noticed Ava and her sunstones which probably didn't help me appear less suspicious. Clearly Ava knew what was expected of her as she played the role of servant, as she stood well back from the jewels on the counter, likely to prevent suspicion of theft. I refixed my gaze on the rubies, unsure how to broach the subject of alexandrite. I looked up at the shopkeeper, who had decided not to take her eyes off us. "

Actually, as a professional jeweller, I was hoping you might know something about a gemstone known as alexandrite?"

"Alexandrite? Never heard of it. It can't be worth much if I've never heard of it. I've got all the best stuff right here; rubies, sapphires, emeralds, you name it. I even have red beryl if you know anyone."

"Ah, well thank you for your time."

The shopkeeper sighed and wandered back to the middle of her stall as we continued our stroll through the arcade. Ava silently followed me as we went, passing shop after shop full of alluring goods only available to the fortunate few who happened to naturally resonate at higher frequencies. The next store we happened upon that we deemed potentially useful, was less of a jewelers, and more of a small sculpture studio that utilised rare and interesting looking stones. This shop was a regular-sized one laid out like a gallery, with some art and slices of large geodes hung on the walls. The majority of the floor space housed pedestals atop which stood little sculptures, some made of elaborately carved jade, and others out of something that made them look like molten lava. We made our way to the back of the store where a man sat behind a desk, sketching. Above him on the wall was a large slice of a geode that looked like thousands of rainbows had folded in on each other and crystallized. The little sign on the bottom left indicated that it was called kaleidoscope jasper. The man looked up from his drawing as we arrived at his desk, happy to see us, but curious of our appearances.

"Hello! And welcome to my studio. Is there anything specific you were looking for?"

He looked at us expectantly, keen to hear what we would say next.

"Well, It might not be something you work with directly, but I was curious to hear what you might know about alexandrite?"

"Alexandrite…" the man stared off into space, thinking. "Nope, I can't say I've ever heard of it. Why? Is it pretty? Should I know about it?"

"No, no, it's not really something you could use in your work, given how rare it seems to be."

"Ahh, I see. Well, if you do see something you like please tell me."

He gave us a sad smile and went back to his sketch before we had even taken a step away from the desk. We turned back around to leave the shop, but I faltered momentarily when I noticed Ava move strangely behind me, moving from my right side to my left, before taking a larger step forward, hurrying me out of the store. Choosing to ignore whatever that was, I continued through the arcade, my thoughts turning back to our search for alexandrite. I could see the end of the arcade now. We had rounded the last corner, and I found myself trying to remember where this particular path came out, recounting the turns we had taken, trying to orient myself. As I was doing this, however, a bright green gem caught my eye. The gem was a large emerald on the counter of a tiny booth at the end of the arcade. The shop had an odd collection of items haphazardly organized, with necklaces dangling from the ceiling, and rings strewn about, some of which even appeared to be carved from ivory. I approached the stall, Ava silently questioning my choice behind me but saying nothing. There was an old lady behind the counter, unmoving in her chair and with long silver braids, wrapped in golden snakes. She said nothing.

"Um, hello?"

"Hello, dear."

"I'm, I mean, I was…"

Something about this woman was off-putting, but in a strange way it felt right, like she was the one with all the answers, but not one to give them away so easily.

"I was wondering what you might know about alexandrite." The woman lifted her head at this, staring at me curiously with her light blue eyes.

"Now that's an interesting tale isn't it."

She looked at me closely, her intrigue only heightening when she noticed my lack of adornments. She smiled warmly, having curbed her curiosity with a theory she would not share.

"There is a story about a girl, the only gem of her kind, who longs for a soulmate but cannot find her match. She is said to roam the city searching, always searching, watching from the shadows, waiting. The gem of the girl is said to be alexandrite, a rare gem. So rare that only one ever exists at any one time, condemning them to eternal loneliness."

The old woman finished, waiting to see my reaction. Her tale certainly wasn't what I expected to hear, nor what I wanted to hear. Now I knew that even if I obtained some alexandrite, I would stand out. The whole point of all this was to blend in. But then again, we had never come here to buy gemstones, only to learn, and I think we had learned more than enough from this woman's story. Plus, I couldn't help but wonder if there truly was a girl out there. Someone destined for me. A soulmate. Or was this woman speaking of a time long past? A girl now deceased, with me taking her place as the only one of my kind. Condemned to eternal loneliness. I pondered this last point absently and for long enough that Ava kicked me in the back of the calf, snapping me out of it.

"Uh, thank you."

I smiled briefly before walking away from the table, flustered, the old woman giving me a knowing look as she sunk back into her chair. I spoke, hoping that Ava would hear me as she trailed behind.

"Did we need anything else here or was that enough."

Ava whispered behind me, "I think that's the most we are going to get."

She seemed uneasy, clearly ready to get out of here. I took a moment to orient myself in this new part of the city. Following the arcade passageway from the outside, I retraced the turns we had taken and soon spotted the big archway that led back into the city's limbs. The two guards still stood silently to the side. We walked out into the limbs of the city, through the archway, not stopping until we turned the corner out of sight of the guards. Ava looked more relieved to be out of there than I expected. She took the lead once again, leading us back to the house.

On the way back, as we reached the top of a slight hill in the city, we could see the edge of the limb and the dunes beyond. Suddenly, a tear opened up in the sky, with gold flames twisting along the edge of an eye-shaped opening. It reflected the earthy patchwork of the sand, superimposed upon unfamiliar stars. In the next instant, the tear exploded into a mass of fiery tendrils and glass. The tendrils whipped back and imploded on themselves, leaving the glass to fall and evaporate before it even hit the ground. Out of the mayhem shot a silver bullet, slowing itself down rapidly as it blasted strange projectiles into the dune ahead of it before crashing. I whipped around to Ava frantically. She frowned at me like that sort of thing was just an everyday occurrence for her, which I suppose it was given that two of us had crashed here in one day. Her eyes went wide with understanding eventually, and she lunged to grab my arm, but I had already turned to run towards the crash site. If whoever this was survived, they could help me make my way back home. I could help them get back home too. I could help them understand this planet even. At least the little bit that I now knew. But nevertheless, I couldn't let them suffer out there in the dunes. I was fortunate enough to be saved and it was time to repay the favour.

I raced towards the edge of the city, glad that I had memorised the maze between the Gehazi house and the inner-city shopping district. I assumed that's what the Earth equivalent of that place was. I closed in on the edge of the dunes. Ava caught up to me, shouting something, but I couldn't hear her over the wind rushing past my ears as I sprinted through the streets. I scrambled up and over the first dune, seeing a thin pillar of red smoke rising from somewhere ahead. As I reached the top of the next dune, Ava grabbed the back of my shirt and yanked me down with enough force that I ended up with a face full of sand. I lifted my head and wiped the sand off my face and shot her an angry look, which turned to confusion as I saw her staring straight ahead, a terrified and disgusted look plastered on her face. I turned to see what she was staring at. It was the downed ship, the thin red smoke rising out of the back end of the silver bullet which remained intact. I couldn't see what Ava was terrified of until I turned my head slightly to the right, seeing a woman dressed in scaly-looking panels folded into a ruffled dress. She was dressed head to toe in red and gold, wearing a myriad of clear crystals all over, the presence of which I could only see from this distance due to them reflecting the evening sun right into my eyes, sparkling as she walked. I ducked down lower, hiding with Ava behind the ridge of the dune. Whoever this woman was, she didn't seem particularly friendly. Not with the six guards decked head to toe in armour adapted for desert conditions that followed her. They all had long spears with different tips; some looking like javelins, others like halberds. No matter the enemy, this entourage was prepared for any kind of foe.

At that moment, squinting into the desert, I remembered my epicode, which I seemed to keep forgetting about. I turned it back on, activating the optical zoom and automated night-vision as it rapidly grew darker with night approaching. Now I could see exactly what was happening down there. The woman had reached the ship and was standing directly in front of it, waiting. A panel on the front half of the ship popped up and rotated to the side. A humanoid creature with dark skin and a black flight suit, with shiny metal plating at various joints, stood up in the cockpit, their mouth moving rapidly and their arms waving around in front of them. I couldn't hear what they said, with my epicode microphone having broken when my ship was disabled. The woman was frowning, looking down at the person that had risen from the ship, despite being shorter than them. She gestured to her guards, drawing my attention to her hands on which she wore long gold claws over her fingers, resembling those of a chryacal. The guard to her right stepped forward, lowering the tip of his spear as he did, and impaled the creature in one swift motion, before stepping back into line, his spear tip now a deep purple. I looked at Ava, horrified, but she hadn't watched. She had turned around and laid down, staring at the sky with a pained look on her face. She knew exactly what was going to happen. It was why she hadn't wanted to come. I looked back to the scene, seeing the woman and her guards leaving the ship and its pilot to dissolve in the dunes. Then I remembered something that Marnie, the lady who sold the healing water, had said. I turned back to Ava.

"That was the crazy priestess I've heard about wasn't it."

Ava looked at me surprised.

"Yeah. I'm surprised you knew about her. Did Achan warn you or something?"

"Actually it was something the lady down by the river said, Marnie."

"Ah, Marnie. I'm not surprised, she's such a gossip."

Ava smiled when she said this, the first time I had seen her do so. As Ava and I talked and the sun continued to set, the world around us grew darker. My night vision gradually adjusted, slowly revealing a figure crouching along the ridge of the dune, much like we were, not too far away. I could see the figure just past Ava's head, appearing only in the darkness. Ava noticed me looking past her and turned around to see what I saw but couldn't without night vision.

Curiosity got the better of me and I started towards the figure, creeping along the ridge of the dune, the sand silencing my footsteps. Whoever it was, they were also afraid of the crazy priestess, but they also cared enough to run out here, just like I had done. The figure did not see us as we approached, just as Ava did not see them. As we got close enough to see each other in only the moonlight or, it wasn't actually moonlight I was just now realising. Now that it was dark enough, I could see the rippling ribbons in the sky that were close to invisible during the day. They were like the ghost of an aurora. A bright green, blue, and occasionally purple, set of bright ribbons that squirmed in the sky, replacing moonlight here instead with a soft, swaying, green glow. I was temporarily distracted by the moving sky, lost in its natural wonder, when the figure noticed me and whipped their head around, facing us. It was a young woman, with unnaturally purple eyes, almost like they reflected the purple of the aurora above us. All three of us froze when we locked eyes. She was the first to speak, her expression unreadable as she spoke.

"You snuck up on me."

"I suppose we did."

I scrambled to point out that we were on the same side, I hoped, before saying much else.

"You were watching the ship too. It appears we were both too late."

She seemed to smirk when I said this, but the smirk quickly turned to sadness, looking back to the ship, "I always try to help them, but someone always seems to get to them first."

She looked back at me knowingly with another sly smile, causing me to frown.

"And what do we have here?"

A voice rang out directly behind me, close enough to immediately send shivers up my spine, causing me to jump as I swivelled on the spot, only to be met with the cold metallic tips of a golden claw. I fell back, holding my face, feeling the burn of multiple fresh gashes slicing my face open. I looked at the dark lines of fresh blood on my hand, before looking up to see the outline of the priestess who I had just seen murder someone, standing over us with a wicked grin.

"A trio of spies it would seem." Her eyes lit up, almost as bright as the rows of clear gemstones she wore, shining brilliantly and reflecting the ribbons of soft light rippling above us. "But I guess that's to be expected of lower gems. No morals, or truth. All lies and deception. I think I'll leave you three to dunes."

As she made her decision, she raised her hands, fingers outstretched like a bird of prey about to sink it's claws into its next meal. She thrust her hands forward, raw electrical energy shooting out of her fingertips and sparking back along the golden ridges of her outfit, lighting her up like white fire. The harsh lighting and scaly red outfit made her look like some kind of demon. The bolts of lightning shot right at us, arcing through the air unpredictably, striking the sand at our feet, turning it to glass and cementing us in place. I tried to lunge out of the way, as did the others by the look of the way they had been pinned by the glass, but none of us had escaped. We were stuck here, rooted to the ground by molten sand, doomed to erode away into the dunes as the glass reverted to fine grains of silicate. The priestess turned away with a satisfied grin, soaking up the results of her carnage and disappearing into the darkened desert. Nobody said anything for a few moments, afraid that she was still there, hiding in the darkness. I snapped out of it first, using my night-vision to check that she was gone. There was no sign of her or her guards. We were alone. I relaxed a bit, glad that she was gone, allowing the tension to leave my body, trying to be calm before worrying about how we were supposed to escape this. As I relaxed, I must've leaned backwards, feeling something poke me in the back. I tensed up again, swivelling around as best I could with both my feet melted into the sand. My feet burned but the night air blowing into the fresh cuts across my face was more than enough distraction. On top of that, what had poked me in the back was the knee of the girl with the purple eyes. Those bright eyes stared back at me, her jaw clenched. I couldn't tell if it was because of the burns on her feet, or the anxiety over the predicament we were in. I leaned forward again, trying not to fall into her. My trying to dodge the lightning had left me awkwardly close to this girl I had just met in the desert of this alien planet. I blushed, not that anyone could tell in the dim, moving light. Ava was a couple of meters away and had somehow managed to end up with only one foot encased in glass. She was sitting up now, almost cross-legged but not quite, given the angle of her glassed foot. The girl began to move, rummaging through her bag and pulling out a small flask. It was similar to the one Achan had given me filled with healing-water but slightly larger and more ornate.

"Here, for your face," The girl said stretching out her arm, handing it to me. When I didn't take it, she quickly realised why, a smirk crossing her face. I was propping myself up on my elbows. I wasn't the most comfortable position, but it was the one that kept me from falling into the girl indecently.

"Here, I'll do it." She smiled, pouring the liquid out into her hand, moving closer to my face to pour it over the cuts. "My name is Nadira by the way." I blushed as she moved her hands to my face, starting to wonder if healing someone before you introduced yourself was a custom on this planet.

"I'm Ender, and over there is Ava."

Ava waved her arm once, studying the glass around her foot, looking for structural weaknesses and not paying any attention to us.

"Nice to meet you both."

We all sat in silence, pre-occupied by something. Ava with breaking the glass around her foot, Nadira with the healing water she was applying to my cuts, and me trying not to stare at her as she stared at the cuts on my face, concentrating on them as she dragged her fingers delicately across my forehead and down my temple. I averted my eyes by studying her clothes, becoming increasingly curious as I noticed that the clothes she wore were nicely made but weren't studded with gems or anything. She also didn't seem to wear many gemstones, but the few she did wear were all different. A rough blue sapphire decorated her right wrist, and a polished rectangular garnet hung from her left wrist. If there was one around her neck I couldn't see it. She noticed me looking at her wrist and her mouth pulled into a straight line. I looked into her face, seeing a clear disdain for this city's obsession with gemstones.

"I suppose you're wondering what my gem type is."

By the tone of her voice, I could tell that she didn't want to explain whatever it was that made her wear different gems, but I didn't really want to tell her mine either.

"I'll make you a deal. I won't ask if you don't." She looked surprised for a short moment before grinning.

"Deal."

I could feel the skin on my forehead weaving back together, my headache subsiding gradually. Nadira moved to the last cut, beneath my eye along the edge of my cheekbone. There were three wounds total, my face now marked forever with scars from giant metal claws. One scar lay beneath my eye, while the other two ran parallel, about an inch apart, extending from my eyebrow to my hairline at an angle, ending just above my right temple. Nadira finished applying the healing-water with a final dragging of her thumbpad across the cut on my cheekbone. A surprisingly intimate gesture that sent a flush of heat through my face, turning it red. Nadira flinched back, blushing now too. She leant back, looking over at Ava, who was still focusing on her foot, before back to me. Now that the excitement was over, I could feel sleep creeping up on me, taking advantage of the lull in excitement and the fact that I was close to lying down on the sand. The hectic, high-stakes nature of the day had expended all my energy. On top of that, I had been awake for well over twenty hours, had burns on my feet, cuts on my face, and broken ribs. I shut my eyes for a moment, noticing how still the night air had become. I couldn't give in to sleep now. I was in the desert, and on this planet that meant I would be a pile of sand tomorrow or soon thereafter. That was the whole point of the priestess trapping us here. I opened my eyes again, seeing Nadira inspecting the glass at her feet, trying to dig the sand out from around them, only to discover that the glass had formed like lightning struck; by branching out, forming smaller and smaller offshoots, essentially forming a large enough root system to stop us from digging ourselves out. I opened my mouth to say something to Nadira, but Ava spoke first.

"Hey Ender, surely that thing in your eye could help us out. You said it had some scanners and stuff, right?"

I turned to Ava, who had still had no luck breaking free, but had dug a decent amount of sand out from around the glass holding her foot.

"Yes, but I don't see what good scanning it will do."

"Well, what else can it do? does it have something like a tone generator?"

"Technically yes but…"

"Perfect, then just find the glass' natural resonance and shoot it with some vibrational tones and break it that way."

"It doesn't work that way. Only I would be able to hear the tones."

Ava mumbled, frustrated, and started trying to smash the glass with her free foot. I turned back to Nadira having forgotten what I was going to say. She was studying the glass, looking for thin pieces to break, but there were none. She sighed and laid back on the sand, her knees stuck sticking up in the air. I closed my eyes again, trying not to give in to sleep. I tried to focus on the situation but the pull of sleep, the cool night air, and how calm about our predicament Nadira seemed to be, was all too much. I tried to keep my eyes open, but all they saw was the aurora above which felt like a dream anyway. My arms were getting weaker, following my eyelids. I couldn't keep propping myself up, I didn't have the strength. I wasn't sure when I fell asleep but my eyelids buckled before my arms did, leaving me asleep in a desert that was slowly killing me and on a strange planet who knows how far from home.

Chapter 4

I woke, my vision blurred, but the vivid colours of the aurora still danced above me. Nadira leaned forward, her face directly above mine, smirking. I froze, my vision slowly focusing. Oh shit. How long had I been asleep in her lap? Was it minutes or hours? It couldn't have been too long as it was still night, but still. I had only just met her—a stranger on an alien world—and there I was, asleep in her lap. My face flushed red as I sat up abruptly, gasping. My joints creaked, grinding like rusty iron, and the rush of air through my lungs grated against my insides, making me cough. Nadira winced and handed me the pearl-water.

"Drink. It'll help, but we don't have long before we won't have the strength to get out of here."

She looked tired. I couldn't tell if she had slept or not, but it was clear that the vibrations of the desert were taking a toll on both of us. I took the flask, making a note of how full it was and only drinking half, before handing it back to her. My joints still ached but breathing wasn't so painful now, and my mind had cleared enough to focus. I looked over to Ava, wondering if she had had any new ideas, but all I found was a divot in the sand and chunks of broken glass.

"She was gone when I woke up. I think she just chipped away at it all night and eventually broke enough off to escape. From the looks of it, though, she would have still taken a big chunk of glass with her, fused to her foot."

I frowned. If Ava had been gone for hours, why hadn't she come back for us? This thought troubled me, but I dismissed it in favour of more pressing matters, telling myself that Ava must still be making her way back, slowly, with one foot fused to a chunk of glass. I looked back to Nadira.

"Have you had any ideas about how to escape from this?"

"No. It seems we're stuck. Your friend got lucky, only having one foot stuck. Us, not so much."

She looked wistfully towards the city.

"I am curious to know more about this thing in your eye that your friend thought could help us though."

"Ah, well, that's hard to explain."

I remembered Ava asking about it, but now that I had had some sleep, I could think more clearly. It might be able to help, I just wasn't sure how yet.

"I'm not sure exactly how it can help, but I think Ava might have been on to something. Maybe I'll find something useful."

Nadira looked at me sceptically, but responded with,

"No time to waste then, get to it."

I chuckled at this briefly, but it turned into a series of coughs, reminding me of our fast-approaching demise. I activated my epicode, cycling through the various scanner types, none of which seemed particularly useful. I settled on a frequency augmentation mode, typically used for radio-based code breaking. In this case, I wondered if I could use it to amplify the desert's vibrations, converting them into the natural resonance frequency of the glass. It wouldn't be a quick escape, but it might mean the glass would erode faster than we would. I matched the epicode to the vibrations of the desert, which was easy when your whole body was already vibrating at the same frequency. As I tuned the output frequency, I could hear the tones in my head as I adjusted the output, slowly tuning it to the natural resonance of the glass. Before I got there, however, one of the tones sang back to me for a brief moment as I passed it. I paused, tuning the epicode back to the tone until I heard it again—a note, a harmony playing over the base frequency, as if something could hear it and was joining in. I turned to Nadira, and the harmony became focused in the centre, rather than off to the side. Something that Nadira had was singing back. But what? She frowned as I looked her over, wondering what I was doing. Her eyes went wide, momentarily confused, and we locked eyes. I wondered if somehow, she could hear it too. She frowned and held up the garnet on her wrist to inspect it. She peered closely at it, before stating,

"It's warm. Like, really warm. Are you doing this somehow?"

I didn't know how to respond, so instead, I adjusted the frequency, the harmony of the garnet no longer singing. "Oh wait, it's cooling down again."

"Then yes that was me."

"What were you doing? And how? With the eye thing?"

"I don't really know *what* was happening, but yes it was with the eye thing, which is called an epicode by the way."

"Okay and? What were you trying to do if not heat up my wrist?"

"Well, I was trying to use the vibrations of the desert against the glass. I was trying to augment them to vibrate at a different frequency when they passed through me, but as I was looking for the right frequency of the glass, I might've found the frequency of the garnet instead. For whatever reason, the garnet harmonised with me like it was singing back to me in repsonse."

"Interesting." Nadira sat back, her eyes narrowed in thought. A small smile crept onto her face, hinting at an idea brewing. She was still piecing together the details, a plan taking shape in her mind.

"Can you play two notes simultaneously with that thing?"

"I suppose I can split the output into two different frequencies, yeah. Why?"

"Play the next note in the sequence."

"The sequence?"

"Yes, the harmonic sequence."

"Oh right, of course." I wasn't a musical genius or anything, but my epicode showed me the wavelengths of each note, making it easy to guess where the next harmony would be. I split the output and adjusted the first to the original frequency, knowing I had found it when the garnet started to sing back. I went to adjust the second one but paused, looking at the garnet on Nadira's wrist.

"I'm not entirely sure what you think is going to happen, but if I'm going to layer even higher frequencies into it, then that thing is probably going to get a bit hot so I'd recommend taking it off."

"Oh I definitely should."

She took it off immediately and placed it on a patch of sand off to the side, as the patch of sand between us was already too cramped, thanks to our glass shackles. I found the next harmonic by guessing and adjusting until the garnet sang back, singing two notes now, all in harmony. Nadira couldn't hear any of this, but her face lit up. She knew it was working as the garnet had started to glow softly, the heat it was building up starting to become visible.

"Okay now add another."

"What exactly is your plan here?"

"Just do it."

I hesitantly added another harmonic, the garnet singing the next one back, before forming a feedback loop, continuing the sequence on its own indefinitely, causing the garnet to glow brighter rapidly. As the feedback loop took off, my sleeve spontaneously combusted, setting it alight, causing me to wave my arm around frantically, slamming my arm against the sand to put the fire out.

"Were you trying to set me on fire or was that just a coincidence?"

"We don't have much time, just shut up and put your hands on the glass and, I don't know think about melting it or something."

As she said this, she grabbed the garnet with her sleeve and quickly shoved it under the edge of her glass shackles, burying it with sand.

"Think about melting the glass? What's that going to do?"

She sighed frustratedly, resigning herself to my ignorance.

"Some garnets have fire magic. I was hoping that since you managed to harmonise with the garnet, you might be on the right wavelength to tap into that kind of magic. I don't know how it works but you already set your sleeve on fire, so I think it's there, you just have to find it and melt the glass." She paused and looked at the mound of sand leaning against her glass shackles where she buried the garnet. "Before the garnet breaks or explodes. It can't heat up forever and I don't know how long it will last, so please hurry."

She locked eyes with me, purple orbs shining back at me, pleading. The sun was starting to rise now, the desert getting lighter, and we were getting closer to our fates as puddles of sand. I reached forward, my shoulders grating in their sockets as I did so, lungs starting to burn against the air. I placed my hands on the glass at my feet, imagining it melting, wishing for it to melt, pleading for it. But nothing. I raised my fist, trying to slam it against the glass in anger, but the stiffness in my joints locked it in place, preventing me from bringing my arm down making me even more frustrated, anger burning my cheeks, and softening the glass under my other hand. As my anger disappeared and I looked down at my hand on the glass, it began to cool again, the heat dissipating with my anger. This was fire magic. Astonished as I was, my aching joints and burning breath forced me to desperation, making anger easy, bringing it all to the surface and channelling it into my hand, melting through the glass without burning my skin. I managed to bring down my other hand too, grabbing melted globules of glass as I pulled them away from my feet, digging in slow motion. It wasn't long before the glass above my feet was thin enough and hot enough that I could move them. Slowly at first, but they were rising out of the glass, breaking free, molten sand dripping off them, cooling into disks on the dune. My feet were free, but as I went to scrape the rapidly cooling molten glass from the tops of them, a muffled explosion rang out, throwing sand up in the air and everywhere, including my eyes, preventing me from looking around for the source of the explosion. But I didn't need to see to know. I had suddenly lost my ability to withstand the heat of the molten glass, as the remains of it on my feet began burning my flesh as it cooled, telling me it must have been the garnet that exploded, breaking the harmonic link. I tried to scream in pain but my lungs didn't want to exhale, fossilising as I slowly turned to sand. I rubbed the sand out of my eyes, the grinding of my joints more painful than the sand scratching the insides of my eyelids. I could see now, Nadira standing beside me, her legs bleeding from cuts that reached all the way up past her knees. The worst ones were on her feet, where the exploding garnet had shattered the glass and sent it flying, ripping through her feet and slicing up her legs on their way outward. She stood, legs oozing blood, dripping on the sand, her breath restricted to shallow wheezing. She stood over me, looking down at me with her now lavender-coloured eyes as she tried to speak. When she couldn't, she held her hand out to me instead. As I took her hand, the rising sun had risen high enough to peak over the dunes, striking Nadira, her eyes turning a bright green as the sun inched its way down the soft lines of her face. It was her—the girl that I had caught glimpses of for the briefest of moments. She had followed me since I crashed, and now here she was. I wanted to ask, to know, to understand, but the pain was too great, and in so many places. The only part of her I could concentrate on was the outstretched hand in front of me, offering to save me. I took it, silently gagging as I tried to stand on the burnt remains of my feet, my ability to cry in pain completely gone. We stumbled down the dune, sliding and limping, leaving trails of blood and leaning on each other as we tried to use our mangled feet. We made our way up the second dune, the last thing that stood between us and safety. We inched our way up, guts writhing in pain with every step. With the first step down the other side of the dune, I fell, taking Nadira with me. We tumbled down the last dune to the edge of the city, where I landed flat on my back on the tiled edge of the maze of streets. My vision still spun but began gaining clarity as the world stopped vibrating. My eyes focused on the bright green eyes staring into mine, barely an inch away from my face. Nadira got up off of me, as fast as aching joints would allow, and shifted her gaze away from me, towards the city. She pushed off my chest as she got up, leaving the warm sensation of her handprint on my chest. She took a few steps towards the buildings, face twisting in pain with every step. She looked back to me, indicating to the best of her ability for me to follow. I did, as I had nowhere else to go, or the ability to think straight enough to form any kind of plan. I stood slowly, Nadira reaching out her hand as I hobbled over to her, the tiles like sandpaper against my raw flesh. We continued like this, clutching each other and trying not to fall, across two streets to the edge of the riverbank. I wasn't sure what good the river would do, but as Nadira let go of me to step into it, she saw the confused scrunch in my face, and pointed to the long trail of blood we had left behind us, all the way from the dunes to here. Of course. Wherever we went, the priestess would be able to follow our trail if she discovered we had escaped our peril. Somehow Nadira still had the strength for strategy when all I had room for right now was survival. As Nadira sank into the river, blood swirling around her and flowing downstream, Instead, I tripped again and fell face-first into the water. The pain lasted only for a moment as the coolness of the water eased the burns on my feet and washed the sand from my eyes. I stood up in the river, my bones still stiff, blinking the water out of my eyes and feeling relieved as the buoyancy alleviated the pressure from my feet. I looked at Nadira whose head was only sticking out of the water by two-thirds, her mouth open and gulping down mouthfuls of river water. I hadn't realised just how thirsty I was until now. It was easy to blame the stiffness and scratchy lungs on the vibrations in the dunes, but dehydration likely played a large part of my condition. I copied Nadira, swallowing mouthfuls of river water, concerned at first about hygiene, but quickly forgetting to care as the clear water hit the back of my throat, reactivating my suppressed thirst. I greedily sucked down the cool liquid. Nadira stood up and explained without prompt in a croaky voice.

"The pearls take water from the river to use in healing magic. Some of the magic leaks into the river itself. It's not very strong, but bathing in it like this might be enough to get us somewhere safe without leaving a trail of blood."

I nodded, understanding, being all too familiar with healing magic at this point. We left the river then, eyes glancing back at the trail of blood, wary of being followed. The new trail we left as we hobbled away from the river was clear, and it evaporated rapidly behind us, leaving only a few visible footsteps at a time. Confident we couldn't be tracked from here, Nadira led the way through the thin stretch of buildings on the outskirts of the city.

We travelled away from the centre, the two streets eventually turning into one, until we reached a section of buildings that looked abandoned. Some were relatively solid-looking, while others were built too close to the dunes and sections of wall had crumbled from the vibrations. On the very tip of this finger of the city, was a two-story structure nearly all intact into which we entered, the inside dark and full of dust. Nadira grabbed my hand, leading me through the dark and up a set of stairs I couldn't see, until she stopped and opened a door, letting light from upstairs flood down into the ground story.

Upstairs was a small room, a living room, that had not been properly occupied for decades. The only evidence of recent occupation was seeing Nadira walk over to a small chest, unlock it with a key, and pull out two pearl-water flasks. She then proceeded to sit down in front of an unlit fire, placing the second pearl-water flask beside her—a clear invitation for me to join her. I walked over and sat down next to her, wincing as I bent down and folded my legs to sit. She lit the fire with something that looked like a large match before she sat back and took a sip from the flask. I did the same, looking down at my feet, the tops of which were raw and charred, the skin around the edges looking like cooled wax melting down the sides of my feet. I held my flask out and dropped a few drops of pearl water onto the tops of my feet. The drops landed and ran through the fresh cracks, leaving behind pink scars in their wake. Satisfied with this and after taking another swig from the pearl-water flask, I looked over to Nadira, who had rolled up her wet and torn pants, to pour the pearl-water down her lower legs. The shallow cuts near her knees quickly turned pink under the water, the clear liquid running down her shins and calves, pooling at her feet. The cuts there took longer to heal, turning a much darker shade of pink, similar to the cuts on my palms when they first healed.

Nadira exhaled in relief, eyelids blinking slowly. It was morning but the nights here were short and the days were long, and neither of us had slept much last night. Nadira looked over at me sheepishly, me pretending to examine the room about us, the morning light streaming through the windows, not having been up long enough to heat up the walls of the building. I started to shiver, apparently having recovered enough to start feeling the cold. Nadira saw this and started to stand slowly, taking small steps to test out the regained strength of her feet. Satisfied, she unrolled her pants and took them off, wringing them out, and laying them over a rack next to the fire, before starting with her coat.

"What are you doing?"

I croaked, surprised by the sudden lack of pants, trying not to look at Nadira's exposed underwear. Nadira smirked, amused by my bashfulness.

"I can't walk around in wet clothes now can I? You shouldn't either. It would be silly of us to make it this far only to die of something like pneumonia."

I couldn't argue with that. Nadira continued to remove her wet coat, and I started removing mine. I was used to undressing in front of people, thanks to the cramped recruits' quarters aboard Cronus, but they were all men. This was the girl who had just saved my life; a woman with bright green eyes and a fierce intelligence, whose green eyes now flickered in the firelight, reminding me of all the questions I had for her.

"You've been following me since I crashed here."

I stated, my suspicion almost greater than the other kinds of feelings that were rising as Nadira continued unbuttoning her shirt, having undone enough for me to realise it was her final layer. I blushed as I tried to focus only on her eyes, waiting for an answer.

"Yes." She paused, hoping that that was enough, but when I didn't move, she sighed and continued, "I go out to all the crashed ships. This building is right at the edge of the city. It makes it easy to watch from, but I never seem to get there first. It's always someone else."

She looked back at me with curiosity, now undoing the last buttons on her shirt, and removing it entirely. This planet seemed to have underwear, but no bras. At least in my extremely limited experience that was based entirely off of this moment. Nadria continued, seemingly not knowing that she was mostly naked, or at least not caring.

"It's very rare that someone makes it back to the city. Even when Jezebel doesn't find them, someone else does, or they don't survive the crash, or I don't find them in time, and they die in the dunes."

Nadira strode over to the small chest, pulled out a thick blanket made of an unfamiliar material, and wrapped it around herself. She then sat down with her back to the fire, facing me. I hadn't really looked until now, as at first it was dark, and then I was about to die, but as her hazelnut hair dried in front of the fire, draped over the back of the blanket, I noticed the streaks of gold running through it, and the way it started to curl slightly as it dried. She raised her eyebrows at me, like she was expecting a response, and I had to recall what she had just said.

"Yeah…wait, who is Jezebel?"

72

She raised her eyebrows at me like the answer was obvious and said nothing, waiting for me to figure it out.

"Oh, that's the name of crazy priestess that tried to kill us isn't it."

"Yes, Priestess Jezebel. The crazy bitch who murders outsiders in the name of purity and would murder anyone who resonates with so-called lesser gems if she had the opportunity."

"But why? Why on Earth would someone want to kill people just because of the rock they resonate with?"

"Because she's a diamond. They all think that that means they're perfect, and that everybody else are sinners. Gemstones have nothing to do with morals, and she's proof."

Nadira was mad now, jaw clenched, looking past me remembering something. She must have had personal encounters with Jezebel before.

"I understand how she can get away with the murder of pilots from other worlds, but she tried to murder us, to murder you and Ava. You both live in this city and are citizens, and you lived to talk about it. Surely she can be brought to some kind of justice."

She smiled sadly at my naivety.

"Trust me, I've tried. But she is a diamond, and even parliament won't go against a diamond. At least not for something as small as *attempted* murder."

"You have parliament here?"

"Well, we have to have some sort of governance don't we? Even if they never seem to focus on what's actually important."

I chuckled, Nadira raising an eyebrow at me as I did.

"That part is pretty much the same as my world."

She chuckled too, and we sat there, smiling at each other, both of us becoming too tired to talk anymore. She looked me up and down, seeing me still shivering, having gotten distracted while undressing, and still wearing pants and a shirt.

"You're going to freeze if you keep those on. You need to take them off."

I blushed as she said this, remembering that she was wearing nothing but a blanket and a thin pair of underwear. She noticed me blushing and rolled her eyes.

"Don't worry, I won't look then."

She laid down in front of the fire facing away from me, her arms poking out of the blanket, exposing her bare shoulders and back. I wasn't sure this was much better, but I stayed silent, awkwardly undressing to my underwear and throwing my wet clothes over the rack in front of the fire. I stood there, unsure of what to do next, but eventually decided to go and look for a second blanket in the small chest Nadira had pulled the first one out of. I walked over and peered inside, finding no blankets.

"There's only one. You'll have to scooch up behind me."

Nadira said over her shoulder with a small grin, looking up at me from across the room on the floor. I was shivering much harder now with no clothes on and away from the fire, the morning sun through the small windows doing very little to warm me. I shuffled back over to Nadira and hesitantly lifted the section of blanket behind her, revealing her bare back. I laid down behind her, just close enough to be under the blanket, but not close enough that we were touching.

"We'll be warmer if we're closer," Nadira said, almost at a whisper. I shuffled a few centimeters closer and stopped. I could almost hear her roll her eyes before she shuffled backwards, pressing her back into my bare chest and her butt into the curve of my hips, our skin touching. I stopped shivering. She reached around and grabbed my hand, bringing it over her and up to her chest, trapping it there. Our bodies were now entwined, skin on skin, with only two thin layers of fabric separating us in the one spot that made all the difference. She was right, this was much warmer, and I no longer had the energy to be embarrassed or scared, as the warmth of her body combined with the fire made my thoughts melt away. The tension eased as I leaned into her and she leaned into me, my mind drifting to sleep.

Chapter 5

I woke, lying on my back on the floor, looking up at the ceiling. For a moment I thought my lungs were still tense from the vibrations in the dunes, but looked down instead to find Nadira with her head on my chest, her breasts pressed into my ribs, making me realise that my broken ribs were almost healed, now only a light bruise, before my thoughts rapidly returned to the naked girl lying on top of me. I tried to move my arm from above my head, only to find Nadira's arm on top of it, stretched out in the same direction like she'd purposefully pinned it there. I found my other arm free, seeing that Nadira's arm was pointed down, running parallel to my side. Her hand was still, but I could feel the tips of her fingers touching my butt. I brought up my free arm, finding that I had no idea what to do with it next. Nadira was still asleep. I didn't have to ponder my next move for very long, however, as all my wriggling about must have woken her up. She moved slowly, without opening her eyes, starting to move her hand away from my butt, but dragged it lightly across my skin all the way from my hip to my peck where she lifted her hand to rub her eye. She blinked her eyes open, lifting her head and seeing me. We stared at each other, her face now just as red as mine. For someone who was so confident getting naked and telling me to strip down and sleep next to her, she clearly wasn't expecting to wake up like this, lying on my chest. It was nice to know that she could feel embarrassment though. I was starting to doubt it.

She got up quickly, her breasts pressing further into my ribcage as she leaned forward to push herself off the floor. She grabbed the blanket in the same movement to wrap around her, leaving me lying there on the floor in my underwear.

"Sorry." She whispered, fiddling with the edge of the blanket. I smiled, watching the sun hit her messy hair through the small window.

"I didn't mind."

She went even redder when I said this, causing me to smile even wider. She got up, turning away, only dropping the blanket when she got to the small chest where she folded it and put it away. I sat up then, taking the opportunity to grab my pants from the rack by the fire and pull them on. They were at least dry now, but the hems had been destroyed. The bottom of the pant legs had been burnt off, making them look more like shorts than pants. Nadira turned around, making her way to her clothes on the rack by the fire. We continued to get dressed in silence, both of us finding tears and burns in our clothes we hadn't noticed before. When we were both dressed and standing there awkwardly, I spoke first.

"How long were we asleep?"

Nadira strode over to the window, sticking her head out.

"About six hours it looks like."

She turned back to me, thinking.

"If we were still in the dunes right now, we would be dead, but we wouldn't have dissolved into sand just yet. If Jezebel was going to check to make sure that we had died, she would do so about now or in the next few hours."

"So, what does that mean for us?"

"I'm not sure."

She looked down at her torn pants, the hundreds of little cuts that now covered her legs, mirrored on her pants.

"But we both need new clothes for starters."

I looked down at my clothes, remembering that they belonged to Achan, and I had no idea how he would respond when he saw the condition they were in. Hopefully, Ava had escaped and filled him in. That is if Ava had made it back to the house. She hadn't come back for us, which had made me worried that either she was too afraid, or didn't care enough to come back, or she didn't make it back herself. I was choosing to believe the more optimistic version where she had come back, but only after our escape. If this was true then she would know we were alive by the trail of blood we left leading to river, but anyone else who went looking would also know that we were alive.

"I borrowed these clothes from Ava's dad. I'm not sure if I can just keep borrowing his stuff, especially now that I've ruined his nicest outfit, but I have to go back and find out what happened to Ava. We're lucky we had each other, but Ava had to make her way *towards* the city alone, and with broken glass stuck in her feet."

"I understand, I can walk with you on the way there, I know the way, but then I have to duck home for fresh clothes—" she brought up her wrist to look at the spot where the garnet used to be, "—and I have some things I want to test out."

She looked up at me, peering into my eyes, searching.

"That… epicode, I think you called it, could be more useful than you think."

Her eyes sparkled, curiously lost in thought. I had nearly forgotten about how we had escaped the dunes. I had used fire magic. I had melted glass with my bare hands.

"Anyway, we should get going."

Nadira piped up. My focus snapping back to her.

"Yeah, we should."

We both paused for a moment in the room where we had just woken up naked on top of each other. I couldn't tell if I blushed or not, but the hint of pink on Nadira's cheeks told me she was thinking about the same thing I was, and we both knew it. She made her way to the door leading downstairs, grabbing a pearl-water flask from the small chest and replacing the empty one in her coat.

"How many of those do you have in there."

"Just enough it would seem," She replied.

We left the old building at the end of the city and headed back towards the centre, trying to avoid unwanted stares at our unruly condition. I was surprised to find that no one seemed to notice us at all. It wasn't as if we were invisible, but somehow, we were remarkably good at blending in, despite our appearances. We made our way through the streets of the city with ease, my joints loose and feeling alert. When we arrived at the Gehazi house, Nadira departed, telling me that she would meet me at the entrance to South-Fork, as she had somewhere she wanted to show me. She told me I could get there by following the river towards the city until I came across the next limb of the city, extending away from the centre on the opposite side of the river. She would meet me at the bridge that crossed the river into this section. Nadira slipped away into maze of streets, leaving me to knock on the door, wondering who would answer and what their reaction would be. And if Ava had made it back.

I knocked, and after a short while, Kalona answered the door with a shocked expression on her face. She hurried me inside and up the stairs where I found Ava sitting at the kitchen table, staring into space rather than engaging with the half-played through game set up in front of her. Her eyes went wide when she saw me. Ava jumped up and, to my surprise, hugged me. When she let go, she looked at me, bewildered.

"I went back. I saw the blood trail. How the hell did you escape? And where have you been?"

"I could ask you the same. You disappeared in the night. Didn't say anything, just left."

I looked at her, eyebrows raised, and she faltered at first, seemingly regretting her choices.

"I smashed the glass off my foot. I was in pain. I wasn't thinking about anything else. All I knew was that I needed to get home, and everything would be okay. Once I got the glass out of my foot and could walk again, I felt guilty for disappearing, so I went back right at dawn, but you were already gone." Her expression darkened, recalling something else. "I should also tell you that I wasn't the first to get there. Cybele was already there when I arrived. It looked like she was picking through the broken glass looking for something. Maybe trying to figure out what happened? I'm not sure."

Ava went quiet, assessing my reaction before asking again, "How *did* you escape?"

"That's…hard to explain. But you were somewhat right about the epicode and the natural resonance frequencies, just not in the way you were expecting."

"Oh?"

I sat down at the table and explained to Ava how I had escaped, my understanding of the connection between the garnet and fire magic, and what happened to Nadira and me after we went to the river. I left out some details about what occurred upstairs in the old house and shared where I would meet Nadira in a couple of hours. Nadira hadn't told me explicitly what she wanted to show me, but I had a feeling it was something to do with my epicode and it's apparent ability to connect to magic.

"Do you really think you can use different kinds of magic this way?"

"I don't see why not. Unless, of course, the gems explode too quickly. The garnet didn't last particularly long, just long enough to escape."

Ava pondered this, eyes sparkling greedily, knowing the different kinds of magic and what they could do, while I sat there having no idea outside of the lightning, fire, and healing I had so far encountered. Lightning magic would be pretty cool, but acquiring a diamond didn't seem easy, and letting it explode would be a waste even if we did. Kalona came back into the room carrying a tray of assorted foods, including strange fruits and more sandwiches.

"You must be starving, you probably haven't eaten since yesterday, have you? Here eat this."

Kalona set the tray on the table, moving some of the sculpted game pieces out of the way as she did.

"Hey! I was in the middle of that."

"Food is more important than games Avarita."

"It's more than a game, Mum."

Kalona walked away, not listening to Ava, and disappeared down the hallway.

"Avarita?" I teased.

"Yeah, that's my full name." Ava replied nonchalantly. I bit into a sandwich as Ava moved the sculpted pieces around on the board. Each piece seemed to melt into the thick wooden surface until only one remained, sitting on a square off the edge of the nine-by-nine grid. A lone piece sitting on an extra square by the board. There was a similar single square on the other side of the board, but it had an ornate carving of a door protruding from it. There had been so many pieces before, and the board had looked so complex. But now it appeared so simple, like a chessboard with only two pieces.

"How do you play?"

"What, proelium?"

"Yeah."

"It's a strategy game. You are this character here, and the goal is to get to the door on the other side, but you have to collect the three things required to open the door before you get there."

"Collect what? There's nothing there."

"Obviously. I haven't started the game yet." She sighed, "I'll show you."

Ava moved the character piece to the first square in front of it, causing a ripple of patterns to spread across the board, originating from that square. Each square now bore some kind of marking—a pattern, a diagram, even a riddle. Additionally, the carved door now had three symbols printed on it, and on the square directly in front of the character piece was a carved chryacal.

"The chryacal is always the first piece. It follows you around the board, trying to land on the same square as you, at which point you lose, but it can only move in an L-shape. Two squares in one direction, and then one perpendicular, or vice versa."

"So what do you do now?"

"We play."

Ava moved the character piece forward on the left diagonal, landing on a square that had some kind of radial pattern printed on it. When she landed, the board shifted, with squares protruding up in a radial pattern across the entire board, giving it a new dimension.

"When this happens, you can't move to the raised squares, but the chryacal can."

After the squares rose, the chryacal moved; forward one and over two, the carved creature now occupying a square by Ava's forward left diagonal. She peered closer at the board, deciphering the symbols and codes on the squares, before choosing the square to her left with the number seventy-eight printed on it. Four columns rose out of the board at the corners of the square she had just landed on, and a roof formed over the character, creating an enclosed doorway with only one entrance. An identical structure materialised on the other side of the board on top of the raised squares. It was the seventh square across and the eighth forward.

The only thing that was different about this structure was that there was no doorway, and the walls were translucent, allowing us to see the character piece inside. The chryacal moved.

"I thought you said we couldn't go on the raised squares."

"I said I couldn't move to them. I didn't say I couldn't teleport there."

Ava stated, not taking her eyes off the board. She grinned, having chosen her next move, and moved the character piece out of the teleporting box. It formed a solid doorway as she chose a direction to move in. As she landed on the next square, a silver-painted sword appeared in the character's hand, Ava's grin becoming more ambitious. The chryacal moved.

The game went on like this, with new pieces sprouting up, and the shape of the board constantly changing. At one point, half of the board turned ninety degrees, causing some pieces to fall while others stuck to it. Near the end, Ava had two of the required pieces to unlock the door: the silver sword, and the tail of the chyracal. While the chryacal was gone, there were four other creatures on the board now, chasing her. One of them was a 'diamond witch' which had a large cone of attack squares in front of her, making her particularly difficult to avoid. The last move involved Ava throwing the chryacal tail into the base of a tower near the final door, claiming she would pick it up on the way out. But on this move, the diamond queen spun around, moving her squares, and caught Ava's character piece within her attack range. This resulted in the witch sending out a spark, knocking over the character piece. Ava dropped her head and groaned.

"Every tiiime." She looked back up again and sighed, returning the pieces to their squares, the board returning to normal as the pieces disappeared. "Didn't you say you were meeting that girl soon?"

"Yeah, how long has it been? I haven't seen any clocks around here." Ava shrugged, probably an hour and a bit. It'll take some time to get there though, so we should get going."

"Oh, you're coming?"

"Of course. You blew up a garnet and used fire magic. I have to see this."

Soon, I had borrowed another set of Achan's clothes and Ava and I were on the way to South-Fork. We found the river and followed it along, getting closer to the centre of the city. Eventually, I spotted buildings peeking over the dunes on the other side of the river. As we neared the city, I saw the bridge connecting the heart of the city to another of its limbs. Ava and I stepped onto the bridge, walking halfway before stopping.

"I haven't been to this part of the city in ages." Ava mentioned.

"I wasn't expecting the buildings to look this old over here." I replied. The buildings on the other side of the river were noticeably older than any I had seen previously. The crumbling buildings at the edge where Nadira had taken me to recover were old, but these buildings, close to the city, were much older and still occupied, their designs hinting at a different way of life. I spotted Nadira making her way onto the bridge, waving with her free arm as she saw me notice her, her other arm wrapped around a bundle of clothes. Ava was looking towards South-Fork and didn't see her until she spoke.

"Hi." Nadira said with a smile, looking right at me. Ava spun around, locking eyes with Nadira. "I see you did make it back after all. How's your foot?" Nadira asked Ava, maintaining her smile, although more forced as she spoke to Ava. I chuckled, Ava raising an eyebrow at me.

"It's okay. And yours? I heard you bore the brunt of some exploding glass. Sounds nasty."

Nadira pinched her pants at the knee, pulling them up enough to expose the crisscrossing cuts covering her ankle and calf.

"Yeah, it was pretty bad, but here we are."

We stood for a moment before I broke the silence.

"Shall we get going then?"

"Yes, it's this way."

Nadira led the way into South-Fork, where the streets were less angular and more curved, as if they mirrored the river's bend in the city's planning. We followed Nadira through the city, with the buildings thinning out before becoming denser again, branching off to the left and right along the river, which seemed to loop back around to meet us. Before we reached the river again, we instead diverted off to the left towards a large building that wasn't particularly tall, but the exterior had large, curved walls, suggesting it was an ovular shape. The exterior wall of the building had a multitude of details in the brickwork, the most pronounced of which were the rows of arches. The arches were set too deep to even see into them, the sun at the wrong angle to penetrate them. We passed under one of the archways at ground level, finding light on the other side after wandering through the dark passage. As we approached the light on the other side, I wondered where Nadira was leading us and what this building was supposed to be. When we finally passed through the archway and emerged into the light, I found my answer, the three of us now standing on the floor of a strangely decorated arena. Rows of seats ran around the edges, following the curve of the wall, each tier getting closer to the ground, the closest row still too high to reach if you jumped.

"Welcome to the city arena. The old one anyway."

"I've never been to this part of the city before, but I've heard about the battles held here. Is it true there were traps hidden all over the floor?"

Ava asked, glancing curiously at Nadira. Instead of responding, Nadira flashed a huge grin and walked over to a nearby patch of the arena floor. She brushed sand aside with her foot, revealing dark lines carved into the ground. Finding what she was looking for, she jumped up and slammed back down, causing solid brick walls to shoot up from the floor, enclosing her in a brick box. I stood there in shock, not sure what to think, but carefully looked down, pushing sand with my foot, searching for hidden traps beneath me. After a few moments, Nadira popped her head above the brick walls, still grinning, before hopping over and sliding down the outside. Ava stared, mumbling something about proelium and history. Nadira began explaining, looking at me, knowing that I had no idea what had just happened.

"There are squares on the floor of the arena. Different obstacles or weapons that either help or hinder you while you battle whoever or whatever you're fighting against. They're old though, so you have to land on them pretty hard." She looked back over her shoulder at the brick box. "I chose this one because I thought we could throw the gemstones in there. It should be able to withstand a small explosion."

"Huh, good thinking. Do you think they will all explode?"

"Given that you're creating exponential harmonies with the gem's natural resonance, yes. At the very least you'll make them fall apart or break, but the ones that can withstand the energy absorption and build up heat will most likely explode."

"Oh, yeah okay that makes sense."

I replied, amazed at how quickly she'd figured out how it all worked. I was still trying to figure that out myself. She held out her hand, a large light purple stone with patches of dark purple and flecks of yellow scattered throughout, sitting in her palm.

"Here. It's cacoxenite. It's the resonance stone of people with telekinetic magic. It's not very strong, but it's a good ability to have."

I took the stone, staring at its yellow flecks.

"Oh cacoxenite, good choice." Ava piped up, having wandered around the brick box before noticing us. I looked at Ava, then back to Nadira.

"Here goes."

I activated my epicode, looking for the frequency that would cause the stone to sing back to me. As I slowly tuned the epicode, I heard a noise, seeing Ava clutch the bloodshot iolite sunstone around her neck.

"Whoa. It got warm." Ava frowned, concerned, "It's suddenly dawned on me that I'm potentially wearing a bomb around my neck."

She looked at me, hoping I knew what I was doing, and that I wasn't going to blow her up.

"Don't worry, I don't think anything will blow up with only one frequency."

"If you say so."

Ava decided to trust me, but continued clutching the sunstone around her neck. I continued tuning, suddenly finding the cacoxenite singing back, the stone warming up in my hand. I held it at arm's distance, walked around to the other side of the brick box, and placed it on the ground. I noticed as I was walking away, that the singing grew quieter the further I went. It cut out altogether once the brick box was between us. I stopped.

"What's wrong?" Nadira asked.

"I think the bricks are blocking the signal, I can't hear it on this side."

"That would make sense." Added Ava, "They are pretty thick, and infused with magic. I'm not surprised they interfere."

Nadira frowned, walking around the brick box, carefully picking up the cacoxenite.

"Maybe we'll just have to keep our distance." Nadira said as she reappeared, holding the purple stone. "Is this better?"

"Yeah, I can hear it now."

Nadira nodded, placed the stone on the ground and walked back over to us. She turned around, facing the stone, then frowned at me.

"Well, what are you waiting for?"

I chuckled, finding it strange how eager she was, and wondered why I wasn't more excited. She was used to this kind of magic after all, and I was the one about to gain telekinetic abilities. I turned back to the stone and tuned the harmonics. After the third harmonic, instead of the sequence taking off, it stopped singing altogether. I frowned, Nadira noticing and squinting at the stone on the ground. It was hard to tell from this distance, but the cacoxenite appeared to be in multiple pieces. We walked closer, Ava trailing behind, wary. Nadira bent down to pick up the rock, the larger chunks of what was left, crumbling into much smaller ones as she did so.

"Looks like I won't be getting any telekinetic powers."

I sighed, having prematurely gotten my hopes up after hearing about telekinetic magic.

"No, I don't think so. But at least this somewhat proves my hypothesis that only stronger gems would be able to last long enough to be useful. I started with the weakest one so we could establish a range of what works and what doesn't, with garnet fire magic being extremely useful, and cacoxenite telekinetic magic not at all."

Ava raised her eyebrows, impressed. "So, what your saying is the next one probably won't work either. That's if we are going from weakest to strongest."

"Probably not, but it might, even just for a moment."

I sighed again. "Ok then, what am I trying next." I said, hoping it wasn't something cool that I wouldn't be able to use. Nadira pulled out another stone, this one was solid black and angular, and a little bit shiny.

"This is obsidian. It's connected to knife magic."

Great. It was a cool one. "Knife magic?" I asked. Ava couldn't help herself, clearly intrigued by Nadira's choice of stone, responding, "Knife magic makes your skin tough enough to block a sword, or a knife, and makes your fingernails act like steel claws."

Dang, this was another exciting ability I wasn't going to be able to use. Ava continued, adding, "For obvious reasons, obsidians are the most likely to find their soulmate, given that they aren't very compatible with others. It can get messy."

Ava grinned, apparently finding this fact fun. I looked back at Nadira, not sure what to think. She handed me the stone.

"Make sure to put this a fair distance away, just in case. Obsidian is insanely sharp and an explosion could be deadly."

I placed the obsidian further away than the previous stone, finding the first harmonic before returning to Nadira and Ava, to make sure that it was still in range. In no time I had found the subsequent harmonics and the sequence had taken off. My eyes went wide in surprise.

"I think it's working. How can I tell?"

Before Nadira could answer, Ava had pulled some sort of knife from behind her back and threw it straight at me. I flinched, not having time to move out of the way. The knife struck me in the hip, deflecting off me with a clang. I looked down at the knife, and then to my hip, amazed at the absence of blood or any kind of damage. I picked up the knife, checking that I still had a connection to the obsidian, before dragging it softly across my forearm, hard enough to scratch the skin, but not hard enough to draw blood. I tensed the muscles in my forearm, the knife point suddenly making a screeching sound as I drew it across my arm, I pushed harder, the knife not even scratching my arm anymore. I withdrew the knife, staring at my arm, grinning. I looked up to see Nadira staring at the obsidian rock, frowning.

"What's wrong, it worked?"

"Exactly. It worked and it's lasting even longer than the fire magic did. I can't think of a reason why that would be the case."

"I'm just glad that it did. If I'm going to keep being hunted. This is perfect for self-defence."

Nadira frowned harder, starting towards the obsidian, but hesitating, knowing that it might explode and rip her to shreds if she got too close. Ava wasn't as concerned as Nadira and instead suggested excitedly,

"Oh hey, go test out the claws on that wall there."

I looked at the wall, and then at my fingernails. They were silver and shiny when I flexed my fingers, but not any longer or pointier. I walked over to the wall eagerly, hoping that my fingertips were sharper than they looked. I stared at the brick wall, suddenly sure that this wouldn't work, despite having seen the metallic toughness of my skin already. I double-checked to make sure I was still connected to the obsidian. I was. I lifted my hand hesitantly to the wall, placing it up high, dragging my fingertips lightly down the brickwork. My fingers didn't feel like weapons, but they left scratches on the bricks. I pressed harder, the grating noise becoming louder and tiny chunks of brick falling from the deeper scratches I was now leaving. I grinned, pressing as hard as I could now, swiping my hand the rest of the way down the wall, generating a scratching sound loud enough to turn Nadira's head. I grinned back at her, Nadira still frowning. Ava was delighted, still egging me on. I raised my other hand and swiped it across the wall as hard as I could, the obsidian taking that same moment to decide to fail, the small explosion muffled by my cry of pain, as my hand became flesh again, grating across the brickwork, cutting into me, rather than me cutting into it. I held my hand out gingerly, examining my bleeding fingertips and sanded-down fingernails. I looked back at the wall. The start of my swipe left four deep scratches and a fifth, shallower one, which all abruptly ended two-thirds of the way across the wall. Thin trails of blood finished the scratches, as momentum grated my fingertips across the brickwork. Nadira rushed over, immediately pulling out a pearl-water flask like it was an instinct. She didn't look at me, only at my hand, grabbing it and pouring the cool liquid into my palm, manually closing my fingers around it. She looked up at me then, those green eyes staring into my own with genuine concern. She blushed, realising how close we were, and I did the same as she turned away, her eyes having lingered on mine a moment too long. I turned my attention back to the obsidian and strode over to it. I unfurled my fist, always impressed at the ability of the pearl-water to heal so quickly. I flexed my fingers, my skin perfectly fine, but my nails still looked gnarled. I followed Nadira, who was standing at the edge of a circle created by flat shards of obsidian, the rock having exploded but only with enough energy to launch pieces as far as a meter and a half.

"Interesting." Nadira said, her frown slowly turning into a grin as her mind worked out a theory. "It's energy." Nadira whispered, explaining when she looked up to find Ava and I staring at her. "It's based on energy. Like just now, the obsidian only failed when you tried to scratch the wall as deep as you could, which takes considerably more energy than deflecting a knife for a split second. That's why it took so long to explode."

I continued looking at Nadira blankly.

"What about the garnet then?"

"Well with the garnet you were melting solid glass with your hands continuously. I have no doubt that uses a crazy amount of energy. So even with the stronger gem, you used so much energy so quickly that the garnet didn't last as long as the obsidian."

I nodded, understanding now. If I was going to try and use magic, I was going to have to figure out how far I could push before the gemstones exploded, ultimately hurting myself and anyone too close. We continued testing the magical abilities connected to the gems. The rest that Nadira had brought were all stronger than obsidian, so they at least did something if not for very long. I was disappointed to find out that pearls were even weaker than cacoxenite, so I wouldn't be able to use any healing magic. The next gem we tried was aquamarine. Nadira choose it only after she half pulled out a pink and black stone from her bag, glancing at me as she did the tips of her ears going red, before putting it back and handing me an aquamarine instead. For this gem, we went up to the top of the arena wall, helping each other up from the arena floor to the first row of seats. We placed the aquamarine a few rows below before making our way to the top of the wall overlooking the river. Nadira pointed at the water, explaining that aquamarine was connected to ice magic, and that it was difficult to use as the water slowly froze once you took control of it. The rate at which it froze also depended on the water density and shape.

"I don't expect you to make anything pretty, as ice magic is usually used for sculptures and entertainment, but I do want to see how much water you can freeze before the aquamarine explodes. It'll be much easier to visualise than fire magic, and it's not far off the strength of a garnet," Nadira explained.

I harmonised with the aquamarine, wary of its distance from us now that I knew the explosion would be close to the same as the garnet's. Before long, I could feel the flow of the river below, rippling ever so slightly as I wiggled my fingers. It was so strange to feel just how different all the kinds of magic were. They all activated in different ways and inspired different emotions. It would be hard to feel truly connected to them all, except perhaps the one I was truly resonant with. Alexandrite didn't seem to have any magic though. At least none that I could feel. Even if it did, there wasn't anyone who would know about it. I moved my hands more now, watching the river below as I felt the water wobble from the invisible pressure I applied. I curled my hand into a fist, clenching it, seeing a large ball of ice form in the river, now floating downstream. I grinned. I tried to fling the ball out of the water by throwing my fist into the air, but it did nothing. I tried again, this time creating a new ball, throwing my fist up as I formed it. The result was a ball that froze as soon as its lowest point left the top surface of the river, releasing itself from my control and plopping back into the river. I blinked, frowning. Nadira laughed,

"Like I said, ice-magic is a bit of an art form. Once the water has turned to ice, you don't have any control. That also means that once you separate it from the river, it becomes solid ice, and you lose control."

I thought about this for a moment, a new idea forming that might work within these new magical constraints. I reached my arms downwards, my fingers spread out, trying to grab as much of the flow of the river as possible. Then, I shot my arms up, my hands still outstretched, reaching for the sky as a large chunk of the river redirected upwards, following the line of my arms. Pieces froze and fell as the flow of the river made its way towards the sky. I continued pushing upwards, directing all my energy into one motion. The spike of ice began to form, reaching for the sky, and gradually slowed down before finally giving out. It was now fully frozen, with its peak protruding above the outer wall of the arena over our heads. The aquamarine gave out at this same moment, exploding behind us as the spike began to fall. Three or four stories of solid ice fell to the ground, slapping the river and displacing a large volume of water as it splashed down, drenching the few people who were standing along the edge of the river. This time, all three of us stared down at the fallen tower of ice, completely ignoring the explosion behind us.

"I hope no one is looking for us right now, because we've pretty much just told the whole city where we are." I said.

"I doubt it. Jezebel isn't one to go looking for the dead bodies of the people she kills." Nadira replied.

I looked at Ava and we locked eyes, realising that no one had told Nadira about Cybele.

"Actually, I don't know if Jezebel is looking for us, but Cybele might be. I don't know what she wants but she knows I'm from Earth, and she knows about our escape, I think. She was searching through the debris when Ava went back to look for us."

Nadira thought about this, then proposed, "She probably just heard the explosion and went to investigate. How else would she have known that we were there at all?"

"You're probably right. It's just strange that it was her of all people."

"Have you seen the museum she runs? It's all crashed spaceships. Of course she went investigating an explosion in the dunes."

"Yeah, that would make the most sense."

Satisfied we weren't being actively chased, we returned to the arena floor. The next gem we tried was topaz. It was the most straightforward of all of them. Topaz was connected to strength magic, which turned out to simply mean that I was really strong for a while, the gem finally exploding when I punched through the brick wall I had left scratches in, toppling it completely. The explosion was surprisingly forceful, kicking sand up and cracking the floor below, the boom echoing around the arena. None of us were harmed, except for Ava, who had a shallow cut on her cheek. After this commotion, Nadira said that she had one left to try but seemed hesitant to tell me what it was. After a moment, she pushed back her sleeve exposing the rough blue sapphire on a cord around her wrist.

"No, you don't have to. I already destroyed your garnet, I've used so much cool magic today, I don't need to break your sapphire just for an experiment."

"No, it's okay. I want to. I need to. This could be important."

She seemed sad but determined. I wasn't going to change her mind, and subconsciously I didn't want to. Sapphire would be the strongest gem yet, and I didn't even know what kind of magic it held yet. Ava just looked impressed, both that Nadira had a sapphire, and that she was willing to sacrifice it. Nadira undid the cord around her wrist, holding the sapphire by the cord out to me. I took it, noting how high the frequency to harmonise with it was, pushing the edges of human hearing. Based on the last explosion, I put the sapphire even further away, before coming back to where Nadira and Ava were standing to finish the cascading harmonies.

From this distance the signals were weak, and it was taking more effort to figure out how the gem was affecting my perception, realising now that Nadira had failed to tell me what kind of magic was connected to sapphires. Instead of asking, I focused harder and took a few steps toward the sapphire, hoping to increase the signal. My mind became clearer the closer I got to the gem, like everything just made more sense all of a sudden—the air, the arena, the floor. I bent down and touched the floor, having been drawn in somehow by its hidden complexity. I couldn't see what was beneath, but somehow, I could feel the mechanisms. I took a calculated number of steps towards the sapphire, rationalising how close I could get and the level of increased risk I was taking based on the suspected energy levels of this kind of magic, and the predicted capacity of the sapphire for greater energy absorption compared to previous gems, based on a linear scale. Then I realised that I don't think like that at all, and wondered if this was intelligence magic, but figured it wasn't because that sounded stupid. I took a few more steps, understanding the risk now, and becoming increasingly intrigued by the arena floor. What was more intriguing than the mechanisms by which the different components rose out of the floor, was the uncertainty of what would arise from each square. Each square didn't have a set item or obstacle hidden within it but something else entirely, or nothing at all yet, but would become something once it was told to. By my apparent subconscious calculations, if I didn't do anything that required more magical energy than I was using right now, I had about twenty-seven minutes left before the sapphire exploded. Plenty of time. I scanned further, trying to decipher some sort of difference between the floor panels that would determine the obstacles that appeared out of them, but continued to find nothing. I did, however, notice one square near an entrance to the arena leading towards the river that was slightly lower than the others. It was lowered about as much as the square that Ava currently stood on, indicating that the tile had roughly the weight of a person standing on top of it—not accounting for the varied degradation across all the different tiles, obviously. Wait.

I deactivated my epicode, disconnecting from the sapphire and switched to optical zoom, forgetting all about the arena floor mechanisms, only remembering the fact that someone was standing there watching us. I zoomed in with the epicode, the stranger walking forwards having recognised being seen. My eyes fell upon the figure of a woman, emerging from her spot in the shadows. It was Cybele. She had been watching us for who knows how long. Maybe she had only seen me staring at the floor as I was just doing, or maybe she had been here since the ice tower fell in the river. It was impossible to tell, but what I did know was that she had a smirk on her face, knew everything about where I was from, and that I could use different kinds of magic, even if it was only temporarily. She strode forward, unnervingly confidently for someone who was outnumbered three to one in an arena made for battle. I found out right then that I was wrong, and she had exactly as much confidence as you would expect from someone who seemed to be on the same side as the numerous chryacal appearing from the shadows at the edges of the arena, stalking out from all sides. I really wish I hadn't blown up that obsidian, or topaz, or any of the stones that might've helped us get out of this. All I had was the sapphire, and that seemed to only be useful for seeing the inner workings of things and understanding them. But perhaps it would make me temporarily smart enough to think of a way out of here. With an army of long-dead creatures and a smirk that sharp, I didn't think I was going to be able to talk my way out of this. I didn't even really know what she wanted from me.

"Hello again, Ender. I see you've learned some magic tricks. I'm impressed. It seems humans are even more interesting than that record made them seem. I mean interstellar probes, petrol, and chicken nuggets? Interesting. But learning fire magic in a few hours sitting out in the dunes and escaping from the most powerful priestess in the city? Now that's something. And I see you've learned ice magic and a few other tricks now as well. How did you manage that?"

Her smirk turned to genuine curiosity, the subtle glow of the red gem around her neck drawing my attention. The harmonic sequence took off as I reactivated my epicode, the sapphire's sequence having been saved for quick calibration. I could feel the mechanisms of the arena under the floor again, the tile beneath Cybele less worn than the one at the edge of the arena, sitting slightly lower. I glanced to the sides, at the chryacal seemingly under Cybele's control, and was surprised to see that they seemed to be too light to weigh down the tiles even a little bit. How curious. I looked back at Cybele, all of her focus on me. Perhaps whatever it was she wanted from me would be harmless. Maybe scanning my gem type would satiate her curiosity, but if that's all that she wanted, she would have no need for an army like this. No, she came here knowing that she couldn't convince me, and that she would have to get whatever she wanted from me by force. Whatever it is she wanted, she would not get. I dropped to one knee, pressing my hand into the thin layer of sand covering the floor panels, I could feel the mechanisms much more easily now, and while I couldn't activate them remotely, I found that I could make some adjustments. I sprang back up, having rerouted some of the circuitry below, falling back through the air, landing hard enough on the floor panel to activate it, but rather than activating its own obstacle, the patterns on the tile beneath Cybele, disguised by the layer of sand, disappeared, a rumbling sound erupting from the other end of the arena. All four of us looked to see what the source of the noise was, noticing a white stream erupting from the wall towards us. As it got closer, I could see the individual droplets that the stream was made of, shooting out of the wall in a line from one end of the arena to the other, passing directly over the square where Cybele stood, and blocking off the exit that she had entered through. She put her arm up to shield herself but cursed as the hot wax burned through the sleeve of her blazer. She snapped her gaze back to us, the chryacal pouncing. Ava began running as the chryacal made their move. She stepped too hard on the next tile and the ground froze in an instant, a thin layer of ice now covering nine tiles including the one Ava stepped on, and the eight surrounding it. She fell, sliding on her ass to the edge of the ice, three of the chryacal slipping too, sliding across the ice towards Nadira. Nadira stared at me wide-eyed, as unsure of what to do next as I was. Cybele had stumbled out of the stream of hot wax, and a line of shadowed figures with an assortment of bladed weapons mounted on poles stood behind the stream, waiting.

I based my next move purely on my statistical analysis of the arena. Watching Ava play proelium showed me how unlikely it was to have four obstacles, such as the ones that had currently arisen, in a row, meaning that statistically speaking the next tile should be useful. A weapon of some kind, or a teleport, or something like that. I shot a look at Nadira, who looked like she knew what I was thinking, and was ready. I faced Cybele again, taking a few quick steps forward and leaping to the next tile between us. I landed, the floor pressing down, a row of assorted spears appearing on one side of the square. I hadn't had much practice with a spear but there was a tiny amount of hand-to-hand combat aboard Cronus utilising poles. We primarily stuck to ranged weapons and ship systems.

Before I had time to reach for the spears, Nadira had grabbed one and was swinging it wildly at the chyracal who had caught up to us. They jumped back, wary of the weapon. Ava was scrambling away from the ice now, roughly in the direction of the sapphire still sitting out on the floor. I grabbed a spear, hoping Nadira could fend off the chryacal while I waited for Ava to look in my direction. She glanced our way for just a moment, and I chose that moment to throw a spear towards her as hard as I could, hoping she could use it. I didn't have time to check if she got the spear, as Cybele was mad now and striding towards us, not running, but maintaining a swift pace. Soon, the shadowy figures behind the wall of raining wax emerged, wax dripping down one side of them. The cooled bits cracked off as they raised their weapons. Cybele stopped. A single tile was left between us. I faced her, the six guards standing behind her and Nadira pinned by a chryacal. Ava was nowhere to be seen. Cybele smiled, seeing no way that I could escape now. I tried to assess the mechanisms in the floor, seeing if I could do something with the tile in front of us, but found that I no longer had a connection to the sapphire. It must have exploded but there had been too much going on for me to notice. One of the guards stepped forward, raising their hand towards me, purple gems embedded in his armour. I couldn't tell what magic he was trying to use, but it had to be some kind of magic, and Cybele was confident we would lose because of it. I had no choice left but one. I sprang forward, fingers crossed, hoping that this last square between us would be something useful, or at the very least something that would separate Nadira and me from Cybele and her goons. Goons that looked strangely familiar. I landed on the tile, Cybele's eyes wide with concern, but soon enough I couldn't see her face anymore as the arena flooded, washing the chryacals and Nadira away to the other end of the arena. I somehow stayed in place, falling over in the water, my face falling beneath the surface, but rising up again to see Cybele standing over me smiling, albeit through blurry vision. The blurry vision didn't leave when my head rose back up out of the water. Instead, it started going black at the edges, my limbs getting heavy. I fell back into the water, my body starting to drift away across the flooded arena, and my mind into the dark edges of my fading vision.

Chapter 6

I couldn't tell where I was when I regained consciousness, but I could tell I wouldn't be leaving anytime soon. I looked around the room, noticing first the leather buckles binding me to an uncomfortable steel chair, a harsh light shining down above me. I squinted into the dark corners of the room around me, seeing blinking lights and the outlines of various pieces of technology, guessing that these were different parts from crashed alien ships, based on the little I knew about Cybele. It seemed all I was to her was another crashed alien relic in need of being taken apart. The lights flicked on, filling the corners of the room with an even warm glow. Cybele entered what looked like a workshop where I was her prisoner. No, her alien relic.

"Hello, Ender."

She approached me, looking me over, shaking her head slightly and chuckling as she noticed the three new scars on my face, inflicted by golden claws.

"I see Jezebel has been knocking you around. I was impressed that you managed to escape her, but she can be a bit rash. I, on the other hand, have seen what you are capable of, and won't be making that mistake. That being said, I don't want to kill you. I'm glad you survived her. I have a lot to learn from you."

I glared at her, trying to be angry, but still feeling groggy from whatever magic her guard had used to knock me out. She smiled, perceiving me consciously registering the grogginess.

"Dream magic. It can put people to sleep, or make them lucid dream, or in some extremely rare cases, predict the future. But of course, you wouldn't know about dream magic. You only use the aggressive, destructive kinds of magic. The kind that's used to shatter glass and topple walls."

She was looking down at me now, with a look not of hate, but of disdain at my choices of magic. Not that I had chosen them at all. I could see now part of the reason why she was so keen to catch me. She saw me as an alien threat. Someone she couldn't understand, from another world, with technology that allowed me to abuse magic. Magic that I had so far only used for destructive purposes. I looked up at her, a sombre expression on my face causing her to frown.

"I didn't understand until now why you kept chasing me. But I get it know. You wanted to know who I was, and the longer you followed me, the more destruction you saw me cause." I bowed my head, realising that maybe it was me who was the bad guy. Every time I tried to play the hero, I ended up only causing more trouble. "Whatever it is you need from me, take it. Scan me, ask me questions, I don't want to be the bad guy, I just want to help." I replied.

Cybele looked at me in surprise, unsure if this was a ruse or not. She slowly pulled out a resonance scanner, and I made sure that my epicode was inactive before she scanned me. She only frowned harder when she read my gem type.

"How peculiar. Alexandrite is such a rare stone…but then again, your abilities are rather unique too."

I lifted my head and stared at her, my eyes wide, "You know about alexandrite?"

"Of course, I run a museum."

She blinked at me. Right, of course she did.

"What do you….what do you know about it?"

She smiled, clearly seeing that I had very little understanding of what it was or what it meant. She grinned.

"Why don't you tell me about how you're able to use different types of magic first."

I sighed but felt that we might be able to come to some sort of understanding, so I obliged.

"I have technology from Earth in my eye that lets me see things far away and use all sorts of scanners. I kind of accidentally stumbled upon a way to use it to augment the vibrations of this planet into frequencies that harmonise with different gems types, allowing me to temporarily use the abilities associated with those gems."

I finished, knowing that I had more details to give, but wanted more answers about my gem type first. "Now what do you know about alexandrite?"

"Interesting."

Cybele stared off into space, her eyes flicking back to me eventually, seeing the hard expression on my face, waiting for answers.

"Alexandrite is so rare, that it is said there is only one alive at any one time. Curiously though right now there seems to be two of you. The other is some girl, in upper gem society somewhere. All I know about her is that her father is in parliament."

There *was* someone else, a girl. I wasn't the only one. The tale the old woman had told me was true, and she was out there somewhere. I was too happy in that moment for someone who was chained to a chair in a historian's basement.

"My turn. This technology in your eye, is it only in your eye, or is it embedded in your brain or elsewhere as well?"

Shit. I could see where this was going. She wanted that tech, and there was only one way for her to access it and that involved her digging around in my brain and eye socket with scalpels and tweezers and the like. I had to do something quickly. The red gem around her neck drew my attention again, its vibrant colour and subtle glow giving me an idea. I looked back down at the floor, hiding my eyes from Cybele so that she couldn't guess why my eyes were moving in strange ways. I used the eye-movement commands to bring up the frequency augmentation mode, using my existing settings to look for the resonant frequency of the red gem around Cybele's neck. I didn't know if she had any magic, but she knew I could make it explode, and that was enough leverage to get me out of here. I started with the sapphires harmonic sequence, guessing that it was some sort of ruby and that it would be close. I found, however, that I had to tune it further down than I expected before Cybele flinched, and a clear note that only I could hear rang out.

"Ah, I see you've finally decided to make a move. How unfortunate. I was enjoying our conversation."

She gave me a sad smile before removing her necklace, walking over to a black rectangular prism located on the bench on the left. She opened a small door on the top of the box and placed the gem inside it, cutting off my connection instantly. She closed the door and locked it with a small brass key she picked up from the bench beside the box, setting it back down in the same spot before walking back over to me, explaining that, "It's the shell of a black box from one of the various spacecraft I've recovered. I think you'll find it's quite explosion-proof, as well as acting like a Faraday cage."

Damn. I should've known she'd have something like this prepared. She *did* just watch me explode a number of gems and now understood roughly how I did it. There had to be something else. Some sort of gemstone hidden within these ships that she overlooked maybe. I continued to tune down the frequency, Cybele looking at me smugly, knowing that I had no more tricks up my sleeve. The lower I got, the less options I had, the tone starting to approach the edge of the gemstones that I knew worked. Cybele moved over to another bench, ignoring me while she unrolled a long piece of leather containing numerous shiny objects. She removed one, inspecting it in the light, and I saw that it was a scalpel. She wasn't messing around. She wasn't even going to attempt some sort of messy surgery, just cut it right out of me while I was sitting in this chair. I started panicking now.

"If you're going to cut me open, couldn't you at least put me back to sleep or something?"

That was a stupid idea, what was I thinking? At least it would be a peaceful death maybe.

"Perhaps. But it's only sleep, so you'd wake up right as I started cutting."

So much for a peaceful death. I pulled at the restraints, testing the strength of the leather, finding it to be much stronger than I was. I looked up at Cybele who was standing over me now holding a scalpel, a still expression on her face, almost conflicted looking, like it was a pity that she had to cut my face open, but she still *had* to cut me open. A strange noise was buzzing in my ear, but I was initially too distracted to notice. When it became loud enough, I assumed it was just tinnitus or the blood pumping through my ears as my heart pounded and adrenaline rushed through me. However, as it slowly got louder, I started hearing the harmony. Having given up hope of escape and seeing Cybele approach me with a scalpel, I had stopped tuning the frequency augmenter, leaving it on the lowest pre-programmed setting: obsidian. Cybele bent down, deciding to make her first incision, across the top of my left eyebrow. The obsidian signal got stronger. Somehow it was making it's way towards us. It couldn't have been one of Cybele's goons. They would know not to bring stones in here, and probably wouldn't have stones as weak as obsidian. Surely it couldn't have been Nadira or Ava. How would they have found me, or gotten more obsidian so quickly? As the harmonies became louder, all I could do was hope that they were strong enough to stop Cybele's knife. She leant down, pressing the tip of the scalpel on the edge of my eyebrow near the top of my nose. I flexed all of my muscles, including my face, as hard as I could, trying to activate the knife magic hoping that it was enough.

"Stay still will you." Cybele snapped as I wriggled.

My muscles tensed and my breath stopped. She cut. The blade dragged along my eyebrow ridge, screeching as it went and not even leaving a scratch. Her eyes went wide with shock, immediately looking up and peering around the room, searching for the source of obsidian she knew had to be hiding close by. Her eyes locked onto the dark entryway, knowing that there wasn't any in the workshop, and that whoever had brought it in had to be lurking close by. She shouted out, glaring through the doorway she had originally emerged through,

"Whoever is there, you've made a grave mistake."

She moved the scalpel back up to my face, the point of the scalpel sitting directly in front of my left eyeball now. Somehow the scalpel felt impossibly sharp. I couldn't explain the feeling, but it was almost as if the scalpel was so sharp that even if it moved away from my eyeball, the air it cut through would become sharp enough to slice my eye open anyway. But that was impossible.

"Your friend here might have knife-proof skin, but his eyes are still as soft as everyone else's. It would be a shame if I had to scoop his brains out through his eye socket just because you decided to intrude on us now wouldn't it."

She squinted harder into the dark, trying to see any kind of movement. While Cybele was distracted, I shuffled my right arm backwards, trying to push the leather band as far up my wrist towards my fingers as it would go. I reached back with my middle finger, stretching it as far down my wrist as I could with a band of thick leather crushing it. Now was my chance. The relief rushing through me at this chance my rescuers had brought was quickly stifled by the adrenaline pushing me to escape and the threat in front of my eye that I couldn't look away from, for fear that the simple movement would slice it open just by being too close. With the knife magic, I could cut my way out of here, but my finger could only reach a few millimeters of the leather band at a time. The band got slightly looser as I cut away at it bit by bit, my hand slowly slipping out of the restraint. This was particularly difficult to do with a scalpel sitting right in front of my eye, the maniac wielding it threatening shadows to leave or she'd use it to carve out my eye and bleed me out through the hole. I stretched my middle finger back, feeling the last few millimeters of the leather strap that was binding my wrist. In one swift motion, I cut the rest of the strap, pushing myself backwards with my legs, and launching myself into the floor. The fall hurt, the hard metal of the chair clanging against the ground, almost winding me, but I managed to keep the momentum in my legs, swinging them through the air as I fell backwards, connecting my foot with Cybele's hand holding the scalpel as it swung through, kicking it across the room over my head. As my legs continued swinging through the air, I shifted my weight to my shoulder, making it easier to flip my head up once my legs had flown over my head, landing me on my stomach on the floor. I looked up, watching Cybele, waiting for her to make her move in the few moments that I lay there on the ground, reaching for my hand that was still bound to the chair to set myself free, but she just stared at me in shock, unmoving. Ava chose that moment to slip out of the shadows, lunging behind Cybele, and flicking her knife up to her throat. Cybele stood there for a few more moments, unmoving. She sighed once I was back on my feet. I was watching her intensely now, not sure if she or I were more shocked at this chance rescue, and with me having the upper hand for once.

"Get on with it then, continue your destructive rampage. Someone will stop you eventually and my death will only make that day come sooner."

I stared directly into her eyes, a hard line drawn across my face,

"I'm not a killer."

And I walked away, hoping that Ava wouldn't kill her, but knowing that I wouldn't be angry if she did choose to. To my surprise, I met Nadira in the doorway, surprised to find her hiding there, and even more surprised to find her eyes glassy and full of tears that hadn't fallen yet. She spoke before I could ask her anything.

"That was so fucked up…I thought you were going to die. I thought I finally… and you were about to get murdered right in front of me because I had come looking for you."

I looked behind me, Ava still holding the knife to Cybele's throat, knowing that if she chose to let her live, we would have to leave very quickly. Of course Ava hadn't come to save me on her own. It was Nadira who led the charge to rescue me, and surprisingly quickly too. Unless I had been asleep for longer than I thought. Nadira grabbed my coat and pulled me tight, uncaring of our precarious situation. I couldn't help but give in to it too, smiling as I wrapped my arms around her, feeling her warmth. I pulled back, snapping Nadira back to the present and catching Ava's stare as she stood there awkwardly watching, with her hands wrapped around a knife and the enemy. I strode over to the black box on the desk and unlocked it with the small brass key next to it, taking out the necklace with the vibrant red gemstone hanging from it.

"You know mine. It seems only fair that I know yours." I said.

Cybele stayed silent as I led the way out of the room, slowing down immediately as I realised I had no idea where I was. Nadira didn't miss a beat, however, keen to get out of there. She pushed past me, grabbing my hand as she did, and led me out of the workshop/dungeon. A few moments later we heard a muffled thump, Ava jogging up behind soon afterwards saying,

"Don't worry, I just knocked her out."

She glanced down quickly at us holding hands but decided to say nothing. We made our way through the dark halls, eventually stumbling upon a dimly lit room, one wall lined with books. The dim lighting emphasised the large bookshelf, making the bare walls of the room seem even colder and more barren. Nadira let go of my hand, a tiny sigh of disappointment leaving me, surprising myself as I realised how much I suddenly missed the shape of her hand in mine. Nadira strode towards the bookcase somewhere over to the left-hand side, searching briefly for a book around her chest level. She found the book she was looking for and pushed the spine in further on the shelf. The shelf clicked and a section of the bookcase in the shape of a door went translucent. Nadira stepped through the translucent bookcase, now standing on the other side in a well-lit and furnished room. Ava followed and I went last, watching the bookcase as I passed through it wondering, when I was on the other side of it, when it had turned solid again. It was just like the little teleporter in proelium. I pointed back at it with a weird look on my face, Ava laughing at me, and Nadira frowning at both of us with a confused smile. I saw the rest of the bookcase from this side, filling the entire back wall of an office that was furnished with a large grain-less wooden desk and an assortment of chairs and cabinets that filled the rest of the room. On the other side of the room, directly across from the desk, was a glass display case. Inside it was a large, light grey rock about the size of a bowling ball. Poking out of the rock were about fifteen large red hexagonal crystals with a few more hidden just beneath the surface, their existence exposed by their impressive vibrance, discolouring the grey rock from within.

"It's red beryl, Cybele's gemstone. This is her office." Ava said, moving to the regular door in the corner of the room. She was holding it open for us, waiting. "We really need to get going." Ava added.

Nadira and I hustled out of the office. I faltered when I realised that we had emerged onto the main floor of the museum. I was just now putting the pieces together, realising why Cybele had an office here in the first place. Of course this is where we were. This was the most obvious place to look, even if the 'basement' was quite well hidden. Nadira and Ava probably wouldn't have found me if I was hidden away somewhere else. At least not while I was still alive. I shuddered at the thought, realising just how close I was to being cut open in the name of science, or maybe just for Cybele's sick curiosity.

We hustled through the museum, from the back wall where we left Cybele's office to the front entrance, past all the exhibits, most

114

of which were alien spacecraft reassembled from their crashes. She really did have a bit of an obsession. We left the museum, all three of us stopping on the front steps unsure what to do next.

"It'll get dark soon, and I think we have some things to talk about." Ava looked at me directly as she said this, clearly wanting to know what Cybele wanted from me. "We should go back to my place and talk there."

Nadira and I both nodded, Nadira more hesitantly than I. The decision being made, we left the museum steps and made our way to the Gehazi household. My mind drifted as we walked, chuckling to myself as I imagined trying to convince Erwin that I wasn't lying to him as I tried to tell him about everything that had happened to me. I wondered If I would ever see him again. For the first time since landing here, I found myself genuinely missing home, or at least a few select people in it. The rest wasn't really worth missing. Not for an adventure like this. We continued winding through the maze-like streets until we came upon the two-tone building where flecks of copper sparkled in the bricks around the windows. Ava led the way through the front door and up the first set of stairs where we found Kalona and Achan both sitting at the table in the kitchen drinking what looked like tea. Kalona stood up when she saw us, rushing over to check that we were all okay.

"You're back, and you found him! I'm so glad you all made it back safe. Does everyone want tea? I'm going to make you all some tea."

Kalona was walking towards us when she got up but managed to pivot halfway through, heading straight towards the kettle instead. Achan stayed quiet, looking for an opportunity to bring up the thing he wanted to talk about. He found that moment once we had all sat down at the table.

"So, Ender, I hear you can use different kinds of magic. How do you manage to do that?"

He leant forward on the table, keen to hear my answer. I chuckled, Nadira chuckling too, realising how that sounded, especially after recent events.

I responded explaining, "It's because of this technology in my eye. I can augment the vibrations of this planet to match the harmonics of different gemstones, allowing me to temporarily use the magic associated with that gemstone." I adopted a more serious look. "That's about as much as I told Cybele when she asked. She saw me as a threat with my different magics. Which is fair enough when so far all I've done with magic is blow gems up and destroy things. Cybele knows the rough concept now so even without my epicode, I think she's smart enough to recreate the technology. Especially with all those ship parts at her disposal."

Ava and Nadira looked uneasy when I said this, but I couldn't read Achan's expression. He looked deep in thought like he was devising some sort of scheme.

"I suppose that's my fault though." Nadira looked up at me apologetically, "I only gave you stones connected to destructive magic."

"That's not true. You gave me a sapphire. It had, well I'm not sure how to describe its magic, but it was more constructive than destructive."

Nadira sighed, giving me a small smile.

"Perhaps. But by the time we got to the sapphire, Cybele had already seen you explode glass, mess up the river with ice magic, and probably punch down a wall."

I sighed, "Yeah, I know." I replied.

Wanting to change the subject and having a ton of questions for Ava and Nadira, I jumped right into them, "So after the guard put me to sleep, what happened to you two? And how did you find me?"

Ava looked hesitant to respond, but Nadira jumped straight into it, saving her from having to.

"Well, once the water took me away, I couldn't see what was happening. I don't know where Ava was, but I floated into the wall of the arena, unable to get up until the water drained. When it did, I found everyone else gone. The only thing left was a number of these little statues."

She pulled out a small carving of a chryacal and set it on the table. I frowned, but Nadira continued, "Cybele is a red beryl. Her magic is extraordinarily rare, but it allows her to make things seem more…real, or important than they actually are. Hence, making these carved chryacal seem much bigger and more real."

That would explain why they didn't seem to weigh enough to lower the floor tiles. Her magic could fool us, but not the arena. I remembered the necklace I had taken from Cybele and pulled it from my pocket, setting it on the table next to the little chryacal.

"Red beryl doesn't actually glow either. The magic just makes it look more impressive than it is." Ava added.

"Anyway, I looked for Ava around the arena, but when I couldn't find her, I came here looking for her. I found her downstairs talking with Achan."

She was watching Ava as she said this. Ava's expression remained still. Nadira looked back at me.

"From here we made a plan to look for you and decided that Cybele's office in the museum was probably the best spot to start. Oh, and we grabbed a few different stones from Achan that we thought might come in handy. Luckily, he had some obsidian which I knew you'd at least know how to use. That reminds me."

Nadira ruffled through her bag under the table, pulling out a shiny black chunk of obsidian, a frosted orange crystal, and a spherical black moonstone, which Achan threaded back onto his bracelet as soon as Nadira gave it back to him.

"Achan, I didn't realise you had magic. What is it?"

He smiled, "Oh it's nothing special, just metallurgic magic. I can separate alloys into their core metals. It's useful to a blacksmith maybe, but not for much else. Nadira here thought it might be useful if you were shackled, or behind bars that weren't pure iron, or something like that. I'm told that you're quite intuitive with new magic."

"I suppose I am."

Achan peered at me curiously. Maybe he was considering me to be his new apprentice? His expressions had been unnervingly unreadable since we arrived.

"Anyway, where was I? Oh right, so we went to Cybele's office, surprised to find it unlocked. Ava was the one who had the idea to check the bookshelf for clues and eventually we found the book that opened the doorway into the basement. It wasn't that hard once we figured that if there was a secret door, then the handle would be at an easy height to reach, so we just checked all the books that were

118

easy to grab, working from the ends inward. It wasn't hard to find you from there but… when we heard Cybele….and saw you…"

Nadira clenched her jaw, and I remembered the state I had found her in just outside the doorway to where I was being imprisoned.

"I know."

I opened my mouth to say more but I wasn't sure what to say. Luckily, Kalona had finished making tea and was placing the cups full of steaming liquid in front of the three of us, distracting us from the turn the conversation had taken. The tea smelled like parmesan cheese and honey. I wrapped my hands around the warm cup, noticing how cold the air had gotten since we first sat down, the sky outside the window slowly turning to night. Kalona sat down next to Achan, seemingly unaware of the conversation, starting up with,

"So, Ender, have you thought about what you're going to do now? Now that you've seen a bit more of the city and even met someone." She indicated to Nadira with her eyes, smiling subtly. "We're glad to have you in our home, but you've got more options than most, what with all your different magics."

Her implication of Nadira as someone I was dating caught me off guard, but she was right. I had no idea what was next. So far I had just been looking for answers and consequently running for my life. I hadn't had much time to figure out how to get home, or to envision my life here. I saw Nadira across the table, her face slightly pink, and her eyes a soft lavender colour now that the sun had gone down. I remembered then what she had told me back in the upstairs room at the edge of the city.

"I'm not sure what's next for me, or if I'll be able to get home, but until I figure that out, I think I want to help other pilots. Those that survive the crash into the dunes."

I turned to Nadira now, speaking to her, "I know you try to help, but can't get there first. Maybe with my magic, we'll be able to help them together."

Nadira beamed at me across the table, Achan's eyebrows raising as an idea sparked in his mind.

"Now there's an idea."

We all turned to Achan, not sure what he meant by this. He elaborated eventually, "Well, as you know, I search the dunes for metals to use in my work. But if I didn't have to go out there, I would have a lot more time in my workshop to make pieces. I'm proposing that instead of me going out there, you guys will, and scavenge precious metals for me from the ships. A lot of the ships are bound to not have any passengers, and you'll be there anyway. I'll help you get set up, get some proper shoes and desert gear, and I'll even pay you for what you bring back. It'll be much more efficient with your multiple kinds of magic, and besides you get to earn some money as well as help pilots. How does that sound?"

Nadira and I looked across the table at each other, smiling.

I added, "We could even use the money to fix up a building at the edge of town, to use as a base and boarding house for pilots."

"I'm not sure how many people we'll be able to save. Probably not enough for a whole boarding house, but those old buildings on the outskirts are outside of the city limits, meaning we're allowed to claim them and build there how we please." Nadira added.

It was all coming together. Maybe I'd even figure out a way back if I could understand how some of the other pilots got here. I was glad to finally have a mission, a purpose, and it was something I could be good at too. With the sun having set, I was starting to shiver. Kalona noticed immediately.

"Looks like it's getting late. Do you live far Nadira? We have a guest bedroom for you to stay the night."

"Oh, I uh…" She looked out the window at the night sky, her eyes a darker shade of purple now. "I live way on the other side of the city actually."

"That's okay dear, I'll go set up your room." Kalona hurried off, up the set of stairs that led to the third story.

"Ava, I think this is an excellent opportunity for you to start working too. I know you have big ambitions, but this will be good for you. Maybe learning about some of these creatures and their planets will help you one day too."

Ava weighed the pros and cons in her head, begrudgingly accepting. Ava frowned at me, the topic of other planets reminding her of something.

"Ender, what's your planet like. I never asked."

"Oh Earth? it's very…complex. Some places look a little bit like this, but most places look like the inner city, but with more steel and glass. Some buildings are a hundred stories high." Ava looked sceptical. I don't think she believed me. "But the places where there aren't lots of people have tons of plants and animals instead. Some trees are so big that some creatures never even leave the treetops. And there's lots of rain there and all sorts of weird fruits."

I sighed, getting ahead of myself. "But the majority of the world, at least where the people live, is all concrete. Like the sandstone bricks in most of the buildings here, but grey."

"How strange."

"Yeah, I suppose it is." I said.

Ava yawned, getting up from her chair, "It sounds like we have a big day tomorrow, although hopefully a less exciting one than today. I'll see you in the morning."

And with that, Ava disappeared upstairs. Nadira and I remained at the table, only heading upstairs once Kalona had emerged back down and beckoned us up. I finished off my tea, liking the taste but not at all understanding it, and followed Nadira and Kalona up the stairs.

"You two will be in here." She opened one of the three doors in the short hallway upstairs. "Ava's room is this one across the hall, and the bathroom is at the end." She smiled warmly, "I'll see you two in the morning."

And she hurried off back downstairs. I leaned my head through the doorway of the room, finding only one bed in the room. I hadn't realised that when Kalona had said she had a place for Nadira to stay, she had meant next to me in the same bed.

"Um, I can sleep on the floor if..." Nadira cut me off with a laugh.

"Don't be silly. You haven't slept without me since you got here."

I went red. She was right. I fell asleep in her lap the first night, and slept basically naked under a blanket with her the second time. If we stayed on opposite sides of the bed, this would be the furthest

I'd have slept away from her. What a strange thought. Kalona had left two pairs of pajamas on the bed. One from Ava's closet and one from Achan's. Nadira immediately began stripping down, facing away from me this time and at a faster speed, not having to deal with cuts and wet clothes. I copied her, facing away, but found my mind drifting thinking about her half-naked form behind me. I turned back around to find Nadira had hopped into bed already, laying on her side, facing my side, but with her eyes closed. I lifted the blankets slowly, and slid under the covers, laying on my back on my side of the bed. Before I could think about anything, Nadira shuffled forward, pressing her body up against mine and reaching her arm across my chest. My initial surprise melted away as fast as it had come. Somehow this really did just feel completely normal. I smiled, looking down at Nadira. I couldn't move my arm that was stuck between us but found that her other hand was resting in the same spot. I laced my fingers into hers and she smiled, not opening her eyes, but she pressed her head further into my shoulder.

Maybe Kalona was right. Maybe I had met someone. Part of me knew that I needed to get home. My family would have gotten news by now of my disappearance. I would've been labelled missing-in-action. They would all think I was dead. But the other part of me, the one with the most amazing, caring, and intelligent woman I had ever met lying in my arms, knew that this was the happiest I'd ever felt in my life. I felt important here, and I had the opportunity to help people, for real, and to do it all alongside someone like Nadira. I didn't really want to leave. I didn't know what this crazy journey would bring next, but if it had just a little more of this, then I would face it all with a smile fixed on my face.

Chapter 7

That morning, I woke before Nadira, trying not to move too much so as not to startle her. Somehow, we had once again become entangled. I was more or less in the same position as when I had fallen asleep, but Nadira had worked her leg over mine, sliding it in between my legs, her thigh lightly touching my crotch. Her arm was still draped over my chest, but it was slipped under my shirt now, her fingers stretched out across the middle of my chest. I smiled seeing her face resting on my chest, her mouth hanging slightly open. Her penchant for ending up on top of me had freed my arm that was between us, her having shifted on top of me enough that my arm was underneath her now, and free to lightly stroke her back. She stirred slowly, and I kept stroking her back, not worried at all about what she might think waking up in this position. Unlike last time, she didn't jump up with embarrassment, but she did lower her leg away from my crotch, and withdrew her hand from my chest to rub her eye.

"Good morning." She said sheepishly.

She laid her head back down for a few moments, sighing when she finally withdrew, getting out of bed and disappearing out of the room. What sounded like a shower turned on a few moments later. I got up and headed downstairs to find Ava and Achan already up and apparently having already been out. There were three brand-new pairs of thick-soled, tan-coloured boots, similar to the ones Achan was wearing when he found me in my ship, sitting in a row by the table. I frowned, seeing the boots,

"How long has everyone been up for?"

"Mmm three hours maybe?" Ava replied. "We just went out and got some basic supplies for the desert. I had a look for some useful gemstones but none of them were strong enough to be of any use. We'll have to go into the city. I was thinking Nadira could help us out with that seeing as she seems to be able to get those kinds of gems. A garnet would come in especially useful I think."

"Yeah, I agree. Wait, is there some kind of speed magic here? That would make it much easier to get to the crash survivors first."

"Unfortunately, no. Topaz would be the closest, making you stronger, but even with the extra strength, the sand would slow you down more than normal ground anyway. You should ask Nadira to try and get a topaz though."

I thought about this, wondering again why Nadira wore different kinds of gems, and why she seemed to have so many different kinds. Maybe, like Ava, her father was a jeweller of some sort, but for some of the upper gems. It was strange how little I knew about her, but I suppose she didn't know a whole lot about me either. I continued to think about this over breakfast but eventually got drawn into Achan and Ava's discussions about our new business. It sounded like we weren't wasting any time.

"You mentioned making a base on the outskirts of the city. Was there a particular place we should start? You did mention before the place you went with Nadira when you escaped Jezebel."

"Yes, I thought we should start there. I don't remember exactly what was there. I think the building itself was pretty stable, but the ground story was completely dark, so I'm not sure what to expect. We'll probably have to fix the windows at least."

Achan made a note of this and we continued planning. Once Nadira came downstairs, we informed her of where we were up to in the plan, and she added that she would go find a garnet and topaz if should could, as well as grab some more clothes and anything she thought might be usefulBefore we departed the house—Nadira towards the city, and the rest of us towards the outskirts—she handed me the flask of pearl-water she had taken out of the chest in the upstairs room of the building we were heading to, telling me to be careful and smiling at me as she departed.

Achan, Ava, and I spent the rest of the day on the outskirts of the city. Achan helped Ava and me clear the sand and debris from the windows of the downstairs room. It was only slightly larger than the room above but housed the bathroom and a small sitting area. We found a building next door with a wall that ran parallel, and we decide we would remove the parallel walls and bridge the gap with sandstone bricks, making the ground floor a large space with two bathrooms and two separate upstairs rooms. We informed Nadira of the plans near the end of the day once she had returned. By that time, I had cut down one wall using the knife-magic of the obsidian to carve out the walls. Nadira had returned with a garnet but couldn't manage to find a topaz. She did, however, say that she already had an amethyst, which she didn't think would make sense to test in the arena. But now that we were building something, it might be useful to help us design the building in some kind of collective lucid dream. I didn't really understand it until we tried it that night.

The amethysts magic was weird, especially when you were using it to put yourself to sleep as well as others. Miraculously I managed to put the three of us into one collective lucid dream. I didn't have much control from there, having to make a conscious effort to maintain the dream, so Ava and Nadira did a lot of the creative work, envisioning what we were going to build on the outskirts of the city. Apparently, neither Nadira nor I could help turning the room where we had slept naked together on the floor into our room. The dream version of the room showed the ghosts of us spooning in a bed that didn't exist yet. It took us a few days to bridge the gap between the two structures with bricks. We had rushed out into the desert when we had seen ships crash, some ships being empty, and others with pilots that hadn't made the journey. We scavenged from the ships, looking for precious metals as well as trying to find out their stories.

After a week, the main structure was finished and Achan had given us enough money for a few pieces of furniture. After we had stocked up on pearl-water of course. The first thing we went out and bought was a proper bed, allowing Nadira and I to stay at the house on the outskirts rather than continue relying on the Gehazi's hospitality. Nadira didn't always spend the day with us, saying that her family wanted her somewhere, or that she was supposed to do something for them. But no matter what it was, I always woke up with her in my arms, even if I had already gone to sleep before she came back from the city. Once we had set up what was to be our room from now on, that first night, I found the same butterflies returning from when I first saw Nadira topless in front of this fireplace. Now this room had a proper bed and I had proper clothes. The fireplace was the same, however, and Nadira was sitting in front of it in only her underwear, making me forget the rest of the world, and bringing me back to the first night we spent together.

I went and sat behind her, kissing her neck as I wrapped my arms around her, seeing her close her fist around something. I stopped kissing her neck, curious about what she could be holding. She spun slowly around to face me, her purple eyes staring into mine with a strange intensity. She looked down at the stone she had clenched her fist around, now revealing its colour and shape. It was pink and black. I recognised the stone I realised, remembering the stone from when she had half-pulled it out of her bag at the arena.

"What is it?" I whispered.

She let out a steadying breath, "I…I don't know what you know about soulmates on this planet but…well. I don't really have one. My gem…I just don't."

She sighed, looking back up into my eyes. I remembered what Cybele said, about alexandrite and the girl hidden in upper-gem society somewhere. I shook my head. Even if there was another alexandrite out there, that didn't make us soulmates. Besides, I couldn't imagine someone more perfect for me than the girl right in front of me.

"On Earth, we don't really have soulmates. Even with magic, it seems silly to think that I would have one here either."

She smiled. "I'm glad we found each other." She held up the pink and black stone. "It's a little bit taboo, but I thought we might be able to use this. I was hoping we could make this first night by ourselves a bit special." She smirked as she said this, biting her lip and waiting for my response.

"What is it?"

"You'll just have to try it and find out."

Her expression was bewildering, developing into a more seductive attitude that was already making me blush. "It's called rhodonite, it should be just above obsidian."

I hesitantly activated my epicode, watching Nadira curiously as she placed the rhodonite in front of the fire and folded her hands in her lap. I found the preset harmonic sequence for obsidian and slowly tuned it up, quickly finding the note. The harmonic sequence took off. Nadira seemingly felt the effect of the magic before I did, her lips parting, breathing in slowly as she tipped her head back, blinking so slowly I thought she had closed her eyes. As I took my next breath, I realised what she was feeling. My skin was suddenly heightened to a state of extreme sensitivity. The flames from the fire spread rippling waves of warmth across my skin and all the hairs on my arms stood on end, feeling the slight breeze rush through the window. I looked to Nadira, my eyes wide, and she smiled, her purple eyes melting my soul and imbuing me with a greater sense of warmth than the fire flickering beside us. She reached out her hand towards me, her wrist loose. I reached out in response, mirroring her, and she dragged a finger hanging from her limp wrist down my forearm towards her, my skin prickling, blood rushing to all sorts of places as the slightest contact set the rest of me ablaze.

As her finger reached my wrist, she grabbed my hand, pulling me towards her, setting my hand on her bare breast, close enough to whisper in my ear, "It's sex magic." At which point, I half understood, and half stopped resisting, giving in to the magic.

I fell forward on top of her, our lips meeting as we fell, her hand shooting up my shirt. The contact created all sorts of chaos inside me, leaving me with only enough room for conscious thought to wonder why I still had a shirt on. I didn't have to wonder long though, as Nadira's other hand joined the first, pulling my shirt over my head, our bare chests now pressing on one another, the fire and each other keeping us warm against the cool night breeze. Our lips only parted once the desperation for air became greater than the forces keeping us stuck to one another. We both gasped for air, using the gap to kick both of our pants off. I put my leg back down, missing Nadira's hip, causing us to roll over on the floor, our grip on each other so hard that she came with me, rolling over on top on me. She came down and pressed her lips back onto mine before we had stopped rolling, my lips parting at the movement, our tongues now tied together. With our tongues locked in the battle that they fought, I might not have felt the rest of me so sensitively, but the rhodonite worked its magic, revealing every square millimetre that our two bodies connected. It was easy to forget through all the parted lips and intensity with which we were grabbing each other, but it quickly dawned on me that we had both just lost our pants, the single muscle between my legs, squished between us, flexing.

Nadira now realised it too. She stopped and leant back, but only enough to look into my eyes, revealing the redness in her face, the rest of our bodies still entangled in one another. With less distractions now, it flexed again, and I noticed Nadira breathing heavily, nodding at me repeatedly, but shallowly. She picked her hand up from its grip on my shoulder, moving her fingertips carefully across my chest and down my stomach, making my breath shudder. She slowed her pace but didn't stop, until her fingers grazed the tip and it flexed again with increasing desire. She slowly wrapped her fingers around it, our gaze remaining locked on each other. She pushed her hips back, releasing the weight of her body on mine, every cell of my skin missing her touch. They forgave her moments later when her skin returned to mine as she slipped the muscle between my legs, in between hers, drawing her hips back to mine until they touched once more, allowing me to feel her from the inside as well as the outside. She laid back down, her chin sitting on my shoulder, wrapping her arms around me, and mine wrapping around her as I realised that this was the closest that two people could ever get.

We woke up naked on the floor on top of a blanket, and in front of the fire that had now almost gone out. After all that effort to put a bed in here, we spent our first night on the floor again. I chuckled, waking Nadira up. She opened her eyes, those bright green gems gazing right into mine, a smile spreading across her face that made me never want to get up. Somehow, even with last night's escapades, we still managed to wake up even more entangled than when we fell asleep. My arm was stuck under her somewhere with my other arm tangled in her hair. Our legs were intertwined, with Nadira's leg on top, her knee bent and her thigh resting across my hip. With our legs entwined this tight and the morning light spreading across our naked bodies, it was impossible to think about anything else but us. With our legs layered and our hips almost aligned, the muscle between my legs started to wake up too, pushing up through our bodies as they lay pressed together, making Nadira chuckle. Without saying anything, she withdrew her leg from my hip, and I assumed she was getting up. Rather than doing so, she instead aligned her hips with mine, pressing her lips into my neck, the manoeuvre startling me and causing me to fall on my back. Nadira went with it and fell on top of me, her hips pressing into me even harder now, her soft skin pressing into the harder part of me that yearned for attention. It stopped protesting as Nadira shifted and it found itself gliding through a slippery channel. Nadira teased me like this momentarily, chuckling as she watched my expression. Eventually, she slid too far forward, rotating her hips just a little until I heard her gasp as she pushed her hips back into mine. I noticed then how different the feeling was as she grabbed me without using her hands, my collective extremities feeling both the inside and outside of her as she undulated on top of me. The expression on her face melted as she closed her eyes and let out a few shallow breaths.

This was starting to feel like a honeymoon.

Eventually, we rose from the floor, both of us delaying putting on clothes as long as possible, until we heard a ship whistling through the sky and we knew we had to go. It wasn't long after that night that we finally managed to get to a ship with the pilot still alive and conscious inside. A week after Nadira and I had moved into the base, A ship crashed right when Ava was leaving. She instead came with us to the crash site where we found a man struggling with his restraints and trying to get out of his ship. We all knew from experience that it would soon explode.

I activated my knife magic and cut through the metal around the windshield, careful not to shatter the glass on top of the pilot. All three of us had to help remove the glass windshield from the ship, the pilot staring at us wide-eyed as we did so. I cut through his restraints next as Ava and Nadira stood on either side of the cockpit, dragging him out of the ship as fast as they could once I had cut the straps pinning him down. The man sprang to his feet, shouting as he knew the ship was about to explode. We all scrambled up the dune, and just as we made it over the ridge, the ship exploded with a force that knocked us off our feet, sending us tumbling to the bottom of the dune. Once we had scrambled to our feet, I locked eyes with Nadira, whose face was beaming with ecstasy at having finally rescued someone. I looked back at the pilot who was dusting himself off. He was a bald man with greyish skin, with rough lumps on his forearms that resembled scales. I was surprised to find that he spoke English, but then became more curious as to why the whole city seemed to speak English. However, it seemed the pilot had the same question about his own language. Ava explained that the magic here didn't favour any particular language, allowing everyone to understand one another regardless of how they spoke. There wasn't even an official language of the city because the original settlers all spoke different languages but didn't realise until much later, ultimately blaming it on the unique magic of this planet. I couldn't believe I had never thought to question it until now. I guess I was just so used to my epicode translating all the languages of Earth for me, that language barriers were hardly a problem anymore.

Nadira extended her hand to the pilot, offering him a pearl-water flask as she explained what it was. The pilot was sceptical until she applied the water to his cuts, leaving him staring in astonishment as they healed.

"But…they're…What's in this stuff, nanobots or something?"

I burst out laughing when he said this, everyone looking at me in surprise.

"I said exactly the same thing when I first got here. But no. It really is magic." I explained.

I extended my hand to him, unsure if handshakes existed where he came from, but to my surprise, he took it.

"I'm Ender, and this is Ava and Nadira. Welcome to…here."

"I'm Araysh, and here is where exactly?"

"Nice to meet you. I have no idea; I got here a few weeks ago. Now, if you haven't noticed yet, there are some pretty deadly vibrations out here in the dunes, so it's best if we get back to the city as quickly as we can."

I smiled and extended my arm towards the city. Nadira took the lead while Ava stayed back to take apart the ship's console.

"I'll see you guys tomorrow. I'll take what I find here straight back to Achan."

"Ok, see ya." Nadira replied.

I followed Nadira and Araysh back towards the base, the downstairs area having been furnished well enough to live in, but not decadently so. Nadira set up Araysh downstairs while I lit a fire. We had built a fireplace downstairs, given that we couldn't get regular lights being outside of the city limits and all. I listened as Nadira excitedly explained everything to Araysh as she set him up.

"So, this here is your bunk. Feel free to move it closer to the fire if you need to. We don't have much in the way of spare clothes yet, but you can borrow some of Ender's for now. I think they'll fit even if they're a bit tight."

"So, what is this place? Why are you being so nice?"

Nadira smiled warmly at Araysh. "This is a… like a…"

Understanding perhaps a little more about this kind of thing than Nadira, I got up and walked over to them from the fireplace.

"Do you have refugees where you come from?"

"Yes."

"We are the people who take in refugees and help them find their way on this new planet."

"Oh." He looked around at the empty room, frowning. "You can't be very good at it. There's no-one else here."

Nadira blushed, embarrassed. I continued,

"Admittedly, we only started doing this two weeks ago, just after I crashed here myself. It was such a rollercoaster when I crashed, and Nadira was already trying to help pilots." I sighed. "Most of the ships that crash here don't have any survivors or have no pilots at all. You're the first who's survived the landing that we've been able to get to in time."

Araysh looked down, pondering this for a moment.

"Well it's certainly not how I saw my afternoon going, but this certainly beats the death by neutron star I was heading for. I'm happy to help you guys out in any way you need."

Yikes. By the sound of it, this guy was having a rougher day than I was when I got sucked here.

"Out of curiosity, how exactly did you get here?"

He blinked at me, "I assume the same way as you, with the whole golden fire, inverted-black-whole-looking mess."

"Right, of course, but do you know what caused it? For me, it exploded out of the inside of a warp travel research facility."

"Oh, wicked. No, for me the anti-matter drive got scrambled by the neutron star and started going haywire. I tried to get out in the escape pod there, but the golden fire portal thing was faster than I was."

"Interesting."

"Do you think there's any way to get back? Preferably not right where I was when I got eaten and sent here."

"I'm not sure. My plan is to figure out how all the pilots keep crashing here and see if there is a way to reverse-engineer it or something."

"I see." Araysh raised his eyebrows, blinking slowly, before yawning. "I'm exhausted. I promise I'll tell you everything I know in the morning." He looked around at the room, seeing the city through one of the small windows. "As long as you tell me more about this place. Especially the magic."

Nadira's eyes lit up, "Actually I have a way we can show you around the city, as well you show us exactly what happened to your ship."

Nadira looked at me and I frowned, taking me a moment to realise what she was talking about. Dream magic. She wanted me to use the amethyst to get a full visual account of what happened to Araysh, as well as show him around without the risk a trip to the museum, for example, might entail. I think we were going to be good at this.

Araysh's dream account of his trip and subsequent crash here was pretty much exactly how he told it. There were weird readings on the heads-up display of his ship, all sorts of sirens going off. He was on the ship with another person, an engineer, who went to check out the engine, but opening the door to the engine room had only accelerated what was happening, causing Araysh to jump into an escape pod which he didn't check the launch trajectory of, finding out too late that he had launched himself into a spiralling orbit that would end with him falling into the neutron star. Although, he didn't have to worry about this in the end, as the golden flaming tendrils snuck up on him from behind, whisking him away to this place.

This account didn't reveal much that I didn't already suspect, but it did make me consider that the kind of warp-speed travel being developed near Saturn could have involved an anti-matter drive. Although I would need more evidence to confirm this, it was a start.

We went out the next day, to find some proper clothes for Araysh, as well as to find the relevant stone for him to wear. It was difficult to explain the whole wearing of one's resonance stones, especially given that neither I nor Nadira wore the proper stones. I had started to wear a flat piece of obsidian around my neck, as that was the kind of magic I found myself using the most, as well as the garnet Nadira had gotten me, around my wrist. Nadira had replaced her garnet by this point as well, and we had commissioned a matching set of silver bracelets from Achan to set them in. While Araysh knew the truth about my magic and Nadira's gemstone ambiguity, we decided to tell any new people that we were both garnets, simplifying the whole gemstone, magic, and soulmates explanation, even though Nadira and I weren't technically soulmates. It was also convenient in explaining that not everyone who resonated with a certain stone had the magic of that stone, as shown by my ability to use fire magic and Nadira's lack of it.

Araysh, it turned out, was an onyx. A black stone connected to shadow magic which was notorious for its use in crime, making it difficult to obtain, but easier to explain why we avoided certain parts of the city. Of course, Araysh knew the truth about everything that had happened, but going forward, we kept the stories quiet, letting the interstellar refugees who found themselves staying with us find their own way in the city. After we saved another pilot a few weeks after finding Araysh, he decided to stay and continue helping us rescue pilots in the dunes and bring back precious metals for Achan. By this point, Achan had collected so much metal that he began teaching Ava the art of blacksmithing—or silversmithing, really—since we had brought back enough silver for plenty of practice, with not enough places to sell it. Silver was a hot commodity but used mostly in upper gem society and they didn't like the idea of buying jewellery from a lower gem. Nadira, however, had a jeweller friend who sold her the rough sapphire she once had, along with other gems that weren't fit to be sold to upper gems. Through this friend, we managed to sell small amounts of silver in the upper gem market and discovered where to obtain onyx for Araysh. Shadow magic turned out not to be very useful in the dunes. It was only useful where there was an abundance of shadows, which happened to be mostly down shady alleyways, and primarily for theft or breaking into places, hence why onyx was connected to criminal activity. Araysh staying out on the fringe of the city with us may have meant he didn't get to use his magic very much, but it kept him from the paranoia and bias that people had against onyx's. Even lower gem society was wary, and they weren't nearly as pious or as bigoted as the upper gems.

The weeks started to fly by. Araysh moved into the other room above the main boarding house, and pilots came and went through the main room beneath. Some people stayed with us for months and others for only a week.

About two months in, Ava had started coming by to teach people proelium, as well as some history of the city. I occasionally played a few games alongside Ava and Nadira, but both of them always got much further than I did. I had been here for five months before I saw Cybele again, and under circumstances more horrifying than I had ever imagined. By this point, I had started giving up on trying to get home. All the pilots had similar stories, but with enough variation that it was impossible to pinpoint exactly what was causing the interstellar portals that dragged us all here. It did, however, seem to be connected specifically to anti-matter-based equipment.

I missed my family, especially my sister Hailey. Though it made me uneasy knowing they thought I was dead, life here with Nadira—helping people get on their feet, teaching them, using magic—was a life better than I could have ever hoped for, even with the vague threat of Cybele and Jezebel hanging over my head. A threat that stayed only in the back of my mind, until the day when everything started going to shit. The day that Cybele successfully recreated the way I used my epicode to use different kinds of magic. Except, she didn't use it to experiment with magic, or maybe she did at first, how would I have known, but no, instead she used it for genocide.

Chapter 8

One morning, five months since I'd first arrived in this city, I was sitting at the dining table downstairs, drinking tea and having breakfast next to Nadira and three pilots we'd rescued from the dunes. I grinned at Nadira sitting beside me, her grinning back with a mouthful of bread and jam. Halfway through breakfast, the fourth pilot who was staying here, sitting over on the couch, stood up suddenly, clutching his chest as he tried to take a few stiff steps towards us, gasping for air that wouldn't enter his lungs. Nadira and I stared at him, our eyes wide. Nadira immediately jumped up to help him, the other pilots swivelling around in their chairs to look. Before Nadira made it across the room, he stumbled and fell, landing on the floor as a pile of pink and brown dust. The five of us all stared at the pile in horror. Nadira turned back to me, shoulders slumped, eyes glassy, but with a horrified look on her face, unsure what to do next. I stood up and walked over to her, instinctively moving to hug her, having no idea what to say, not sure there was anything to say given how little information we had and the suddenness with which it had happened. The other three at the table continued staring at us in horror, starting to get uneasy like they were expecting it to happen to them at any moment. In the silence of the room, I heard hard footsteps landing outside. Someone was running towards us. Not sure how to react, I activated my epicode, holding Nadira close as her head whipped around to face the door, hearing the footsteps too. I had fire magic immediately ready, having lit the fire with it minutes before. The new refugees thought I only had fire magic, as I had explained the magic here using the matching garnets Nadira and I wore. Araysh had left earlier that morning to do something in the city. He didn't tell us what, but by this point, he was as much an independent citizen of the city as we were. The footsteps got closer, not slowing down much as they reached the door. The door swung open hard, Ava standing in the doorway, panting, her face red. She went to speak, but froze, noticing the fresh pile of dust near the lounge, and the expression on Nadira's face. Her expression softened, knowing the pilot who had just died. They had had a heated proelium competition the day before, with him getting closer to beating Ava than anyone else had, including Nadira, who previously held second place to Ava. Ava sighed,

"It's not just him. Everyone that resonated with talc has turned to sand. All of them. All at the same time. I ran here to tell you… but…"

She looked back to the pile, her eyes glassy but her mouth pressed into a hard line. Nadira instead pressed her face back into my shoulder, trying to disguise her crying, but I could feel the warm drops landing on my collarbone.

"How can something like this even be possib…"

142

I trailed off, staring into space. Nadira picked up on what I was thinking, looking up at me through glassy eyes.

"No, It's not your fault Ender. No one could of imagined she could use it that way."

Ava picked up her meaning, her eyes widening, hearing her whisper, "Cybele."

I clenched my jaw. She finally figured it out. She'd worked out how to augment the vibrations of the planet and tune them to different frequencies. I sat down at the table, everyone staring at me, my chin buried in my fists. I chose to focus on the puzzle rather than the fact that it was all my fault, and that my coming here, and telling Cybele how my epicode worked, is what led to this…instant genocide. She now had the ability to wipe out any kind of gem she wanted. But no, the real question was why. Why would she want to destroy a whole type of gem, especially talc? She wasn't eliminating any kind of dangerous magic, and she didn't seem like the genocidal type. Cybele was crazy, but she had reasons. Her reason for detaining me was to protect the city from my destructive magic, and then she tried to kill me to get the technology that allowed me to do that. Maybe blaming my destructive shows of magic was just a guilting technique to get me to talk, but still, why would she spend so long building this technology just to do something like this. This didn't align with her ideals at all. Unless I had her all wrong and she really was just an elitist psychopathic bitch… oh, of course. It had been so long I had almost forgotten. Cybele and Jezebel had some sort of strange relationship, and Jezebel would absolutely systematically murder half the city, especially starting at the bottom of the ladder, in terms of resonant gem strength, that is. But why would Cybele build such a weapon for her? Did she just not care about consequences? Or maybe she didn't know the destructive power it held. No that couldn't be it. If she was smart enough to invent it then she knew exactly what it was capable of. There were just too many variables. We were going to have to do some investigating. Even if that meant getting closer to the people we knew could now turn us to dust in an instant.

I looked up from my thoughts, finding the refugee pilots frozen in their chairs, and Ava staring at me intently, trying to figure out what I was thinking. Nadira watched me, concerned, knowing that I blamed myself, which was fair, considering it was all my fault. Before I could summarise my thoughts out loud, Araysh burst through the door.

"What the fuck is going on out there? Everyone is going crazy!" He trailed off on that last word, seeing the pile of pink and brown sand between the couch and dining table. "Don't tell me that's Tzargen."

None of us replied, the refugee's faces still frozen in fear and the rest of us with pained looks on our faces.

"Fuck." He turned around for a moment, gathering himself. When he turned back around, he wasted no time, "Alright so what are we going to do about all of this? Wait shit, do you think this is because of that...y'know."

His eyes flicked to the pilots, then back to me, knowing that they didn't know anything about our past encounters with Cybele or Jezebel.

"I think so. I'm just trying to figure out why she would do this."

One of the pilots spoke up, "Who did this, and can she do it again?"

I let out a barely controlled breath, not wanting to think about how frequently this could happen, and how many more times it would happen, all because of me.

"I don't know anything for sure. I only have a suspicion that a dangerous woman named Cybele invented this technology and has potentially given it to an even more dangerous psychopath. Both of whom have tried to kill me at some point."

Nadira jumped in, proposing another answer, "Maybe this was just a test fire, like when you first used fire magic and the garnet exploded."

I pondered her suggestion.

"Cybele's much smarter than me and she already knew that the gems could explode if the magic is overused. She has invented this technology from the ground up so she knows exactly how it works and what it does. It's possible that this was a test fire, testing it out on the easiest target before going for more strategic ones, but what could she be after?"

No one replied, having no idea what Cybele could want either.

"If Cybele isn't after anything, then I think she might've given this technology to Jezebel, whose motivations for an attack like this, while corrupt, are at least not a mystery."

"But what would Cybele's motivation be for giving this to Jezebel? She must've known this is what she would do with it," Ava asked.

I thought some more, only coming up with more questions and no answers.

"What I want to know is what's currently being done to stop another attack." I said.

Nadira scoffed. "By who? Parliament?"

Ava and I both looked at her, dead serious about her suggestion.

"You can't be serious." She shook her head. "Parliament won't do anything about this. They never do. If it is Jezebel, they definitely won't. She's a diamond. She'd have to do much worse for them to make any sort of move against her, and if its Cybele, well, it won't really matter anyway because chances are they won't ever find out about this attack."

"Why wouldn't they find out?"

"They don't care about lower gems. They might be less obvious in their distaste for and distrust in lower gems than Jezebel, but they'll all be secretly glad that there's less 'lowers' to worry about. Besides, no one would even tell any of them that this happened."

"That's absurd, a whole type of gem turns to dust, and they won't even hear about it?"

"That's politics for you."

"Then we'll go tell them."

"They won't listen."

"How do you know?"

Nadira sighed frustratedly, "Because, my father is in parliament and he's an elitist asshole. They all are."

"Oh."

"Yeah. So just trust me when I say they won't do anything about this."

"So… is that why I've never met your father? Because you hate him?"

"What? No, I don't hate him, we just… don't agree on very much. He's a decent father, aside from being away a lot at parliament. I hardly think my relationship with my father is top priority now though."

Her face was a little red now. I wasn't sure if it was from being angry or embarrassed.

"You're right, but maybe you could convince him to hear us out. A weapon like this isn't just a danger to lower gems, but to all of us. Maybe if they knew that, they'd take a little more action."

It was Ava who piped up now, "You can't just talk to parliament. You might be able to talk to individual members like Nadira's father, but the actual location of parliament is a secret. Even if you did somehow manage to find it, you wouldn't be able to enter without completing the trials."

"What trials?" I asked.

Nadira went strangely quiet now. Ava however excitedly delved into it.

"Parliament is supposedly a group of a hundred individuals, each of whom completed a series of trials that tested their intelligence, strength, and endurance in order to join. Completing these trials means that you become part of an elite group with such impeccable judgement that the individual has just as much power as the group to exercise their will over society. No-one really knows how to find parliament or what the trials are, but people in upper gem society can typically find someone to give them enough hints, or some sort of endorsement to help them get there. I'm not entirely clear on that part as lower-gem society is severely deterred from even trying to join parliament given how many upper gems die trying. It's considered a death sentence for lower gems to even attempt the trials."

"Wow, that's very different to Earth. Does parliament even vote on stuff?"

"Vote? On what?"

"Nevermind."

I turned to Nadira, who clearly knew exactly what I was about to ask.

"Nadira, unless you have any ideas to how we can stop this, I think we need you to talk to your father."

"I…the trials are dangerous. I don't want anyone to die, and so pointlessly. Even if you manage to join parliament. Then what?"

"Well, I suppose we would start by arresting Cybele. If Jezebel is so untouchable because she's a diamond, then we can just force to Cybele tell us everything. Maybe she even still has whatever it is she built and we can shut it down right there."

"I suppose that's true."

She thought about it for a moment, looking at me concerned. She sighed.

"I'll see what I can do, but it's likely not going to be enough. She stood up. "If we're going to do this, we'll have to be quick. I don't know how long it will be until they strike again, so I won't have time to go all the way to the other side of the city, and you and Ava will need to come with me. Araysh, you stay here and look out for these three."

"Yes ma'am." He responded.

She sighed, then pulled the amethyst out of her bag and handed it to Ava.

"You'll need to fit in where we're going, I think this matches your iolite sunstones closely enough that no-one will question it if you pretend like you belong there. We'll meet you outside in a moment. Ender and I are still in our pyjamas."

I had almost forgotten we were in the middle of breakfast. My tea was cold now, but I downed the rest of it and followed Nadira up to our room. She kept a pained expression on her face even as she changed out of her pyjamas and into her city clothes. I didn't have any clothes specifically for the city, but I did have my standard everyday gear, which had been designed with the help of Nadira and Achan, to be suited for the dunes and for combat. The vest had a removable strap with a small compartment sewn in, which housed a number of useful gems for combat and for quickly removing people from exploding ships. So far, I only had black moonstone, topaz, and aquamarine in there, as well as the obsidian around my neck and garnet on my wrist. It was designed, however, to be able to easily slide back what looked like a large flat buckle, to reveal the gemstones hidden there, which could then be easily plucked out and thrown to use as grenades, or if they were about to blow me up. I hadn't had to do that yet, but it sounded like I might have to soon enough.

I picked out the nicest shirt and pants I had, wearing them beneath my vest, making sure to match colours as best I could, knowing how weird upper gems were about fashion and accessorising. Ready, I turned around to find Nadira purposely procrastinating by feigning indecision between two pairs of shoes. I walked over to her and hugged her tight, which was clearly the right move as she leant her head on my chest and squeezed my arm.

I could only guess what she was thinking right now, let alone feeling. She looked up at me.

"This is a terrible idea." She whispered. "But I guess we have no other choice."

She looked off into space, absently leaning on me now. She picked up her head and sat down to put her shoes on. Moving with haste now, and a little bit of anger, "But I won't let groups of people just be murdered all at once. Whole magics even could die out just like that."

She stood up, slinging her bag over her shoulder with passionate purpose, "Let's go."

Nadira, Ava, and I made our way towards the city. Given that we had built our base at the very tip of one of the longer limbs of the city, it was a long walk before there was any kind of transport available. We made it to the entrance to the shopping district of the inner city, the same archway Ava and I had passed under to search for answers about my gem, alexandrite. I hadn't even thought about my true gem type in so long. As far as I was concerned, I was a garnet, and I was Nadira's soulmate, and she was mine. We entered the inner city, Nadira leading the way through the arcades and connected building lobbies, eventually emerging out onto a street that was unusually straight for this city. What was more intriguing though were the five large structures arranged in a semicircle at the very end of the street closest to us. The other end of the street looked like it went right into the centre of the city, marked by the tallest building in the skyline with a big pointy spire and a collection of reflective materials, evidenced by all the different shades of sunlight being reflected back at me.

"Here, this one here will take us to Norwest-Wedge."

Nadira said, pointing to the second closest box structure to us. I squinted at it, recognising the design.

"Is this a teleporter? It looks just like the little ones in proelium."

"Sure is. Just keep walking straight through it and you'll end up on the other side of the city."

"These would make way more sense in the actual limbs of the city, rather than just to cut through the inner part."

"Well, when we make it to parliament you can do exactly that. Probably. I don't really know how they decide who gets to use what resources."

I laughed, although it was short lived and felt strange given the kind of day this was turning out to be. We walked single file through the teleporter, nothing feeling different as I walked under the archway of the little structure and out the other side, nothing having changed except the entire scenery.

"Huh. I thought it would be more… teleporty than that."

Ava scoffed at me. "Teleporty?"

She wasn't impressed, and Nadira was too focused on where we were going to acknowledge that I had said anything. We continued in silence, presumably towards Nadira's house, or at least where her parents lived. We soon came across a courtyard, before we had left the inner city and entered Norwest-Wedge. At the other end of the courtyard was a building that, at first glance, looked like a six-storey version of the museum, with suspiciously classical architecture, columns, and golden chryacal and all. We started up the front steps. I frowned.

"This… isn't your house… is it?"

Nadira let out a long breath. "No… I… I thought that you and Ava should start looking for clues about parliament here. It's the oldest library in the city, and it's in the inner city. There's bound to be some clues here on an old map, or in a bit of history from the early years of the city. Anyway, I just have to talk to my dad alone. My parents are… difficult. I'll meet you back here when I'm done. I'm not going very far into Norwest Wedge. I'll see you soon."

Ava was frowning at Nadira as she spoke, but as soon as she turned to head off, Ava smiled and waltzed right into the library, leaving me standing there, bewildered at both of their behaviours. Was Ava not concerned about what Nadira was walking into? I suppose she did have a better grip on parliament and the history of the city. Maybe I didn't need to be so worried either. Either way, we had work to do.

I strode into the library after Ava who took a second to take it all in. I copied her when I saw that the very centre of the library was all open, a six-storey tall open space enclosed in rows of books, all the way to the top of the vaulted glass ceiling. Ava looked overjoyed, too excited given the circumstances.

"You do remember why we're here right?"

"Of course, I just…have always wanted to come here. It's always been so far, and I didn't have the right kind of clothes, or gemstone to make it here without being escorted out. But now, with this amethyst and these decent clothes I can finally afford, now that Dad's business is going really well and he's paying me too, it's all come together—just not under ideal circumstances."

"I get it. We do have work to do though."

"Luckily for you, I'm obsessed with this library enough that I already know my way around. Come on, I think we should start on the fourth floor with the architectural history of the city."

"Sounds about right."

I followed Ava up the main staircase that wound its way up the floors, hugging the edge of the rows of books around the central void. On the fourth floor, we hooked right, moving around the edge of the central void still, until Ava took us right into the stacks, stopping at an intersection between four bookcases.

"It's right about this area, so grab something that sounds like it could help and—" she peered around the edge of one of the bookcases, before pointing down the row at a set of desks, a study nook built hidden in the maze of bookshelves, "—take it over there."

I nodded and Ava instantly disappeared. Not seeing which way she had gone, I strode over to one of the four bookshelves at random, tilting my head sideways to read the words on the spines: *A History of Brick-making, Dunes and How We Built Upon Them, Chladni's Architecture*. None of these seemed useful. These titles described how the city was built, not what was built and where. I slowly passed my eyes over the spines of the books, looking for something that might give us some insight. Then I landed on one: *Institutional Architecture and its Role in the City*. Institutional architecture, meaning libraries, museums, cathedrals, and hopefully parliament. I took the book off the shelf and found an image of the same library we were in, printed on the front cover. I quickly scanned the rest of the shelves on the other side as I made my way towards where Ava had pointed, but didn't see anything else of note.

I found Ava sitting at one of the tables in the hidden study nook between the rows of shelves. She had a stack of three large books, the first of which she was scanning the table of contents already.

"Wow, you found three already? What are they?"

Without looking up, Ava half closed the book she had just opened to read the cover, before reading the spines of the other two.

"This one is *Secrets of Ancient Arenas*, and those two are an atlas of the city, and a collection of old stories, like folklore."

"Why would folklore be in this section?"

"It wasn't, it was just sitting on that table over there, but I grabbed it because I thought it might help."

"Oh."

I sat down, opening the book I had chosen, and searched the contents for any mentions of parliament. I got distracted however, when I came across the blueprints of Cybele's museum. I scanned the plans, finding that it looked pretty much exactly as it did now. Where Cybele's office was, however, there was an artifact storage room the size of the office as well as the empty room behind it. At the back of this room was a door than led down to what should've been more artifact storage but was currently a hidden workshop where a new weapon of mass murder had just been created.

I shook my head, slamming the book shut a little too aggressively, earning a stare from Ava as she reminded me we were in a library, and a library that she wasn't exactly supposed to be in. Not that there were actually any laws against it. I pushed the book away from me and took the book full of old folklore from the pile, wondering what kind of old stories people who used magic every day came up with. I scanned the list of stories, none of which immediately sounded any more or less interesting, so I started with the oldest one. It was a short tale, about a man who had crashed into this planet long ago. The city didn't exist at this time. The few who survived their ships crashing managed to set up tents along the river. At the time the man came to inhabit a tent by the river, the village was only but twelve strong. It was there that he met a woman, a ruby, for the villagers had discovered the magic of the planet by this time and had built resonance scanners out of the wreckage of their ships. The man himself resonated with painite, a rare gem that the villagers had not seen before. It was soon discovered that painites did have a connection to magic, specifically blood-magic.

The man put this skill to work as a doctor, helping the village prevent blood loss and performing transfusions and the like. One day however, the man and the woman had a child, a child which cried on the day that it was born, unknowingly tapping into the blood-magic of the painites, causing the whole village to drop dead from heart attacks. The newborn was left alone in the desert with no one to care for it.

"Eesh that was dark. It's not a great sign that that the first story I read from this book ends with everyone dying."

Ava looked up from her book, thinking, "Oh the one about the painite baby? Yeah, that is strange one, some say it's a prophecy."

"A prophecy?"

"Yeah, like as in that one day a child will be born that causes mass destruction one way or another. But prophecies can't be taken literally, and no one has seen blood magic in centuries."

I stared at her, unblinking.

"Don't worry about it, it's probably not true, and if it is, then chances are there's still a few centuries to go before it does happen. Our current problem certainly wasn't caused by a newborn, so there's no need to worry about it."

Even after five months, I was still surprised every time I learnt a new insane bit of history. Shaking it off, I moved to the next story, and the next, learning about ancient creatures and dead kinds of magic, even a story about a diamond and a sapphire who fell in love, but went mad, building themselves a fortress in the dunes out a glass, a huge tower rooted to the ground by the glass branches that snaked their way through the sand. The tower collapsed within two days, taking the pair with it. It was concerning how many of these stories involved people dying, with all evidence they ever existed, besides these stories, dissolving in the dunes. I closed the book, unsure what to think about what I had just read. The only practical thought I seemed to be left with was that the city must be younger than I thought.

"Ava, how old is the city anyway?

"It's hard to say given how much the population used to fluctuate, but the museum and the library are both about a hundred years old, maybe a little bit more. If I had to guess though, I'd say about three hundred years. Before that it was mostly tent villages spread out along the rivers. It wasn't until some of these got too big that people started venturing outwards. Some explorers from the south river and the northeast river met in what is now the centre of the city, and they started a proper civilisation."

"Maybe that means parliament is right under the centre of the city?"

"I mean it might be, but there's enough history and significance there that it's quite a hotspot. I think parliament will be more hidden. If it was under the centre, more people would find it easily."

"Yeah, I suppose you're right. Maybe a map of the city around the time the museum and library were built would help. This book shows the plans for those places as well as some others, but not parliament. Maybe there's a spot on the whole city map from a hundred years ago that looks suspicious."

"Actually, that's not a bad idea."

She opened the atlas, flipping through the pages until she found a map of the entire city from ninety-years ago. For comparison, she also marked a map a few pages further in that showed the city one hundred and sixteen years ago. As Ava and I examined the two maps, we noted their differences, like the empty plots where the museum and library should be in the older map, but both buildings were already built in the slightly newer one. There were plenty of differences just like that, as there was a clear implementation of infrastructure around a hundred years ago, but we didn't even know if parliament was the same age as these buildings. The cathedral, for example, was in both maps, and it was further north of the city than I was expecting, making me wonder how old it really was. Just as Ava and I were giving up on these sets of maps, Nadira appeared between us.

"It looks like you guys started down the right path without my help."

I swivelled in my chair to find Nadira almost smiling. I beamed back at her, glad that she was back and instinctively reaching out to hold her hand. Ava frowned, "We are?"

Nadira spoke as she sat down.

"My father had a lot of questions as to why I was looking for parliament, but eventually he told me that I should start with maps. Then he said that was all he could tell me, and that he was sworn to secrecy, and that the magic involved in such a vow was not to be messed with. Also, I should probably mention that he made me vow not to try to enter parliament myself. He was very adamant about this and used some kind of binding magic, so I don't think I'll be able to enter if we find it."

I had prepared for this anyway. I had access to different kinds of magic, and I was the one responsible for this whole mess. It had to be me. It was my fault and I had the best chance of survival.

"That's okay, it should be me anyway. I can use multiple magics, so I'll be able to handle a wider array of obstacles, whatever these trials throw at me."

Nadira looked at me worriedly, but resigned, knowing that logically I was the best option. I couldn't decipher Ava's face in that moment. Nadira slid the atlas across the table towards Ava, flipping the pages right to the very end, finding the oldest map in the book. The map was from two-hundred and fifty years ago, and yet the cathedral was still there, unchanged. The only difference now was that it looked enormous compared to the rest of the city which didn't quite fill the inner city area yet. There were a few indications that people still lived in the original villages along the two rivers, but none of the buildings there had been drawn on this map.

"Wow, how old is that cathedral? is it still there?"

"Yep, it's still exactly how it was two hundred and fifty years ago. I have no idea how they keep it in such good condition though."

158

Ava flicked her head to face Nadira, frowning.

"You've been to the cathedral? I thought that place was only for priestesses and devout rich people."

"It is, but I went there once with my parents when I was a kid. I don't remember why, but I was old enough to remember what it looked like at least."

Ava shook her head with a slight smile on her lips.

"You are frustratingly mysterious at times, you know that?"

Ava teased. Naira smirked back at her. We returned to the map, looking it over. I squinted, still thinking about the cathedral.

"Is there a map of just the cathedral at this time?"

Nadira flipped through the last few pages, finding one that showed just the cathedral, although a decent amount of the floor plan details were blotted out.

"Huh that's weird. But I suppose they wanted to maintain the privacy of the residents, so I guess it makes sense."

Nadira said upon seeing the cathedral plan. Did it though? All the other building plans were intact. Ava frowned again, and I started to think she just looked like that now.

"Hang on." Ava oriented the book to face her. "The pattern in the dunes, it almost forms a square. Maybe the missing bits in the cathedral create a puzzle, like the ones on the squares in proelium."

"Not everything is a game, Ava."

But the missing parts of the cathedral's floorplan were only absent within the almost-square created by the dunes, while the rest of the cathedral's plan was perfectly legible. Ava wasn't listening to Nadira's criticism, lost in the puzzle as she often was with proelium, trying to figure out what it could be trying to tell her. I watched her intently, her mind working away, and Nadira gave up, watching her too, wondering if she could actually be right. After a few minutes, Ava's head hit the table, groaning. Nadira and I sighed, having hoped she was onto something. Then, Nadira raised her eyebrow, a soft, "Oh." escaping from her lips.

She reached into her jacket pocket and pulled out a tiny, dark blue sapphire.

"I stole this from my father while I was there. He has them stitched all over his clothes, so he won't miss one this small, and it's small enough to fit in Ender's compartment too."

She handed me the gem, my jaw hanging open slightly, knowing how severe the punishment for theft of one's resonant gemstones could be in this city. Perhaps that's why Nadira hadn't done this before, only now when we were desperate for answers.

"Maybe we're not smart enough to solve the puzzle, if there is one, but there's plenty of sapphires in parliament, too many if you ask me, so I figured that this would help us in some way."

I held the tiny blue crystal in my hand, having not used a sapphire since that day in the arena. I looked around those in the study nook, satisfied that they were too entrenched in their respective literatures to notice me. I slid back the compartment slung across my chest, revealing the row of various stones set inside it. I slotted the sapphire into the next available space, slid the cover back into place, and tuned my epicode to the sapphire's harmonies.

A strange chill settled on my wrist, the constant warmth of the active garnet I'd grown accustomed to now gone. I focused instead on the map, staring at the plans and the missing sections. I knew the sapphires magic was working when the legend made a lot more sense suddenly and I found myself constructing a three-dimensional model of the cathedral in my mind using the dimensions on the plan.

I shook my head, trying to focus instead on the flat images, the missing sections. What was being said by the pieces that could no longer speak. I deactivated my epicode, the plan reminding me of something that the sapphire hadn't revealed to me, but my own recent memory.

"Ava, can you pass me the book of folktales?"

She silently handed me the book, looking at it eagerly, trying to think of what I'd discovered. I opened the book to a tale I had read barely thirty minutes ago; *The Wanderer and the Three-Pointed Star.* The story went like this: A wanderer travelled through the desert. No one knew for how long or what he was doing out there, only that one day he came across a village on the brink of becoming a small town. He stopped there for a drink of water. A woman who had seen him approach out of the desert asked,

"From whence did you come, stranger? There is nothing out there but sand."

"Yes, but sand sings songs. Songs much older than any bard in this village could know," he replied.

"Sand doesn't sing," she countered. "What else doesn't sand do?" The woman had no response. "Sand sings, as all the desert, and the next tale it will sing to me requires a long journey. One that starts right here."

The man bent down and drew a four-pointed star in the sand, then pushed sand over one of the points, leaving behind a three-pointed star with uneven spacing, resembling an arrow. He turned and headed out into the desert in a straight line, exactly in the direction of the middle point of the three-pointed star. The woman shouted after him.

"You'll die out there, and this star will fade into the sand!"

But the man didn't respond, having already disappeared over a dune. The woman remained in the village, occasionally remembering the strange man, and walking out to where he had drawn the three-pointed star, amazed every time to find that it was still there, unchanged by the desert's vibrations. Taking this as a sign, she built herself a house over the star in the sand, eventually forgetting about the man. Many months later, the man returned to the town, arriving from the exact opposite direction that he had left. The woman ran out to him on the edge of town, but stopped as she met him, having no words left. The man continued as straight as before, eventually crossing town and entering the woman's house, stopping in the doorway. She had something to say to him now.

"What are you doing? I don't know how you survived out there for so long, but you can't just come back and stand in my doorway!"

The man said nothing but picked up the mat just inside the front door, revealing the three-pointed star still recognisable underneath.

Then he spoke, "I have walked one hundred and seventy-six-thousand four-hundred and thirty-two steps around this planet, and the sands have told me the story of the world."

"What is it?" Enquired the woman.

He responded, "It is not a story for me to tell, but one for you to listen."

With that, the man crumpled into sand, filling the grooves where he had drawn the star, which disappeared along with him.

I closed the book, knowing that Ava would understand where I was going with this. Ava knew immediately why I had read that whole story, the tale revealing more than I had anticipated when I had decided to read it again.

"What's going on?"

Nadira asked, Ava all too eager to answer, jumping straight into it.

"I was right! For the most part. This story solves the puzzle. You see, the square in the dunes only covers three of the four wings of the cathedral. The three in the square form an arrow, like in the tale. I think if we follow the arrow made by the cathedral and take the same number of steps as the man in the story said, then we'll make it to parliament."

Nadira thought about this, me just sitting there watching her mind work, enjoying the quizzical expression her face made when she was thinking really hard.

"Wouldn't a hundred and seventy thousand steps be nowhere near enough to walk around the whole world? Let alone take him many months. We could do that in a few days."

"Exactly. It's a metaphor, but with real numbers thrown in. That's what makes it stick out, at least usually. Ender just got lucky that he happened to read that right before looking at the cathedral plan."

Ava pouted at me, trying to blame my find on luck to hide her disappointment at not being the one to figure it out. She was right though, that book was just here. It wasn't even supposed to be in this section. Nadira smiled.

"Looks like we've got a trip to prepare for then."

She stood up, taking one of the three books with her, but not moving any further with it, realising that she had no idea where to put it. Ava laughed, "I think the staff just come by and re-shelve them from here."

"Oh, okay. Wait. How do you know so much about this place? Have you been here before?"

Ava chuckled, "No."

But she didn't elaborate, enjoying being 'frustratingly mysterious' for once. We left the books on the table and headed out of the library, the inner city looking just as it had on our way in.

Once we got closer to the limbs of the city, however, we noticed a strange atmosphere hovering over the street. We made our way towards the archway marking the boundary between the limbs of the city and the inner-city shopping district. We couldn't discern what was happening until we passed through the archway and saw the new strangeness of the streets from the inside. There were twice as many piles of pink and brown sand sitting about, and fresh grief etched on the faces of passersby.

Chapter 9

"No, NO. Already? Fuck."

Nadira looked at me frantically, knowing only that a new group of people had just been murdered, by the machine whose creation I was responsible for. We didn't waste time asking around to figure out which gem had been targeted. Instead, we raced home. Ava and I practically chased Nadira all the way to our place on the outskirts of town. Nadira burst inside and dropped to her knees, crying with relief when she saw everyone still alive. Araysh had gone out when the commotion started, finding out as much as he could. Other than discovering that it was selenite that was targeted, he discovered nothing. Ava started thinking practically,

"At least now we know that we're being targeted from the weakest gems upwards. Plus, we now know how to get to parliament."

Nadira jumped up, "Yes, we do. We need to go there now. The longer we wait, the more people will die."

She started towards the downstairs chest full of pearl-water, but I stopped her with my hand. She knew what I was going to say before I said it.

"We can't just go there unprepared, you know that. This is parliament we're talking about. We'll have to face trials and many days in the desert. So many people die trying to do this, we can't just expect to knock it out in a few hours before more people die." I sighed, Nadira looking up at me, teary eyed, "If we die trying to save a few people, then who will be left to save the rest of the city?"

She knew I was right, but she didn't want to have to accept that more people were going to die before we would be able to save anyone. She planted her face in my chest, and I wrapped my arms around her, hating both Jezebel and Cybele, if for nothing else than the fact that they made her cry. Ava was the first to suggest a practical plan.

"I think… we should leave at dawn. That'll give us enough time to prepare, as well as let us leave while it's still cool outside. I'll see what Dad has that might help us survive the dunes." She adopted a pensive look. "I think I need to go check on them too. I know that they're still alive, but who knows how something like this will affect the city. I will see you at dawn. I'll… meet you here."

Ava left, and I thought it strange how she paused like she did, but I quickly forgot about it when Nadira pulled her face from my chest.

"Right, well, we should go buy some tents then." She suggested.

So, we went out and bought tents, and food, and bags big enough to fit it all in. I found it ridiculous with all this magic around that there wasn't a way to make everything temporarily lighter, or smaller, or fit into a magically bottomless bag. There were plenty of options, this planet was just stubborn. It was almost dark by the time we returned. Nadira tried to focus only on what was in front of her, turning her attention to menial tasks, making sure Araysh knew what to do while we were gone, as if he hadn't helped us run the place for almost as long as we'd been here. Despite her efforts, the weight of the day's events pressed down on her. Each task was a desperate attempt to distract herself from the gnawing anxiety and grief that threatened to overwhelm her. In the quiet moments before bed, Nadira sat in front of the fire, staring into it with glassy eyes, her expression a mix of exhaustion, sorrow, and hopelessness. The fire's flickering light highlighted the tear tracks on her cheeks, though she had long since run out of tears to shed for the day. The weight of their mission, the death they had witnessed, and the uncertainty of what lay ahead all converged in that moment, leaving her feeling utterly spent and despondent. I sat down behind her, wrapping my arms around her. She didn't move but continued staring into the fire. I whispered in her ear, "We have to get up early tomorrow and it's going to be a long day. We should get some rest." She stood up slowly, her hand fiddling with her waistband. She said nothing as she laid down in bed. I couldn't tell if she'd managed to banish her thoughts all together, or if they were drowning her instead. I laid next to her in bed, staring at the ceiling as she lay facing away from me. I knew we were supposed to be trying to get as much sleep as possible tonight, ready for tomorrow, but sleep wouldn't come easy. Not knowing that people might die in the night, and especially knowing how hard Nadira would take it if they did. I wouldn't say I was used to death, I certainly wasn't, but joining the navy required a certain acceptance that it could come for you or your friends at any time. I closed my eyes, trying not to think of anything at all, but found my mind uncomfortably wandering to the piles of pink sand by the entrance to the inner city, the people within jovially going about their day, while the people a few steps away grieved the loss of their loved ones. I was getting too angry to sleep. I didn't know if Nadira sensed it or if she was just too tired for her thoughts anymore, but she rolled over, stretching her arm across my chest. Her warmth and the thought of her next to me was enough to banish everything else running through my mind, leaving only the shape of the girl curled up in my arms.

The dawn came with an odd sense of calm and preparedness. I woke to find Nadira already lacing her boots. Swinging my legs out of bed, I did the same. Downstairs, we drank tea in silence while the refugee pilots slept soundly in their bunks in the corners of the room. We waited for Ava through the dawn, my frown getting deeper as time passed, and Nadira's breath getting shakier. Araysh came downstairs, finding us still sitting at the table with cold tea. He spoke quietly to not wake the others,

"What are you guys still doing here, and where's Ava?"

Nadira and I looked to each other. It was clear now that something must have happened for Ava to have missed the dawn, especially on a day like this. I had thought Ava was excited about finding parliament, especially since we had unanimously decided that I would be the one to fight in the trials. Maybe she had gotten

168

caught up in something. Maybe she had turned to dust. With this last thought, I pressed my mouth into a hard line. Out of the corner of my eye, I saw Nadira's eyes widen, knowing she had picked up on what I was thinking. She stood up aggressively,

"We have to find her."

"We'll go pick her up from her house then. But if she's not there…"

I didn't really want to finish that sentence, but Nadira and Araysh both knew that we had to go, especially if Ava was in trouble. Araysh spoke up before anyone tried to put the worst into words.

"If she's not there, you guys have to go, but I will search for her until I find her, in whatever state she might be in."

There was a moment of silence as we all imagined the all too likely possibility that we would come across a pile of sand in Ava's bedroom. I let out a breath, and grabbed my desert camping pack, Nadira doing the same and leading the way out the door. We began speed walking at first, but the suspense was unbearable. We broke into a jog—me drawing strength from the topaz's magic, and Nadira driven by anxious adrenaline. We stopped at the doorstep of the Gehazi house, dropped our packs, and knocked hesitantly. Kalona opened the door, her initial look of surprise quickly twisting into an unreadable expression.. She stepped back, letting us in, not saying anything. That wasn't a great sign. We filed into the kitchen where Achan was sitting, working away at something. His jaw clenched. Achan spoke, seeing the looks of distress creeping into our faces,

"Don't worry, Ava is fine."

We collectively let out a sigh of relief, Achan proceeding to ask an odd question,

"What do you know about Ava's ambitions for her future?"

Sensing this was going to be a long conversation, we sat down at the table. I responded, having known Ava the longest, if only by half a day,

"She was never particularly clear about what she wanted to be, but I assume some sort of proelium grand-master, or a historian. Maybe run the big library in the city, even if she doesn't have the right gem for it."

Achan chuckled, "No, but you're right about one thing: she doesn't have the gem to be what she wants to be. But thanks to you two, that doesn't matter now." He paused, not sure how we would react, "Ava has always wanted to be in parliament, to change the rules of this city, to be something greater than what the city tells her to be. Which is why she left yesterday. Right as she got home, she told me everything and left. She's going to make it through the trials and prove to this city that you don't need to be a diamond to be worthy of power, or decency, or money."

Fuck. She was going to get herself killed. Probably before she even made it to the entrance to parliament. How could he not see that? Nadira seemed relieved that she was still alive, but worried still, knowing that it likely wouldn't be for much longer. In an uncharacteristically severe tone, Nadira blurted out,

"You've sent your daughter to die."

Achan got visibly angry but kept his voice calm.

"Ava is talented. She's strong, stronger than those bloody sapphires and rubies that sit around in their palaces all day doing who knows what."

Araysh jumped in too, "I think she can do it. Ava is crazy smart, and stubborn as all hell. If she thinks she can get into parliament, I think she can too."

Nadira stared at the both of them, shocked.

"We had a plan. The three of us can survive the desert better than one of us alone. If she was smart, she would've waited until we got there at least to abandon us. She's reckless is what she is." Achan couldn't keep his voice as calm now, standing up at the table, leaning both his fists on it,

"I hope you do make it there. I genuinely hope you can fix this shit happening to the city. But I believe in my daughter, and if you don't, then I think she made the right decision to leave without you."

I felt like I should say something "I…"

They both looked at me, an intensity about both of them, "I…we need to go. None of this matters now. She's gone. Maybe we'll catch up to her, but I doubt it. But we still have to go. Even if she does make it into parliament, we can't sit around for her waiting for it. Besides, two of us can fix this quicker than just the one."

Nadira seemed like she still wanted to protest, but Achan cut her off,

"It's settled then. Go."

He sat back down, now ignoring us. Nadira stormed out, frustrated, letting it out once Kalona had closed the door behind us.

"I can't believe she would do this. We were supposed to be doing this to save the city from Cybele's machine, but she's just used us, and pursued her own self interests."

"We can't worry about that now. Maybe we can't catch up to her, but we at least—"

Araysh gasped, drawing our attention. He had a look of horror on his face as he realised what was happening.

"NO!" Nadira shouted at him, frantically trying to pull out a pearl-water flask from her coat. As she struggled, Araysh's expression softened, croaking out a whispered, "Good luck." before he dropped to his knees, and crumbled into a pile of pink and brown sand, swirling now around our feet. I stared in shock. They weren't following the ascending strength of gems anymore. My breath was uneasy. Araysh was the first person we had saved from the dunes. And now he was gone.

He was gone. Tzargen was gone. Ava had run off and Nadira was crying into the sand that used to be Araysh. Everything was going to shit. It was falling apart right in front of me. I thought I had finally found my place in the world, even if it wasn't actually *my* world. And it was all happening because of me. If I had never come here, these people would never have died. My breath shuddered again, and I felt a hot tear run down my cheek, my eyes going blurry, filling up with them. Araysh was like a brother to me. I had never had a brother, but this tall, grey man had been nothing but a friend to me since he arrived. Now he was dead, all because I had given a villain the secret to mass murder, and he happened to resonate with a gem associated with criminals. That's why they wiped out onyx next, and not whatever gem was next up the ladder. They'd skipped a few just to take out a couple of criminals. I'll admit it would have been a smart move, but they weren't all criminals. Probably very few of them were criminals, and certainly not ones who deserved death. But one of them was Araysh. I didn't care if it was Jezebel or Cybele pulling the trigger; they both deserved to die for their part in this. Nadira felt my tear land on her shoulder, and she had looked up at me from the remains of Araysh on the ground, surprised to see me crying, the look of surprise on her face reminding me that I hadn't cried once since I had come here. She'd never seen me cry. When I was with her, I had very little to cry about. But this was a breaking point, as my sadness turned to anger, Nadira standing up to wrap her arms around me, shocked when I pushed past her, slung my pack over my shoulder, and trudged towards the city. She quickly donned her pack and rushed after me, her face a mix of concern and shock as she took in my tear-stained cheeks and clenched jaw. No thoughts remained, only anger. I trudged through the streets with Nadira silently trailing just behind. As we approached the inner city, she spoke softly.

"We'll have to go around the inner city to the cathedral. We can't walk through there like this."

I silently obeyed, taking a left and slowing down slightly as I reached the edge of my familiarity with the streets closer to the inner city. Nadira took the lead, and I fixed my gaze on her, feeling slightly better. However, my face remained immobile, locked in place until Araysh was avenged. We made our way around the outskirts of the inner city, eventually moving away from the city once more, down the Norwest-Wedge.

Nadira explained, "The path to the cathedral bottlenecks. There's only one way to it unless you cut through the dunes."

"It's like an island." I replied, but she didn't seem to know what I meant.

She continued, "Luckily, based off the map we saw in the library, we should be able to travel along the dune ridges from the Norwest-Wedge to right in front of the northern point of the cathedral. We'll have to start crossing the vibrating parts of the desert from there though."

The dune ridges that she was talking about were the ones that made up the almost-a-square that framed the cathedral as a three-pointed star. I tried to distract myself with the fascinating collection of buildings in the Norwest-Wedge. Large mansions, all squashed together, seemed to grow taller as the space around them vanished. It felt strange to think that Nadira had lived somewhere in this maze, or at least used to. However, the architecture wasn't enough to distract me. My thoughts kept drifting back to the image of Araysh, reduced to a pile of sand on the ground. The immediate anger had subsided, simmering below the surface now. It still consumed all my energy, leaving me feeling empty, my face a blank mask that clearly worried Nadira even more than my tears. We left the Norwest-Wedge, scrambling up a dune with our heavy packs, getting some questioning stares from the upper gems that were milling about. It was harder to distract myself out here, with nothing else to focus on but Nadira and the sand. She led the way along the top of the ridge. From here, we could vaguely see the dune snaking through the desert, with the cathedral standing alone in the sands ahead of us. We trudged through the sand, feeling the strange stillness of the desert beneath our feet. Most of the desert's still parts had been built upon, becoming the city, but this stretch between the Norwest-Wedge and the cathedral remained untouched. We came to a bend in the dune, the ridge now heading directly towards the middle of the cathedral. Nadira stopped, looking out into the desert. She pointed.

"We need to get to that one there, it should bend around in front of the cathedral until we are directly north."

I nodded and followed her as we clumsily slid down the dune, the added weight of our packs making it harder to keep our balance. The sand began to vibrate beneath us, and while the thick soles of my boots helped, they weren't perfect. They wouldn't prevent us from turning to sand if we stayed too long. The gap between the dunes was small, but that only made the sides of the dunes steeper, the second dune requiring us to climb with our hands and feet to make it up the incline. We stopped at the top briefly to catch our breath, before we continued along the ridgeline, eventually finding the bend in the ridge that took us to a point directly north of the cathedral. I used the zoom on my epicode to determine when we were looking at the point dead on. I understood then why there were so many sapphires in parliament. It would be nearly impossible to walk perfectly north from here in a straight line, but sapphires could mentally measure the spacing of the cathedral, aligning themselves perfectly before setting off into the desert. Lining it up with the naked eye alone was extremely difficult. Even the slightest deviation, after approximately one hundred and seventy thousand steps, would put you too far from your destination, and you'd turn to sand before you could correct it. I hoped Ava knew what she was doing. She was smart, I knew that, but braving the desert alone with little more than the hope that you were going the right way, would be a challenge for anyone. A challenge many died trying to attempt. I didn't know what was in store for me during the other trials, but I imagined that this one alone dealt out a lot of the death attributed to the parliamentary trials.

I calibrated my epicode to serve as a compass. The planet's magnetism was all over the place, so I had to adjust it manually using our position from the cathedral. If only Ava had stayed with us, it would have been so much easier for her. Nadira was right. She was reckless, even if I believed she was strong and smart enough to make it on her own. She was making it much harder for herself than it needed to be. Part of me thought she really could do it, but another part knew I was probably kidding myself. Maybe I was simply delusionally believing she'd be okay, not wanting to lose any more friends. I took a deep breath and a step northward, off the dune's ridge and into the desert. I had thought that the vibrations would be our biggest problem, but after seven straight hours of hiking up and down sand dunes, my legs were killing me, pulsing with every step, until we came to the bottom of a dune that neither of us could walk up. Strength magic might have allowed me to carry two tents on my back, but it wasn't meant for endurance. Nadira and I both collapsed into the sand in the middle of the day. We lay on our backs, sweating and panting, shading our faces from the sun.

"How many steps—" She gasped for more air mid-sentence, "—have you counted so far?"

"Forty-eight thousand—" I gulped down more air, "—Six hundred and twelve."

"Good. I've counted six-hundred eighty-four."

It was barely midday. I wasn't sure how long my legs or lungs would last, but I believed we could make it there in two days. After twenty minutes of lying in the sand, my legs still ached, and resting my head directly on the sand had given me a headache and caused my vision to blur. I sat up, waiting for my vision to focus, finding Nadira looking back at me when it did. I gathered my thoughts.

"If we can just do another forty-thousand steps today, then we could probably reach parliament by mid-afternoon tomorrow."

Nadira looked drowsy already, but nodded, standing up before I did. We continued through the dunes for another seven hours, this time taking a series of small breaks along the way. I had hit eighty-six thousand steps, or thereabouts, finding the singular focus on counting my steps to be a good distraction from all the dark thoughts hiding in the corners of my mind. The last dune we travelled up for the day was a still one, a spot along the surface of the planet where the frequencies vibrating its surface cancelled one another out, granting us somewhere to sleep without decomposing overnight. This last incline was the longest we had taken to travel the shortest distance all day, both of us shuffling bit by bit up the dune, our legs stiff, only swinging a few degrees at a time before stepping again. Nadira reached the top before I did, as I had had to deactivate the topaz earlier in the day when I felt it getting too hot, threatening to explode on me. As soon as I did so, the extra weight I was carrying accelerated my exhaustion, my legs and back crunched between the tents and the sand. I collapsed on the top of the dune, resting there for a moment, enjoying the stillness. Nadira started setting up the tent before me, handing me pearl-water as I sat up, easing the stiffness in my legs, but not granting me any more strength. Once the tent was up, we all but passed out inside it on top of one another, the stillness and the shade a welcome combination that felt like strangers after the long day we'd had. As we rose just before dawn the next day, moving was painful. Every muscle, from my toes up to my legs, spine, and neck, was stiff and sore, already worn out after the first half of the long journey. As we packed up the tent and prepared to leave the dune, I noticed a drawing in the sand. I moved closer to it, smiling when I recognised it. It was a three-pointed star, drawn in the direction we were headed. I could only hope that Ava had drawn this to orient herself when she rose again. It seemed unlikely she would've slept here on this same ridge unless she had pushed herself well into the night, only resting at dawn. I knew this marking might've been much older, but I chose to believe it was from Ava and that she had made it this far, still perfectly aligned north.

We continued on our way, the strength magic of the topaz easing my sore legs, letting them bound down at least the first dune with ease. It only got harder from there. On my count of one hundred and seventy-five thousand steps, I spotted a tent pitched on a wide ridgeline directly ahead of us. It was a large tent, big enough for someone to live in permanently. As we got closer, I could also see two smaller structures standing apart, one of which was perfectly aligned north of where we were. The initial excitement, or possibly relief, of finding such a structure in the middle of nowhere was enough to make me relax just slightly, causing my foot to sink further into the sand than I should have let it, the jelly legs that were barely holding me up unable to deal with the imbalance, and I fell, rolling down the dune rather than walking. The sun burned my face as I lay at the bottom of the mound of soft sand, watching Nadira try to hurry after me, herself tripping, but only landing on her knees, sliding a short way down the last steep incline of the slope. I debated just sleeping right then and there, even as the sun burned my face, and the vibrations made my vision blur. I thought I almost saw Nadira smile as she helped me up. We continued to hold each other up, hobbling over to the tent. We found the entrance and hobbled inside, discovering a series of elaborate furnishings. Some were too large to have been carried all the way out here, but many were old, hinting at previous inhabitants. Each item appeared to be from a different era than the one next to it. A young man, wearing most of the armour of a cathedral guard, appeared.

"Oh hello! I wasn't expecting more wanderers today! Two in a week is freakishly frequent, but three in a day? That's got to be some sort of record."

Three? So Ava did make it, at least to this tent.

"You said three... was there a woman here earlier today?"

"Yes! Just this morning. Why? Do you know her? I suppose that would make sense. It's unheard of for so many people to show up on the same day. Did you get separated on your travels? If so, she's quite a bit faster than you. Seems like her odds were much better than yours, and that's saying something considering she was only a sunstone. What about you two? What are your stones?"

Wow, this guy could really talk. I couldn't decide if I thought that the isolation had made him a bit crazy, or if he was sent out here because he was already a bit crazy. Nadira had some questions for him of her own.

"Are you a cathedral guard? Why would a cathedral guard be protecting the entrance to parliament?"

"Oh, now that's an *old* question, the answer to which I'm not privy, nor allowed to reveal if I was."

This guy was already annoying. I felt Nadira tremble, her legs weak. The guard seemed to see it too and offered us a seat. I couldn't tell if this was the comfiest chair I had ever sat in or if I was simply so grateful for a soft chair that I was exaggerating its qualities.

"So," the guard began, "Do you both wish to attempt to enter parliament?"

I started to say no, but Nadira cut in with her own question,

"What happens if we don't?"

The guard smiled, "Plenty of people come this far, and don't have the strength to continue. I assume you saw the two teleporters outside?"

We both nodded.

"One of them leads to parliament, the other back to the city. These are both one-way trips, however. If you enter parliament, there is no backing out. The same goes for returning to the city, although in that case, you could always walk back." He chuckled at himself. "I should also mention that both teleporters are enchanted with binding magic, making you unable to reveal the location of parliament to others, or discuss certain other details, which I'm sure you will discover in time.

"Now, I must know if both of you wish to attempt parliament, as you won't be allowed to enter together."

Nadira had no more questions now, so I answered.

"No, just me."

"Excellent, Then I suggest you both make your way towards the teleporters, I assume you know which is which. If not…then I would urge you not to risk your life at parliament."

The guard stood up, but I was too comfy, and my eyelids were heavy.

"Are you sure I can't just stay here for a little bit and regain my strength?"

"I'm sorry, but no."

He pointed to a large hourglass sitting on a table in the middle of the room. I felt like that was something I should've noticed earlier.

"The timer is almost up, at which point, this tent and both teleporters will stop existing until the next wanderer comes along."

The hourglass had a quarter of its sand left in the top, slowly draining from one to the other. I sighed and stood up, drinking the remains of my pearl-water flask, Nadira offering me her half-empty one in exchange. I paused, knowing I didn't have much time, but I had to know something.

"How do you just stop existing? Do you go somewhere else and hang out until the next person comes along? How do you change shifts with the next guard?"

"Ah, well the thing about only existing for a few minutes a week, perhaps a month, is that you don't age very quickly. I have been doing this job since the beginning. For the city, I think it has been a few hundred years, but for me it has only been three."

"Three years?" I looked around the tent. "How'd you get so much stuff then, and from all different eras by the look of it?"

"Wanderers leave them before they enter parliament. They don't need tents and cooking pots in there."

"Oh."

The guard glanced at the hourglass, moving us with haste now,

"Enough now, you both have a decision to make, a door to enter, and a goodbye to say. Get going."

And with that he pushed us out of the tent, closing it back up. I looked at Nadira and then to the teleporters. Neither of us seemed to have any words. Nadira silently took my pack from me and dragged it over to the teleporters, not sure which was which. The one closest to the tent heads to parliament." I said.

She dumped the packs in front of the furthest teleporter, then came back and stood facing me, looking up with those bright green eyes, the sun catching the tears welling in them. She grabbed the front of my coat.

"You have to come back. If you don't, there'll be no one left. Araysh is gone. Ava might be dead."

She rested her forehead on my chest.

"I know, I promise I will, and I'll find Ava too."

She looked back up at me, her face telling me she didn't want me to go, but she knew why I had to.

"You promise?"

"I promise." I tried to give her a reassuring smile, but I wasn't all that confident in myself in that moment either, my eyebrows twitching in their indecision. She let out a long breath, then stepped back, glancing at the teleporters, wondering how long we had left.

"Good luck," she said finally. Then she turned around and hurried off through the teleporter, dragging my pack through after her. Right. Moment of truth, I guess. I took a deep breath, turning towards the teleporter. I tried to prepare myself to face whatever was on the other side, not being able to see anything through the doorway. I debated switching to fire magic, to light my way if it was as dark as it looked on the other side, but decided against it. I didn't have time for this. Strength magic was probably my best bet. Besides, I was worried that if I deactivated it now, then my legs would buckle beneath me. I took another deep breath, knowing that I had stalled too long, and stepped forward into the darkness on the other side of the teleporter.

Chapter 10

I was engulfed in darkness, no trace of the teleporter I had just stepped through. Tentatively, I took a step forward, struggling to identify what the floor beneath me was made of. If this place was anything like the desert, then moving in a perfectly straight line was probably my best bet. Unless. These trials were supposed to test all sorts of attributes. Maybe for this part, I'd need to navigate through a dark maze or something. I stretched out my hands, trying to feel the walls on either side, but there was nothing. With no other information, I took another step forward, and another. After the fifth step, I felt a shift in the air and noticed the change in the echo of my footsteps. I was now in a much larger room. I couldn't gauge the size of either room, but this second one was spacious enough to have its own weird kind of weather. I couldn't quite describe it—air currents swirling around me, some thick with electricity, others carrying the scent of... tea? I thought I could hear a buzzing sound, like the hum of electricity through the walls of a spaceship. I took another step, the buzzing now unmistakable, but it was secondary to the enormous doors that began to open, flooding light into the cavern I seemed to be standing in. To my surprise, the doors resembled the hangar doors aboard Cronus, but they were much larger, opening into a hangar that was filled with sand. A plain sandstone grid was carved into the floor. I approached the edge of the hangar, watching as the massive doors slid out to the sides, disappearing into the cavern walls. The sandstone tiles resembled those from the arena in South-Fork, but these were free of excess sand and lacked any markings.

I held my breath as I took a step into the hangar, onto a sandstone square. As I did so, the square in front of me squirmed and a sand-coloured chryacal jumped out of the ground, its sedimentary skin turning to flesh as it escaped the sandy floor. It stood before me, poised to strike. A deep hiss emanated from its jaw, reminiscent of a cat's, but many octaves lower. I froze, but the chryacal stayed in its square. While I was focused on the beast before me, I hadn't noticed the changes to the rest of the board. The eighty-one squares now adorned with patterns and symbols hinting at their secrets. I peered past the chryacal, recognising the game and spotting the intricately carved wooden door directly across the board. A smile crept across my face—not because I was a master of proelium, but because Ava was. If anyone could make it across this board, it was her. I wasn't so confident in my own abilities, and I had a feeling this was going to be much more challenging than a regular game— and far more lethal. It was hard to focus on anything other than the chryacal mere metres from me, a hungry look in its eyes, but I had to choose my next move. I remained perfectly still and flicked my eyes to the square next to the chryacal, and then to the other side. I had four options total: a lotus flower, a Penrose Staircase, a frog, and a cube surrounded by rings, similar to Saturn's. Wait. These symbols were unlike anything I was used to seeing on a proelium board. The usual ones were cultural, mathematical, or something along those lines. But these? These were all from me. This planet didn't even have frogs, lotus flowers, or, as far as I knew, rings. The board was pulling these images from my mind, creating puzzles it knew I could solve, because I had the answers. But was this board powerful enough to conjure up the image of a species like a frog, just from the pictures in my brain? I had no idea, but it seemed more likely that these symbols had to be connected to things that I knew were already possible in proelium. Or perhaps not. There was only one way to find out, however risky it was.

I made my choice, walking over and stepping onto the square baring the ink-stained image of a frog. Nothing seemed to happen, except the chryacal leaping over me and landing on a square behind me. The board remained unchanged. I looked at my hands. I didn't seem to have changed either. Damn. Maybe this board wasn't expecting such foreign concepts that it instead did nothing. In that case, this was about to be all too easy. But that seemed a little too easy, especially on a planet teeming with universal foreigners. I had chosen the square directly to my right, and the chryacal had landed on the next square to my right, severely limiting my options. I was left with three choices ahead of me: the cube with Saturn's rings, what looked like a warped infinity sign—perhaps more like a diagram of a wormhole with two large spheres at the ends—and a tessellating triangular pattern. It was difficult to make a strategic decision without really knowing any of the rules, but for this set of symbols, there was only one that I could even begin to guess what it might do. I glanced at the chryacal before making my move toward the square displaying the image of a cube surrounded by Saturn's rings. As I landed, everything happened at once: the squares lifted off the ground, whizzing into the air. I caught a glimpse of the chryacal leaping, but I couldn't see where it landed, my vision blocked by the tiles rearranging themselves mid-air. I looked down, wondering when the tile I stood on had started to lift me up into the air.

When the chaos settled down and I could get my bearings, I found myself on a three-by-three grid floating in the hangar. I blinked stupidly, looking around for the other tiles, counting a few as they floated past, seemingly orbiting the platform. I scoffed at myself. Idiot. I was standing on the cube from the image, the extra tiles that didn't fit, now orbiting it, including the carved door I was supposed to be trying to get to. Right. Now it was getting interesting. I looked down at the five tiles around me on this face of the cube, and leant back over the edge to see the remaining three that I could move to. Whichever one I chose this round was risky, not being able to see the chryacal and figure out where it could move to. I smiled. Game on.

The game continued, the chryacal chasing me around the cube. When I stepped on a solid black tile with an empty square in the centre, the cube turned itself inside out, causing the tiles to spin around. The chryacal and I were now trapped inside the cube, with floor pieces dropping out each time I made another move. Inside of the cube, as I stood on the wall, or what could have been the wall given that all the walls had their own gravity and I couldn't see the actual ground anymore, I stood within range of a square that depicted a hooded figureI debated for a while whether it was worth the risk, as the figure looked like an assassin. I decided that either meant an assassin would come after me if I chose it, or, and this is what I was hoping for, that it would grant me the weapons of an assassin. Of course, I had been pretty hit and miss so far with the tiles, so I could be very wrong about either of those. In the end, I went for it, jumping to the tile on the wall in front of me, not sure how the gravity switch would work, but it did, landing me on my chest. Before I could react, the chryacal sprang off the wall, landing on the square I had just vacated. It twisted mid-air, its claw catching in my hair and slicing my scalp open. Blood poured down my face and into my eye. I clutched my head, shouting in pain as I slammed into the tile I had chosen, which decided at that moment to fall out of the cube and join the rest that were in orbit. I sat up, reaching for my scalp to feel the wound, but instead found my hand already wrapped around something that had been there before. I stared at the two objects now in my hands, blinking away the blood that carved a river down my face and dripped off my chin. Two silver daggers with sculpted handles and a subtle curve were now in my hands. My face lit up with a beaming smile—I had the weapons of an assassin. Maybe I could finally fight the chryacal. But as soon as the thought crossed my mind, my head throbbed, and the idea of attacking that creature filled me with nauseating dread.

I reached for the half-empty flask of pearl-water that Nadira had given me, the magic liquid being enough to stop the flow of blood down my face, but not properly close up the wound. I stood slowly, trying not to pass out, and looked over my next set of tile choices. Unfortunately, the nature of the orbiting tiles meant that only two of them were viable to jump to, and one of them was the door. I was close enough finally to be able to see the symbols on the door properly. Fuck yes. One of the three symbols on the door matched the daggers I now held in my hands; the other two were the chryacal's tail and what seemed to be a chameleon. My joy quickly faded when I noticed a fourth symbol, located two-thirds of the way down the door, separate from the others. It was the image of a man's face. I shuddered. I was really hoping the face was some sort of metaphor or something like that.

Collecting myself, and touching the wound on my scalp delicately, I turned around to see my only choice of tile left, a giant leap away. The blood drained from my face. The image was easy to decipher, as it was a drawing of a chryacal. It only took one claw of that beast to rip me open, and now I was potentially about to introduce another one of them. Two chryacal to chase me around the board and cut me open. Unless it was indicating something to do with the other one? I let out a steadying breath. It didn't really matter. It was my only choice either way. I leapt, smacking my knee into the edge of the tile, but otherwise landing alright. At least, I thought I had, but the tile was falling down to the floor of the hangar and I was falling with it. I landed, hitting the tile half a second after it had hit the ground. The cube we were orbiting collapsed in a puff of sand, which fell and filled the hangar, concealing all the other tiles and the chryacal I knew I had to find as soon as possible. The cloud of sand dispersed, revealing the chryacal in the middle of a completely new arena. The original grid remained intact, but the edges of the board rose from the ground, walling us in like mountains. None of the tiles had patterns anymore. They were all blank. I didn't get time to wonder why, as the chryacal began running, bounding straight for me, and I suddenly understood what the tile had meant. It leapt at me, and I ducked, rolling to the side as it crashed into the mountainous wall behind me. I got up and raised my daggers. The chryacal let out a deep hiss, stalking me as it searched for its moment to strike. I was terrified. This thing had clawed at me, run at me, and it now had the chance to attack me however it liked. And it hadn't even tried to use its tail yet. Its tail alone looked like it could decapitate me with a short flick. I was sweating now, my sweat beading and picking up dried blood from my forehead as it ran down my face and into my eye. I lifted my wrist to wipe it away but the chryacal used the opportunity to strike. I only saw it for a moment, but the beast crouched lower as it ran at me, so I jumped. I realised how stupid that was as the beast dove under me, its tail coming up to meet me like a spear. I did the only thing I could do in mid-air and scrunched myself into a ball, putting my blades as well as the thick soles of my desert boots between the rest of me and the tip of the ancient living weapon about to impale me. It hit, slicing into my boot, and sliding down my blade, causing me to spin off to the side, landing flat on my back. I was winded, but I got up as quickly as humanly possible as the chryacal turned to face me again. I adopted a fighting position, only to find that the entire heel of my boot had been carved out by the creature's tail, which threw my balance completely off. I had to kill it now. I couldn't do this for much longer.

I took a breath, hoping that the remaining pearl-water was enough to keep my legs steady, and I switched the tuning on my epicode from topaz to obsidian. I felt heavy. My limbs all felt like they were made of lead, and I was certain that I wouldn't be quick enough to dodge another attack like this. But with the knife magic, I might not have to. The chryacal bounded again, showing even more of its teeth as it ran towards me. This time I didn't run. I held my ground, hoping that I could take the chryacal down swiftly enough that the obsidian wouldn't splinter and I'd get myself mauled to death anyway. I adjusted my stance lower, recalling wrestling moves I had learned in the navy. Obviously though, they weren't designed with a massive, fucking reptilian cat with a crazy axe-looking thing for a tail in mind.

I tensed every muscle I had, dropping to one knee as the chryacal leapt at me. I dropped the daggers—they were too long for an attack this close. Dropping to my knee allowed me to pivot to the side and beneath the chryacal. It twisted, swiping at me with its teeth gnashing, chomping the air where my head had been a moment before. Its claw connected with my face, the sound of screeching metal ringing in my ears as I blindly shoved my left hand toward its belly. Its scales provided some protection, but not enough to stop my own claws from burying themselves in its insides. The beast's own momentum sliced up its organs as I held my fingers out, flexed and stationary, inside its belly. The chryacal landed with a slide, hitting the edge of the arena and turning to sand as it failed to rise, leaving its petrified tail behind on the sandstone tile. I sat there panting as the mountains crumbled, the patterns reappearing on the tiles. Everything was scrambled now, with the blank tiles I had already activated scattered around the board. I remained sitting there for a few minutes, catching my breath as I got used to the extra heaviness in my limbs without the topaz active. It was then that I remembered the sapphire Nadira had stolen from her father for me. I hadn't received a new gem in months and had nearly forgotten about it, tucked away in the hidden pocket of the strap across my chest. Standing up and examining the new board, I decided to switch to the sapphire. The moment I did, it became clear that this should have been my first move, as the board suddenly made a lot more sense. This board, however, was infinitely more complex than the arena, where I had slightly disrupted the mechanisms. The sapphire's powers would contribute little beyond some initial understanding, as the puzzle images, drawn from my own thoughts, were not any more obvious. I sighed, switching back to the topaz, and trying to decipher my tile options.

The board felt strange with the chryacal gone, but now I had two of the three things I needed to open the final door. Now I just had to find something that looked like a chameleon. Did the board take that from my memory too? I looked down, and made my choice, the board shifting and throwing obstacles at me with each subsequent decision. It wasn't until a strange tower had risen on the far side of the board that I noticed something odd about a tile I had previously thought was blank. By that point in the game, the board was also populated by a sandworm that surfaced every two turns, and a pair of sentient shadows, commonly associated with onyx magic, all intent on my demise. At first glance, the tile appeared blank, but as I squinted at it, I began to notice a slightly different shade of sandstone etching lines into the surface. When I shifted my focus from the individual lines to the entire near-invisible image, I found that I recognised it. It was a chameleon. Without a second thought, I confidently stepped onto the chameleon tile. When I did, a pedestal erupted out of the tower, upon which sat an actual chameleon. I wasn't expecting that.

The next moment, the shadows made their turns, but not how I expected. The shadows typically stretched five tiles forwards as their attack, but only moved two tiles in that same direction. I was expecting them to move towards me, stretching past their marks in a predictable way, but they didn't. They instead moved away. Then the sandworm erupted from the ground, not at all where I was expecting. The sandworm's movement was hard to calculate, but as long as I kept track of it with every move, I had so far been able to avoid it. Now that something had changed, I had no idea where it would appear next, and it moved in patterns, meaning that it could pop up on any square of the board, regardless of how far it was from its previous position. I hesitantly took a step towards the chameleon in the tower, onto a blank square. The shadows moved again, but in the same direction I was travelling. Oh shit. The shadows must've been trying to get to the chameleon as well. If they killed it, I would lose. And under these circumstances, I was pretty sure that meant death. I smiled seeing my current tile choices.

"Looks like it's time for the Penrose Staircase."

I said out loud to no-one, stepping onto the image of the infinitely ascending stairs. To my surprise, a straight set of stairs appeared, leading from the tile ahead of me, right up to the top of the tower. The shadows moved and the sandworm erupted out of the ground right behind me. I stepped onto the first tile that made up the stairs, all of which were blank, to my surprise. The shadows moved. I rose another stair, the shadows moving closer to the chameleon, and the sandworm erupting out of nowhere that I could predict anymore. I took another step, and then another. It was only after the shadows had reached the base of the tower that I realised that I was still standing on the first stair somehow. I slapped my palm against my forehead, wincing as pain shot through my scalp from the claw wound. They were *infinitely ascending* stairs. I was never going to survive this game. I just kept making stupid mistakes and had only gotten this far through luck and magic. As long as Ava made it through, maybe she and Nadira would be able to fix all this without me. I'm sure they could, they were much smarter than me after all. And if Ava was in parliament already? Then what did I need to survive this for? I sat down, tired, and not knowing how to proceed. The shadows were about to climb the tower and I was still stuck at the bottom of a useless staircase. For all I knew the sandworm would swallow the chameleon in the next turn and I'd be dead anyway. I had sat down too long now, the long trek through the desert and subsequent running and battling a chryacal, among an assortment of other insane obstacles, and I was ready to pass out from exhaustion. My eyelids fell, and I made the conscious decision to stand up to avoid falling asleep, but my legs had already gone to sleep, so instead I fumbled over the side of the stair, falling onto the tile off the side of the staircase, having no idea what secret it held. It turned out to be a metal box. A box which was now slowly crushing me to death. How original. I went to switch to the garnet to melt my way out of here but stopped. The metal felt too thick, the garnet would certainly explode if I tried to melt that much metal. Maybe the sapphire could reverse the box? No, not in this arena. The only other option I had was the black moonstone. Metallurgic magic, capable of separating alloys into their elemental metals. I just had to hope this box wasn't pure iron, or an illusion made of sand. I pressed my hand up to the shrinking wall, my knee getting constantly closer to my face, and felt for the metals, separating them into bands. The copper was the easiest to find, and to see. I pushed as much copper as I could into one wall of the box, trying to thin it out, making it malleable enough to deform. Pushing this much copper though was too much for the black moonstone, the magic dissipating as the rock exploded. Luckily, it was only a weak stone, and the force felt a bit like a punch to the sternum as it exploded within the confines of the strap across my chest. If that was the garnet, I would be dead. But the copper was soft enough and thin enough now that I would have enough energy to melt through it with fire magic. I switched to fire magic as quickly as I could. With my neck crammed against the ceiling, I slammed my hand against the wall, pushing, the copper moving outwards, and eventually melting, a hole opening up in the wall. I tried to shuffle out, but I was too crammed now, my head against the ceiling and my spine curling around the inside of the box. With my last bit of strength, I unstuck my leg and pushed against the opposite wall with my other hand, pushing the rest of body out of the hole in the wall, hot copper dripping onto me as I passed through. I lay on the edge of the tile now, panting, making a conscious effort not to touch the adjacent tile that I was dangerously close to.

The shadows had started climbing the tower. Fuelled with a new rush of adrenaline, I jumped up, knowing that if this didn't end soon, I'd end up falling asleep in the mouth of the sandworm.

"Ok, what are my options now?" I said aloud, finding it helpful for staying awake. There was the lotus flower again, some kind of messy squiggle, an explosion, and a ruined tower. It wasn't looking good. The ruined tower and the explosion were immediately out, posing the greatest risk of death to the chameleon. The squiggle could be anything, and the lotus… what was the symbolism behind the lotus? I must know it. If the board pulled it out of my brain, then I must know its importance. What culture was it from? A religion? I groaned, frustrated with myself. Maybe it was just a regular flower, and the tile would give me a nice bouquet just for choosing it. I chuckled. Now I was really losing it. The exhaustion was getting to me. Then it clicked, and I remembered the single word I knew associated with lotus flowers—rebirth.

It wasn't much in the way of helping me strategise, but I think I was long past that at this point. Whatever rebirth meant in this game, I hoped it would somehow reset the shadows and the sandworm. I didn't know how, but it sounded much more promising than a squiggle or a ruined tower. So, I stepped forward. The ground was immediately wet beneath me, and the water rose so fast that it was already above my head when I thought to look at the chameleon. I squinted through the distortions on the surface, not seeing much, and quickly realising that I wasn't floating. Not even a little bit, like the water had had its buoyant qualities surgically removed. The water continued up the tower, swallowing the shadows, and would soon reach the chameleon. Could chameleons swim? I suppose it didn't matter. I'd just killed both of us anyway. I would be out of air soon, and the chameleon would drown the instant the water rose too high. This was it. I was finally going to die playing this stupid game. I wanted to scream, but instinctually didn't want to let go of the little air I had left. The water was almost at the top of the tower now, and my vision was going black at the edges. What a stupid way to die. I didn't even get to figure out what that frog symbol at the start meant. Wait. I looked down at my hands, but they looked the same, I looked closer, at my skin, but there was nothing. Dang, so much for breathing under water or swimming abilities, but the water was almost at the chameleon now, and if frogs were known for anything it was their legs, so, as the edges of my vision gave up on me and my lungs started to burn, I had one last thought—jump!

My hands closed around something, I couldn't see it, couldn't feel my limbs, my thoughts slowed as my mouth drained of water. It was draining though, and my vision began to return, my limbs understanding that that they were pressed against sandstone. I lifted my head off the rock, feeling the strange material in my hands, surprised to find the sea-glass coloured skin of a chameleon staring as me, slowly turning to sand. I panicked, remembering how the chryacal turned to sand when it died, but the chameleon remained, having matched its skin to the colour of the floor.

Oh. I looked around, finding myself where the base of the tower used to be, on the far side of the board. There stood the door right in front of me, the symbols glowing as I held each item up to it, seemingly dissolving into it like the key was the sand that they were made of. Finally, the door swung open, and I saw out of the corner of my eye as I walked through, the fourth symbol of the man's face glow.

Sure enough, ahead of me was a man, approaching slowly, his hands clasped behind his back and his robe adorned with sapphires. The floor in front of me, between the man and I, had formed a sandstone grid without me realising, and I whipped around to see the door still open, the board now on this side of the door. I swivelled back around to face the man—my final obstacle. He stopped on the other side of the board, surprising me when he yelled out my name,

"Ender! I had hoped I would finally get to meet you. Perhaps you are worthy of my daughter after all if you're capable of making it this far."

He studied me a moment, the blood draining from my face. This way my last obstacle? Nadira's father? No, he must just be here to welcome me, but why did the board move?

"I wasn't sure I was going to get to meet you when I saw your friend come here first. I thought perhaps, well, you're here now, that's all that matters."

He saw Ava?

"My friend that came before me, is she with you? is she here?"

He adopted a more sombre look, "I'm sorry to be the one to tell you this, but she didn't quite make it past the last trial."

I didn't even know how to process that information. Ava was… No, Nadira's father was standing in front of me, the last obstacle on this upscaled proelium board

"What now?"

"Now now, not so hasty. This is after all our only chance to get to know one another."

"What do you mean?"

"I think you know exactly what I mean. If you didn't, you wouldn't have made it this far."

198

I did know, but I didn't want to believe. Why of all people did I have to fight Nadira's father for this last battle?

"I know what you're thinking. Why him? How did I end up in a fight to the death with my girlfriend's father?" He laughed, "Well, let me tell you how. I chose to be the one to fight you. As I'm sure you know, there can only be a hundred parliamentarians, and so any challengers have to take their position in the arena. I heard about you from Nadira—an outsider who barely survived his crash here. She was so embarrassed by you that she wouldn't even tell me your gem. And after that performance, I still can't discern it. Would you mind indulging me?"

"I'm not dying today."

"We'll see about that."

The ground began rumbling, the tiles beneath my feet all activating at once. Was he doing this? This was totally unfair if he could use the entire arena against me. But if he could control the board, then maybe I could too. The tiles shot up from the ground all around me, distracting me from using my epicode. They spun around in the air, finally settling in a tunnel-like formation, a single row of tiles left on the ground leading to Nadira's father. With the tiles still now, I switched to my sapphire, Nadira's father too far away to feel the effects of the frequency augmentation in his own sapphires. The tiles lit up in my mind, their secrets revealing themselves to me. I could even see the hold the man at the other end of the tunnel had on them, strangling them to his will. I had the advantage with him not knowing I could see this, and didn't plan to give that away any time soon. I saw a signal flash between him and three of the tiles closer to me above my head. I watched them, trying to figure out what they would throw at me, knowing that even Nadira's father wouldn't be able to predict it. The instant the tiles decided, I grinned, it was my lucky day, and the man at the other end of the tunnel had no idea what I was capable of.

The water bucketed down from the tiles, a solid wall of water falling right on my head. In those half-seconds between the water falling, and it hitting my head, I switched to the aquamarine, to ice magic, just quickly enough to split the water as it reached me. The tsunami crashed down around me without a single drop landing on me. As it hit the ground, I felt its flow, grabbing it, and vaulted it down the tunnel, spinning it as I did so. I hadn't practiced very much with ice magic, but I was exceptionally good at making icicles, and this one was particularly deadly, the spin I gave it flicking off water droplets as they turned to ice, leaving behind large icy spikes along the edges of the massive projectile. At the other end of the tunnel, a boom rang out, the ring of tiles around the edge erupting into pillars of rock, crashing together and forming enough of a wall to stop my icy projectile, shattering it to pieces, the remaining water inside it not enough to reform and attack again. The rock pillars crumbled to dust, revealing Nadira's father panting, wide-eyed.

"So, an aquamarine are you?" He scoffed, "Ice magic. Known for its artistry and elegance. Not exactly something that's useful in a fight, although whatever that was was impressive, I'll admit." He grinned, "But now I know your secrets."

He stood up straight and pushed back his hair, his overconfidence in his inevitable victory misplaced. I grinned myself, ready to surprise him again. What would Nadira think of us? The thought distracted me as he attacked me again, this time more strategically, activating a collection of tiles at once, but cancelling their effects as soon as they were revealed, only retaining the one that he thought would kill me the quickest. He was wrong again, hurling a series of arrows after me, shocked when I used knife magic to catch them, and then strength magic to throw them back at him like darts. This time he dodged my attack with surprising agility. Looks like I wasn't the only one with tricks up my sleeve. His face grew redder with every attack and every surprise counterattack I launched back at him. He cursed under his breath and shouted, "Who are you?!" without giving me a chance to respond, all while sending the tiles themselves spinning towards me.

Before I could switch back to sapphire, the tiles reached me, and I discovered their properties the hard way. The artificial gravity of each thrown tile lifted me off the ground, pulling my limbs in different directions. Even with the strength magic, there wasn't much I could do while suspended in mid-air. Nadira's father smirked, walking towards me now, believing he'd finally got me. I let him walk forwards, having switched back to the sapphire, waiting for him to join me in the arena, unaware that we shared the same abilities. I waited until he was close to me before using the sapphires magic, connecting to the tiles that he was using to pin me in the air. He gasped, stopping in his tracks, presumably feeling my grip on the tiles as I tried to pull them from his control. He whispered under his breath as he stared at me.

"Not possible."

He almost looked afraid as he yanked back control of the tiles, keeping me suspended in air, and starting to test the limits of my borrowed magic. We both strained against each other, the forces in play invisible to everyone but us. I felt my chest get hot, And I knew I wouldn't win this tug of war. I flexed my hands, testing the way the tiles pulled on me, and found the forces to be purely gravitational. I smirked, letting go of my hold on the tiles, just long enough to be distracting, straining to reach for the compartment on my chest, sliding it back, revealing the row of stones embedded within it. Nadira's father's face twisted into an unreadable mess.

I plucked out the sapphire, burning my hand as I did so, my hand snapping back towards the tile pulling at it. A sense of sadness washed over me as I realised what I was about to do.

"I'm sorry," I whispered before I flicked the sapphire towards him, putting all of the energy of the sapphire that I could draw on into one tile, the one closest to Nadira's father, ripping that tile from his control and placing it between us, the motion putting the sapphire past breaking point, causing it to shatter in a crystal-blue explosion right at his feet. The shards ripped him apart in a cloud of sharp dust.

Silence fell over the arena, before the tiles began to fall, crashing down on top of me, with no sapphire left for me to move them with. I switched to knife magic as quickly as I could, preventing the tiles from slicing me open, but still burying me under their imposing weight. In the silence, buried under a cozy pile of rubble, the exhaustion finally found its opportunity to descend, sending me into a semi-comatose slumber.

Chapter 11

When I woke up, the first thing I noticed was how well rested and relaxed I felt. I had thought for sure after a long trek through the desert and a series of endless puzzles and battles, I would be too stiff and too tired. I sat up, flexing my perfectly healed fingers, only now just realising how weak they had gotten by the time I had had to fight Nadira's father. The blood drained from my face. Oh shit. I killed her father. What would she think of me now? Maybe she would understand? No. Even though I had no choice, even though he chose to fight me, and even though it was possible Nadira might have known something like this could've happened, given her hesitation to let me do this, this wasn't something you could just get over. Nadira was forgiving, but she could be vengeful, and for something like this…She was happy to go after her enemies when they attacked her friends, but how would she react when someone she loved killed another that she loved? I was so lost in my thoughts that I didn't see the old man approach the hospital bed I appeared to be laying on.

"You're awake. Can you stand?"

I looked up at the old man who stared at me sternly with an itching curiosity behind his eyes. I swung my legs over the edge of the bed with ease and stood.

"I definitely feel much better than I thought I would."

"Ah, well, two days in bed and a pearl-water bath will do that to you."

It was then that I noticed the robes I was wearing. A dark green fabric embroidered with gold, flowing over the top of a matching dark green leather outfit, the tight sleeves and occasional adornment of shiny scales on places like my shins and forearms telling me it was designed for battle. The old man wore a similar set, but dark blue and adorned with sapphires like Nadira's father's robes were. I lifted my sleeve to examine it, startled when the sleeve flashed purple and back to green as I lifted it to my face.

"Ah yes, it was tricky to make that fabric you know, we didn't exactly have iridescent green-purple silk on hand. Sorry about the gemstone adornment too. We didn't have any alexandrite on hand. You are quite rare."

As the man spoke the words 'alexandrite' I locked my eyes on him, remembering that he said I had been in bed for two days. Shit, so much could have happened in two days, and here we were standing around talking about weird fabric, which curiously reminded me of Nadira's eyes. She couldn't be alexandrite, could she? No, that couldn't be right, she would've told me. And she would probably have a gemstone at the very least. But then again, even the all-powerful parliament didn't seem to have any. I was getting distracted.

"How did you know I was alexandrite?" I blurted out, trying to get back to some sort of topic, unable to focus yet on whatever I was supposed to be doing.

"Well, we scanned you while you were asleep."

Obviously. I looked around the room, trying to figure out my next move, only finding one set of doors on the far wall, of a design unlike anything I had seen around the city so far. The man caught me looking at the doors and suddenly remembered what he supposed to be doing.

"Right, of course! Welcome to Parliament! This is only the recovery centre of course, but if you'll follow me, I'll show you to the main hall."

The man started towards the doors, and I followed, finding myself admiring the new robes I was wearing, thinking about Nadira's eyes every time the colour of the fabric shifted. She must think I died in here, having been gone for two days. The doors opened and we left the recovery room, turning into a metallic corridor that reminded me a little bit of the U.E.S Cronus, but this one was much more gold and decorated, a bit more like a luxury cruise ship. We turned again, coming across a set of three boxes shaped like the teleporters in the city, but these were all metal and looked more mechanical, with wires and things that looked like giant magnets wrapped in copper in the ceiling and floor. The old man pointed at the leftmost one, explaining that,

"This one heads upstairs to the command floor."

He then proceeded to step through and disappear before I could ask any questions. I followed, stepping into the box and suddenly finding myself in a similar corridor, except this one had a taller ceiling and the wall was lined with portraits, the individuals all wearing different coloured robes similar to the ones the old man and I wore. He began speaking as we walked past the portraits down the hall.

"These are the portraits of all the past parliamentarians and, as you can see, everyone has a custom battle robe made to suit them. Yours is rather unique though, as there's only been one other alexandrite in parliament."

My focus snapped towards him.

"What? There has? Can you show me?"

He smiled, "Of course, she's right over here."

He took a few more steps down the corridor before stopping before a portrait on the wall of a woman wearing a dark green robe and a silver necklace clasped around a large square gemstone, with hints of purple hiding in the corners of it. The woman's face was strange in that her skin tone seemed to match the background, making her green eyes stand out unexpectedly. Holy shit. This had to have been Nadira's ancestor or something. Their faces weren't at all similar, but the eyes, and the colour… Maybe it was just an alexandrite thing. But I didn't have that. I wondered what Nadira's mum looked like.

"She was a parliamentarian one hundred and thirteen years ago." He said as he looked at the portrait lost in thought. As interested as I was in finding another alexandrite, even a long dead one, I had a mission, and I had already lost too much time. Who knows how many had died while I slept. I'm sure Nadira had made the effort to find out exactly how many. I cleared my throat, drawing the man's attention, flicking my eyes further down the corridor and back.

"Right, onwards then. We're almost there."

He continued down the hall, the portraits coming to an end. The man turned to the right towards a large set of ornate doors that didn't quite fit the decor of the rest of the space. As we walked by the last of the portraits, I glimpsed the figure in the final one, Nadira's father, in his blue robe adorned with sapphires. A wave of guilt washed over me. The old man looked back at me with a smirk before flinging the ornate doors open, revealing the chamber inside. Awe completely took over any feelings of guilt. The room inside was quite different from the metal corridors, the furnishings resembling the style of the upper gem society in the city. It wasn't something I was particularly familiar with, but the soft sandstone tiles and ruby-red fabrics and gold trim were pretty recognisable.

Inside the room was a series of stepped seating, resembling a small colosseum. The seats were filled with a sea of colours—blue, red, purple, and amber, to name a few—all of which stopped to stare at me as we entered. This was parliament. The faces turned towards me, with a noticeable majority wearing deep blue sapphire robes, most of them looking at me with distaste. The other colours, however, seemed to stare at me a little more fondly, some even with an unabashed curiosity that made me feel even more out of place, realising that my robes didn't match a single person in here. I was once again the odd one out, and just when I was starting to feel like I belonged in this city. The old man approached a pedestal in front of a large window. Unsure whether I was supposed to follow him or take a seat in the stands, I hesitated. Then, he waved me over to join him, so I followed. As I walked, I noticed the view out the window of the proelium arena below in the hangar. The board had been reset, and the doors were closed, waiting silently for their next victim. The man stood on the podium and, as the whispers quieted, he started to speak.

"Welcome friends. Today we introduce a new member of our society. A unique soul that has earned his place amongst our ranks. Today we welcome you, Ender Herman, resonant with the rare gemstone of Alexandrite, to Parliament. If you wish to make a statement you may do so know. If not, I ask you to take a seat amongst our ranks. You belong here now."

He looked at me expectantly. This was my chance. This was why I had come to parliament. Well, close to it. Nadira didn't think they would help us, didn't think they would fight against Jezebel, against a diamond, and so our plan was to use my power gained by being a parliamentarian to stop her. But I was here, and I had the opportunity to ask for their help. I couldn't understand why they wouldn't help, why they would just stand back and watch the genocide of the masses. If nothing else, maybe I would found find out why. I approached the pedestal, the old man stepping back as I did so. I looked around the room at the assortment of expressions and coloured robes. I took a deep breath, preparing myself for rejection, to be immediately cast out of parliament. But then again, why would I want to stay in a group with the power to stop mass murder, but the refusal to do so. I found some anger to use to project my voice to the room.

"Hello. I'm not usually one for speeches, but I came here to parliament looking for help, for the power to help me defeat an enemy of this city who you may or may not know, has already murdered entire gem types. Three whole kinds of stones had been eradicated when I set off on my journey here, and that was at least three days ago by now. Who knows how many more have died."

The faces of parliament were more tense now, but I couldn't tell if it was guilt or disgust that I saw on their faces.

"I came here to ask for your help, and to ask why and how you can stand aside while so many die and entire kinds of magic are wiped out in an instant."

My voice broke at the end, and I knew I was done. I had at least made my case. I stepped back from the podium, and the old man stared at me, bewildered, clearly not expecting such a performance. Instead of taking the podium himself, he turned to face me, his expression becoming blank as he initiated a debate.

"We have reason to believe these attacks were carried out by the priestess Jezebel, who is a diamond, and therefore can't be judged in the way that others can. We may be parliamentarians, but diamonds are pure. She must have good reasons for doing the things she does, even if to us they seem… questionable. She did, however, eradicate shadow magic by removing those resonant with onyx, freeing our city from the stain of crime they tortured our city with. Her plans may not be clear, but good can be seen in some of her actions, if not all."

I stood there shocked. He spoke as if diamonds were gods, their will purely good but often undecipherable.

"How do you rationalise the murder of the countless others she's murdered then? When I came here, only Talc, Selenite, and Onyx had been wiped out. How many has she 'removed' now?"

I mocked his use of delicate language, pretending that murder wasn't murder.

"They were weak gems. Our city is stronger now, with tougher gems like us and less of those with weak souls. They were prone to theft and lies and deceit. Her methods may be questionable, but Jezebel has undoubtedly made our city stronger, safer."

The more he spoke, the less I could believe the words that came out of him. He seemed so nice when we first met, and now he was spitting acid, praising Jezebel for the eradication of lesser gems. I was too stunned to say any more. The old man sighed adding,

"You are a parliamentarian now. We can't stop you if you wish to go against her, but now that she has become the High Priestess, I think you'll find it rather difficult to get close to her. Parliamentarians have power, but people tend to lean on their beliefs when equal powers find themselves at odds."

He was disappointed in me, I could tell. But the disappointment of a dogmatic, elitist old man wasn't really on my list of things to worry about at the moment. Also, did he say High Priestess? When did that happen?

"High Priestess? But I thought that was someone else, the woman who carries the petrified chryacal tail as a staff?"

"Ah, yes. Her name was Annabelle, two soulmate rubies that had merged permanently to lead the Fovan Church. She set an example for all those that wished to follow her path. She was quite a woman, and Anna and Bella, the two souls that she was made up of, were quite the characters as well. It's unfortunate that they had to die, but it's hard to argue her removal when a diamond should've always been the High Priestess. It was quite unusual that Annabelle rose to the position in the first place, but that just shows you how much she was admired."

Had to die? These people were insane. The faces of parliament all seemed to be nodding, like they agreed with the old man, although whether that was for Annabelles character or Jezebel's right as a diamond to kill her, I wasn't sure. My face got hot with anger.

"You people are cowards."

And with that I stormed out, many in the crowd standing up, anger on their faces, outraged at the disrespect of my insult. The old man simply clenched his jaw and raised his hand, hoping that the angry robed figures would all stay in their seats.

"I will escort Ender here back to the city. I'm sure he has other places he wishes to be."

He moved swiftly, catching up to me before I reached the exit, taking the lead, and entering the corridor without looking back, expecting me to follow him. I did, knowing I had to get back to Nadira as soon as possible. We stopped in front of the set of three teleporters, the old man raising his hand to the edge of it, a holographic map of the city popping up in the doorway of the centre teleporter. He turned to me, explaining with a blank expression,

"This teleporter can connect to any other within the city. Just select here which one you'd like to go to." He clenched his jaw again, as if unsure whether to continue, "And if for whatever reason you wish to return to parliament—" He raised his left arm and pushed his sleeve back, revealing a tattoo around his wrist, of two loosely braided cords; one a navy colour, and the other a deep purple. "—Simply take your middle finger and draw it around your wrist here, and down your other middle finger. The teleporter will pick up the signal and bring you here."

I looked down at my left wrist, bringing it up to examine it, wondering how I had not noticed that I now had a magical tattoo. Sure enough, the same two dark-coloured cords were tattooed on my wrist.

Having finished speaking, the man gestured to the teleporter, apparently not leaving until I had stepped through it. I looked him up and down one last time, a combination of disappointed and mad that I had gone through all this for nothing, and that I had slept while Jezebel killed the High Priestess and taken her position, making herself even harder to get to, apparently out of the reach of parliament even, not that they would ever move against her anyway. I scoffed.

"Thanks I guess."

Before I clicked on the group of teleporters that we had initially entered on our way to the library. I stepped through, and all of a sudden I was there, the noise of the crowds initially deafening, making me realise how strangely quiet the corridor had been. I blinked into the sunlight, my eyes adjusting to the rippling, watercolour sky and the streets around me. After orienting myself, I set off towards our outpost on the outskirts of the city. I spent the entire journey worrying about what would happen when I saw Nadira again—half of me dreading her reaction to the news about her father, and the other half wondering if Nadira really was an alexandrite, and what that would mean for us. Could we be soulmates after all?

Eventually I came to the outpost, itching to get out of these robes after getting an uncomfortable number of stares outside of the inner city. I reached the door and for some strange reason I felt compelled to knock, rather than walking straight in like I usually would. I heard footsteps, and the door swung open, Nadira's face meeting me in the doorway, her smile so wide it managed to outshine her eyes for the first time ever. She ran at me and hugged me, practically jumping into my arms, and I buried my head in her neck as we embraced in the doorway, both of us unable to speak through the flood of relief seeing that the other was okay. She pulled back.

"Your stuff appeared on our bed, all your clothes too, and I didn't know if that meant…" she trailed off, clearly assuming the worst,

"Why would they send the clothes of a dead man back?" I asked.

"I suppose, but the blood all over the shirt, and the boot… whatever carved into that could have easily killed you."

Her eyes widened then, just now noticing the long cut on my scalp, parting my hair awkwardly.

"What happened!? Tell me everything."

And so I did, starting with the hangar doors opening into the cavern, and ending with my swift return, having been unofficially shunned by parliament. I did leave out a few details, saying that I had to fight and defeat a parliamentarian to take their place, without mentioning which one it was that I had to kill. I also left out all the bits about alexandrite, saving it for last to finally reveal to Nadira that we might actually be soulmates, that all this time we ignored our gems thinking we were the only ones of our kind, but had managed to find each other anyway. I didn't get time to make these revelations known however, as Nadira started thinking out loud, planning and trying to figure out our next move. She was pacing back and forth, not paying any attention to me now.

"Right, so I already knew that Jezebel had forcibly become the new High Priestess, which I think is why she hasn't killed any more gems since onyx, she's been too busy executing her plan to become High Priestess, that being said, now that she's there the genocides will probably continue."

She paused for a moment, thinking, and I went to speak, but she continued, "And parliament won't help, not that we expected them too, but now that Jezebel is the High Priestess, it'll be much harder to get to her. The only real chance we'd have would be to break into the cathedral, but it's one of the most heavily fortified buildings in the city. There's no way we could get in there just with your parliamentary power. We might get past the first few checkpoints, but after that, we'd just be surrounded and we'd have no chance at all." She looked up at me. "My father must have been in parliament. I wouldn't expect you to recognise him, but he knows a bit about you. Did he seek you out at all? Did he say anything that might help? He wouldn't say anything to me, even as his daughter, but now that you're a parliamentarian, he might've confided in you something that he knows might help us."

She looked at me, waiting for an answer, and I knew the truth would shatter the beautiful vision of her as she stood before me, her big green eyes looking hopefully up into mine. My eyes went glassy, and I choked on my lie,

"I didn't... well, he did introduce himself. He said you wouldn't tell him what gem I was, so he tried to discern it for himself."

I tried to chuckle, but Nadira frowned at my odd attempt at humour. She then froze, her expression blank as she mumbled, not looking at me.

"He sought you out..."

She looked up at me, starting to understand. My expression told her everything, words failing me as my mouth opened and closed. She whispered more forcefully now,

"He didn't... that arrogant bastard."

I wasn't used to seeing Nadira like this; it was a specific kind of anger that I couldn't quite place, leaving me staring at her, shocked. She saw my expression and was immediately offended by it,

"Why are you looking at me like that? You killed him. You killed my father..."

Her voice broke, and the anger dissolved, a wave of sadness dropping her to her knees. She slapped my arms away as I tried to comfort her, to hold her. She instead jumped up and ran out the door without another word. By the time I crossed the room and reached the door to run after her, I could no longer see her. She had managed to disappear in that way that she does, but her eyes weren't looking at me this time, so I had no way of finding her. I shouted her name after her, but even the wind wouldn't respond to me. I looked back to the empty room.

Ava was gone. Araysh was gone. And Nadira had run away. I was alone. I looked down at my dark green robes, ripping them off me as angry tears fell from my eyes. The pursuit of parliament had only gotten my friends killed. No wonder Nadira despised it as much as she did. All they did was bring pain and death, and refuse to use their power for good to at least try and justify it all. Now I was alone, and it was all their fault. I stared at my torn robes on the ground, the folds exposing the hidden purple iridescence along the ridges. I kicked it away and stormed up the steps and into Nadira and I's room. But being there was too much. I had come back in the hopes of telling Nadira about being an alexandrite, fantasising that everything would suddenly be okay, and we could be proper soulmates, but all I had come back to was pain. This room was too much for me right now. Too much had happened here and I couldn't spend a night alone without Nadira. I hadn't yet since I first got here, and I was becoming increasingly terrified that this might be the first. I snatched the strap housing the compartment of gems from the bed that had apparently been teleported here, but chose instead to throw it at the wall, the remaining gems falling out, remembering those that I had broken in my fights on the proelium board.

I left the house altogether and went towards the city, wishing not to be seen, and finding myself surprised when no one really seemed to notice me despite wearing the dark-green parliamentary leathers—A battle outfit—that should've stood out significantly in this part of the city. I continued, relieved to be ignored, and approached the Gehazi house. I didn't know if they knew about Ava yet, and I really didn't want to be the one to tell them, especially not without Nadira's support, but I had nowhere else to go, no one else left to talk to, and they deserved to know what had happened.

I hesitantly knocked on the door. Kalona opened it, relieved to see me. That was a good sign at least, but it meant that they probably hadn't heard about Ava yet. Kalona invited me in, and I rose the stairs to the kitchen to find a less relieved looking Achan, whose stare bored a hole in me, glancing behind me for a moment looking for Ava.

"Where is she? I thought she'd be back by now. Is she still in parliament?"

His questions were calm, but the strain of maintaining that composure was evident. I sat down tentatively, unsure how to respond but knowing that I couldn't lie.

"Technically, yes, she is."

He held off his relief, anger rising in his voice as doubt took hold.

"Technically? What do you mean, boy? Spit it out, where is she?"

"She made it to parliament, across the dunes."

I paused and took a steadying breath.

"But she didn't make it through the next trial."

I froze, fearful of his reaction, which I was right to be, as he stood up forcefully, bumping the table into my ribs.

"No. There's no way Ava failed at something you could do. She was better than you at everything. You're lying. What was the trial? Go on, tell me."

I tried to oblige but found myself choking on the words, eventually replying.

"Binding magic. It won't let me tell you. But when I discovered it, I thought for sure that Ava would have made it through."

"And how do you know she didn't then."

His calmness was momentary, hoping to have found a hole in my lie.

"The parliamentarians, they told me, and I saw them all there afterwards. Ava wasn't with them."

His jaw was clenched too tight to respond now. Kalona had run off to their room, with her hands over her face. Achan continued to stare at me, supressing some kind of urge, that was revealed the next time he spoke. It was at a harsh whisper now.

"Get out. This is all your fault. Your quest has gotten my daughter killed. I never want to see your face again, or I might just kill you myself."

He refused to look at me now. I didn't know Achan had this inside of him, and I still wasn't sure as I backed away towards the door, staring at him in shock. As I reached the top of the stairs, I suddenly believed him, as he looked up, locking eyes with me and hurling his chair at me. It crashed into the wall as I broke eye contact and raced down the stairs, the door automatically swinging shut behind me.

And that was it—the last place in this city where I might've found some comfort, some relief from the growing terror in my chest, and the anger screaming at me to tear this city down. I had no reason now to ever go back to see the Gehazis. It was just Nadira and I, and the only thing holding back my anger was knowing that she was somewhere in the city, and letting that anger out would only prove Cybele right—that I was dangerous and destructive. Instead, I walked into the city and downed a few of this planet's versions of cocktails. I sat there, wallowing, racking up a tab. The bartender, recognising my leathers and tattoo, was too afraid to ask me to pay or cut me off. He was likely wondering what kind of supreme judgement I possessed that led me to spend my time this way. I chuckled. Yeah, me, with superior intellect and judgement. Me, the mediocre boy from Earth, the little mudball turned concrete jungle. I chuckled again at the sheer absurdity of it all. I joined 'Hit-Me' to escape my parents and do something useful with my life, but I couldn't even pass the final exam. My failure took me even further away, to this distant corner of somewhere, where for a moment, everything was perfect. I felt like I had a purpose. I was someone. I had magic, and I could help people. I even successfully made it to parliament; the most prestigious achievement one can attain in this city. And yet, it's all just led me to a bar, with dead friends, and no way to get home. How I missed home right now.

I sighed and stood up, catching myself as my legs wobbled beneath me. I chuckled again, finding it funny for some reason, and finding a little bit of joy in my inability to walk straight, although I couldn't figure out why.

I continued down the street, wandering towards the heart of the city, seeing an arcade entrance and randomly deciding to walk down it. I had no direction. Only an avoidance of the nothing that I had left. I walked past stalls and shops, many of them closed now, the ones that were open selling some of the more intriguing items. One stall in particular I found selling rhodonite and a wave of unwanted feelings washed over me, instinctively making me reach for the bracelet around my wrist that housed the garnet. I was surprised that parliament had left me with it as they had taken all the rest of my clothes off of me. I stared at it, only making myself sadder. I forced myself to look away, suddenly craving another cocktail. My eyes caught on an aquamarine sitting on the table instead, and I became lost in a fantasy, of making myself a little boat out of ice, floating away on it down the river and disappearing into the desert. Perhaps I'd come across another settlement where I could start again. Surely this planet didn't only have one city. I missed home. Immersed in the fantasy, I strode over and picked it up. A voice from somewhere on the other side of the table echoed, "Looking for a gift are we?"

I replied clumsily, "Uh, no, for myself actually."

"Oh really? It doesn't seem like your type, but who am I to question you."

I smiled. She seemed bold. I wondered if she treated all parliamentarians like this, or just the drunk ones too clumsy to notice her subtle digs.

"I don't have any money, but I can offer you this in trade."

I said, taking the garnet from my wrist, trying not to look at it as I held it out to the shadows on the other side of the table. She emerged, taking it and examining it. She was shorter than I expected, but it was too dark to make out many of her features, not that I tried very hard before my mind returned to the daydream of me floating down the river in a boat made of ice.

"A good trade. The aquamarine is yours."

She disappeared into the shadows, and I scoffed as I took the light blue stone. I mumbled to myself, "

A good trade for you maybe. That bracelet was worth way more."

But I was glad to be rid of it, set in my plan to start again. For some reason, I found my way out of the inner city at South-Fork, deciding to cross the river and wander towards the old arena. I stumbled up the steps that rose up through the stands of the arena. I made my way to the top, to the very same place where I had first used ice magic. I sat on the edge overlooking the river, unsure how high I was, but it was too high to be this clumsy, I knew that much. I closed my eyes, enjoying the cool night air on my face. A small shiver ran through me, making me temporarily wish I had my garnet again to conjure a fire, but regretted the thought, being content with the warmth the alcohol provided.

I looked down into the dark waters of the river, following them with my eyes through the buildings and under the little foot bridges on the outskirts of the city. I could barely follow the dark line as it carved its way through the dunes out into the desert. I sighed, waving my fingers, playing with the flow of the river below, making little shapes and watching them float down the river. I sat there playing with the magic, erasing all other thoughts from my mind and trying not to think about where Nadira had run off to. To where she had gone to find comfort, away from her father's murderer. No. No thoughts, just little magical ice canoe floating away down the river.

I found myself surprised at my ability to make anything that looked remotely like a canoe.

"Ender!"

A voice rang out below from the arena floor. It was Nadira's voice. The sudden noise startled me, and I lost my balance. Instinctively, I reached out with magic to steady myself, but quickly realised that it was probably safer to let the water catch me rather than conjuring ice. I plunged into the cool river, my shoulder jarring painfully as it struck the surface first, followed by the rest of my body. The aurora rippling on the surface of the water was pretty from underneath. The added waves my body had created as it broke through the surface made the scattered light go crazy in unpredictable ways. By the time it had settled into something more predictable, I realised I was running out of air. I swam upwards, reaching for the ripples of light, becoming aware of just how strong the current was in this section of river. It was much faster than I had anticipated. I attempted to use ice magic to propel myself out of the water and onto the bank, but I inadvertently froze the water around me instead. My feet became encased in ice, causing the buoyant ice to flip me upside down. My lungs burned as I struggled to hold my breath. Desperately flailing, I couldn't even manage to right myself to breathe. In that harrowing moment, a grim thought crossed my mind: What difference would it make if I died? Everyone back home thought I was already dead, and everyone here was either dead or despised me. I wouldn't be missed. And so I stopped struggling, using the last moments of conscious thought to make peace with my impending death. As my vision left me, the last thing I felt before I died was something wrapping around my arm.

Chapter 12

The aurora rippled above me as I felt the gritty sand beneath my fingers. Slowly, I sat up, the block of ice still encasing my feet. My legs were cold and numb—worse than numb; I couldn't feel them at all. Nadira kneeled next to me, staring at me with worry. She leapt at me after seeing that I was alive, wrapping her arms around me and pushing me back into the sand. I was still in shock, surprised to be alive, but the new warmth in my body and my soul was enough to bring me back to the present, smiling as I squeezed her so hard I couldn't help but wonder If I was hallucinating, if this was a conjuration of my brain as it shut down, freezing to death underwater. She whispered in my ear, her voice shaky.

"I already lost my father, I can't lose you too, not now."

Tears streamed down my face as I sobbed into her shoulder. The warm liquid made it even more evident how cold I was becoming, the block of ice slowly freezing me. I croaked out a word to Nadira,

"Fire." And she understood, pulling back and quickly pushing back her sleeve, revealing the garnet around her wrist. The matching one of which I had traded for the very magic that had put me in this position. Idiot.

I was weak and stiff, and Nadira could see that, lifting my hand to the block of ice. I switched to the fire magic, immediately warming up, the ice beneath my hand starting to melt rapidly. As the final bit of ice melted away, I finally lifted my gaze to meet Nadira's. The guilt etched on my face felt out of place against her expression of forgiveness and concern. We stared at each other in silence, unsure of what to say. Suddenly, a rush of panic surged through me as I remembered all the things I wanted to tell her before she ran off. It felt like if I didn't say them now, I might never get the chance.

"I'm alexandrite." I blurted out, surprising her with my abruptness. "And I think that you are too."

I continued in a whisper, averting my eyes from hers, unable to accept her forgiveness fully when I hadn't forgiven myself yet. The look of shock on her face gave way to a smile, and finally, she chuckled,

"Of course we are. What else would make sense."

I chuckled too. I suppose she was right, but still I frowned.

"But my eyes, they're not like yours, and if that stealth thing you do is alexandrite magic, I can't do that either."

Her smile widened,

"You weren't born here. The magic hasn't affected you in the same way that it has me. As for my magic, its chameleon magic, and you've found yourself a different way of blending in. Not visually like me, but magically."

"So you think I can only channel different magics because I'm alexandrite?"

"Well, not exactly. Otherwise Cybele's machine that uses the same concept wouldn't work. I think it's more like you were drawn to using different magics as a way of blending in here, *because* you're an alexandrite, like it's part of your nature."

I thought about it and realised that she was more right than she knew. Blending in was so engrained in my nature that it was the thing I strived for as well as hated about myself. On Earth I was just mediocre, a nobody, the very middle of the pack in school and in HITNE. I didn't stand out at all, no matter what I tried to do. And yet, now that I was here where I could blend-in with magic, I had somehow managed to do the opposite, making myself a target, a parliamentarian, a friend, a killer.

Nadira saw me lost in thought and snuggled up to me in the sand.

"I think it'll all be okay now. I know we don't have a plan, but I might have an idea now." She said, sighing. She looked up at me from in my arms, "That being said, today has been emotionally exhausting, and neither of us are in any state to walk back to the city. We've drifted too far out."

I looked out across the dunes, unable to see any sign of the city over them. It was just us, the river, and the sand.

"Tomorrow, we stop Jezebel and destroy that machine. We better get some rest." She continued, smiling up at me, "It's not like we haven't slept out here under the stars before."

She lay back down, curling up in my lap as I remained sitting up. I smiled too, this was just like our first night, sleeping out under the stars, only this time we were finally going to stop Jezebel instead of running away. That, and we were by the river where the sand was still, making it much easier to sleep, knowing we wouldn't wake up half turned to sand.

The garnet remained active all through the night, keeping us warm out in the desert, a chilling breeze occasionally blowing across the river. The morning came and I felt an immense amount of joy just simply watching the sunrise change Nadiras eyes slowly from a deep purple through to a bright green. Our first night together as proper soulmates, and we had spent it just like our first. That day was pure hell, but now, all I could remember was that it was the day I met Nadira. Meeting Jezebel, her attempt to kill us, and abandoning us to die seemed to fade away in comparison.

Nadira sat up, stretching her arms out, smiling at me. She rose her hand to her collarbone, to a necklace under her shirt, to fiddle with the stone. I frowned, and she noticed, taking it out from under her shirt and letting it glint in the morning light. It was a rather fancy silver necklace with four-pointed-stars dispersed along the chain. The single gemstone in the centre was a dark-green princess-cut gem, a square shape, with hints of dark purple hiding in the corners. My eyes widened, recognising the necklace from the portrait of the alexandrite parliamentarian.

"It's not exactly a family heirloom, but because there's usually only one alexandrite alive at a time, it gets passed down from one to the next. Rarely in person, but it makes its way to us one way or another. My mother gave me this when I was eleven." She looked down at the necklace. "I haven't been wearing it because I liked pretending I was your garnet soulmate with you, and being with you felt more right than being an alexandrite." She smiled now, "I'm not entirely sure what made me want to wear it now, but I think maybe seeing you in that dark-green robe made something click in the back of my mind, and suddenly being an alexandrite felt more right than it did before. I love you, Ender, and I know this journey hasn't been easy, but if we don't have each other to go through it with, then what do we have?"

I was starting to forgive myself. I wasn't there fully, but Nadira knew how to sway my emotions better than anyone.

"I love you too Nadira."

For some reason I thought about something that Nadira had said the night before, "You said yesterday that you might have an idea, to stop Jezebel. What is it?"

She smirked, "I'll explain once we get home."

Home. As far as I was concerned, Nadira was my home. Regardless, the word still made my thoughts drift to my parents and my sister, Hailey, as we walked along the river, back towards the city. It was nearly midday when we arrived at the edge of South-Fork, and just past it when we finally made it home. Nadira was eerily silent during the journey, and I imagined that she was thinking about her father, or Jezebel, or both. Even if she said she had forgiven me for it, the grief over the loss of her father was still present and would always remain no matter what I did. We made it back, and I immediately asked about her idea the moment we walked through the door, having not been able to figure it out, or come up with anything of my own during our silent journey. Nadira spun around to face me, smirking, her eyes scanning the room to see if we were alone. We were. She walked up to me, dragging her fingers up my arm and lacing her fingers together around the back of my neck. I couldn't tell if it was just me or not, but this sudden change of pace felt a bit forced. Perhaps it was a distraction for her from everything else going on. Either way, I couldn't help but fall for it, real or not. She spoke only when she had taken my hands and spun herself around, pressing her back into my chest, wrapping my arms around her.

"I'm sure you've heard of soulmate fusion by now, but do you know how it works?"

"I…n-no" I stuttered, taken aback by her sudden mood change. I could feel her smile at me, knowing that I was blushing. She didn't turn back around.

"First, you have to ensure your bodies are aligned, hence why I'm facing the same direction as you. Then, you focus on each other, on your love, or so I'm told. From there I'm not really sure. You're supposed to just kind of melt together, in a way."

A slight rush of panic went through me.

"Is it like… permanent?"

Nadira chuckled, "No, it's not. It's just a way to be closer to each other, as well as in our case, enhance our magic."

In our case. She said this like enhanced magic was the only reason we were doing this. Technically I suppose it was *why* we were doing it. She still hadn't explained how it was supposed to help. But I thought she would at least acknowledge wanting to do it for… y'know, other reasons. She took my hands again and stretched out our arms, our bodies matching each other's positions as closely as possible, my eyes just seeing over the top of her head. I laced my fingers with hers as our arms were outstretched, and she leant back into me. I closed my eyes, trying to focus on this feeling, on our love, on what she meant to me, and wished with all my soul, to just melt into her. It wasn't until Nadira took a deep breath and let it out shakily that she started to feel extra warm, the places we touched all feeling like skin on skin for a moment, despite the layers of clothes between us. The next moment was something else entirely, like I could sense Nadiras thoughts, and her emotions came rushing through my mind, however fleeting. I wasn't Ender anymore. I was both of us. But before I could open my eyes, a rush of emotions slammed my consciousness; grief from the loss of my father, a sense of isolation, missing my family back on Earth, and a thorough sense of shock that we both had to have been feeling to be this strong.

We split apart the next moment, having been unprepared for such a connection to each other. We sat on the floor, staring at each other. I understood it now, and I think Nadira understood me a little more now too. She was trying to hide it, but the grief she felt was intense, and being here with none of our friends around, many of them now gone too, wasn't helping. Even after being connected with her like that, I still didn't know how to help. Or if I was even the person who *should* help. She surprised me when she spoke.

"I didn't realise how much you missed Earth."

I smiled. "So much has been happening, I don't think I even realised it myself. Not until everything started breaking down here anyway."

A moment of silence followed as we recounted the tragic events in our heads. "I…" I began but wasn't sure what to say. Nadira spoke up.

"I suppose I should explain. Maybe it'll work better if we both a have a clear goal. Something to focus on, to align our thoughts so that they don't clash together when we fuse."

I wasn't sure that was entirely the problem, but it was a rational solution to something that would take months to sort out the hard way, and we didn't have that kind of time. Nadira continued when I nodded.

"So, chameleon magic helps us blend in right? And fusion enhances magic, so I'm hoping that the enhancement will make us even more invisible, allowing us to sneak into the cathedral. Of course, to get over the bridge we'll have to use your parliamentary access, but once we're in, we can just disappear into the cathedral. They'll know we're there that way, but there's not really any way to sneak across the bridge, we'll have to be let through the gate."

I thought it over, finding my thoughts drifting to wondering what it would be like to pull off this mission, letting Nadira guide me from the inside, making unfamiliar buildings familiar through her eyes, knowing exactly what to do when I knew myself that I had no idea.

"Wait but how do we find Jezebel once we get in?"

"Well, I figure that she'll probably be somewhere in the priestess quarters wing. I was just going to look for the biggest, fanciest room. She is the High Priestess now after all. If that fails, then I was going to look for the place with the most security."

I was nodding, "That should work. I mean, I have no idea what the cathedral even looks like, but I trust you, so if you think this will work, I'm all in."

She smiled, "Try again then?"

I nodded and she stepped closer to me, spinning around and leaning into me. I restrained my thoughts to everything she had just said about the mission and leant into her too, feeling the now somewhat familiar sensation of our souls merging, becoming both of us. This time, we remained together, our thoughts no longer colliding. Instead, I found myself able to vividly picture the cathedral and its grand halls. I knew exactly where to look first and could remember the imposing presence of the gates at the bridge. I glanced down at my hands, my gaze catching the floor first. I noticed I was a bit taller—not just from Nadira's perspective of seeing from Ender's height, but both of us were now a few inches taller than Ender too. The image of Annabelle crossed my mind, and I recalled how tall fusions always were. It made them noticeable in a crowd. Hopefully, my robes still fit. I noticed my clothes then and couldn't help but chuckle.

My parliamentarian leathers were the less malleable of our two sets of clothes, resulting in the leathers and scales looking relatively normal, but the areas between where I had grown when we fused, were now a patchwork of my other clothes, of Nadiras outfit, filling the gaps between scale shin pads and leather bands. I found myself thinking about parliament, the trials I had gone through, and the people I had met, and the battle with my father. I remembered killing him myself. The next moment I was on the floor again, Nadira sitting across from me in tears. I instinctively shuffled over to her and wrapped my arms around her. She didn't run away from me this time but let me comfort her. Her face was warm and wet in my shoulder. When she stopped sobbing, I heard her whisper,

"He really didn't give you a choice. I… I felt everything that you felt when you were fighting him. You tried so hard… but you didn't have a choice. I'm sorry."

I clenched my jaw, remembering the emotions flooding through me when we were fused, feeling Nadiras reaction to seeing me kill her father through my eyes, feeling like she was killing him herself. I couldn't imagine how that would feel, except, I kind of had.

"Don't apologise. You've already been more forgiving than anyone should be for what I did."

She pressed her face into my shoulder, and we sat in silence for a few moments. Slowly but surely, the tears ran out. When Nadira was ready, we fused once more, both of us focusing solely on the mission ahead, determined not to dwell on our past or present, or anything that might cause us to separate again. The sun was getting low and we were running out of time to figure out how to stay together for long enough to pull this off. You'd think magic based on being soulmates would be easy, but apparently not.

Eventually we had fused and remained calm enough to try on my parliamentary robes in this larger form. They were loose and flowy, making them adjust to my size easily. The damage I did ripping them off me earlier was minimal and not too noticeable, but I couldn't let my mind wander to that. Onwards. I estimated that I'd get to the cathedral before sundown if we left now. If we entered any later it would raise suspicion, or they might not even let us in all together. That meant that we only had the trip through the city to figure out this enhanced alexandrite magic. It was difficult to gauge if it was working, as the only way to confirm our invisibility would be to ask someone. I had likely gotten the hang of it though, since it wasn't much different from how I usually navigated the town. Watching myself through Ender's eyes via his memories was intriguing, and I hoped this form would conceal our eyes. I didn't have a mirror, but I imagined our combined eye colour would dull the brightness of the green. Although they'd be purple soon anyway which made them much harder to see in the dark.

Nearing the cathedral, after having made our way to the inner city, taken a teleporter to the north, and then made our way northwards, I decided to test our invisibility. I purposefully bumped into a person on the street, hard enough to make them turn around and look for someone to shout at. They had shouted but stopped abruptly, seeing no-one there, despite us standing right there, eyes staring right at them. I smiled. We were completely invisible. Even my eyes didn't show. We were ghosts in this city right now.

Spotting the gates on the bridge leading to the cathedral, I calmly veered off towards a building on the edge of the inner city, staying out of sight of any guards or priestesses. Not that they could see us anyway, but we didn't need the attention from suddenly appearing out of thin air when we un-fused.

Confident that no one was watching, I un-fused, separating once again into Ender and Nadira. I stood across from Nadira, a smile spreading across my face, relieved that we had managed to figure out this whole fusion thing—at least to some extent. My smile broke into a laugh when I saw Nadira wearing my robes. I couldn't help but find her cute with the look of confusion on her face, staring at the robes on her.

"I guess we put on the robes while we were fused, so they didn't know who to return to." Nadira posited.

Magic was weird. But at least we weren't naked. I'd seen plenty of movies where stuff like this would leave everyone naked. Nadira stuck her arm out towards me, holding the robes in one hand. I took them and put them on, Nadira fixing her hair and trying to make herself look as formal and nice as possible. She was stunning. She caught me staring and blushed as she waved her hands at me, gesturing me towards the gate. I obliged, adopting a bit of a pompous expression as I approached the gate. The guards clearly found me curious, Nadira even more so as she trailed barely behind me, but they didn't argue as they opened the gate. I didn't even have to say anything. They had just looked at my robes and moved to let us through. I glanced backwards once while we were halfway across the bridge, just to check, and I found the guards still watching us.

Night was fast approaching now and there were priestesses outside the cathedral lighting fires in various places along the walls and in the gardens. It was harder to remember the images of the inside of the cathedral when I wasn't fused with Nadira and hadn't experienced it for myself yet, but I thought I remembered there being a covered area between the front entrance and the inside, like whatever the cathedral equivalent of a porch was. I made it just past the entrance and veered off to the left, the fires on this section of the wall along the porch having already been lit. I turned to Nadira, trying to hurry, but finding her more prepared than I expected, as she continued towards me when I turned around, spinning and falling into me softly in one fluid motion. We fused just like that, having found our flow. I was now a little bit taller and completely invisible. Able to remember where I was going now, I entered the main hall of the Cathedral and took a sharp right, following along the inside wall of the main hall, behind the various platforms designed for different kinds of offerings. Before I reached the front half of the hall, where the pews sat facing the lectern, and the large statue stood behind it of a woman, of Varanasi, I turned right, into an antechamber off the main hall. I caught my breath, seeing the two guards standing there on either side of the large door at the entrance to the east-wing. The priestess quarters. But how were we supposed to get past the guards? I stood there thinking about it, eyeing the door and guessing that even if I drew them away, the door would still make a fair amount of noise when I opened it. It looked old and heavy. Luckily, I noticed the gemstone of one of the guards was an amethyst and realised that I could put the two of them to sleep if I tapped into its dream-magic. I moved to activate my epicode, finding the feeling strange, unsure if that was because of my new physiology, or just Nadira's feelings, not understanding what the epicode felt like. As I went to activate the epicode, I hesitated, unsure if it would even work with us fused like this. But I suppose there was only way to find out. I activated my epicode, trying to remain calm, the part of me that was Nadira uncomfortable with the feeling of it and how it displayed images in my vision. I activated the frequency augmentation mode, and set it to amethyst, fighting harder to remain calm now as Nadira's discomfort grew with the activation of a new type of magic, like half of my body wasn't used to it, wasn't quite compatible with it. At the same moment, the guards both stared straight into my eyes, and I realised I was no longer fully invisible. I heard one of the guards whisper,

"What is this creature…" while the other shouted at us, raising his spear,

"Who are you, you shouldn't be in here!"

But before he could lunge at me, pointing his weapon directly between our eyes, I tapped into the dream magic, and knocked both of them right out, putting them into a deep sleep. I went to deactivate the epicode immediately, to become invisible again, but the part of me that was Nadira recognised their reaction somewhat, and knew that they had only seen our eyes. Only our eyes had become visible when I had activated the epicode. If I had to guess, I would say that the enhanced magic we were taking advantage of while being fused, was limited. It seemed to work surprisingly linearly, like two people equalled twice as much magic, allowing two of the same gem fused to have twice as powerful magic. In our case, however, this meant that we could use one persons worth of magic to remain semi-invisible, and the other persons worth of magic for whatever other kind of magic we chose. I had a strange feeling then, as the part of me that was Ender did a double take, like he thought we might've inadvertently activated a sapphire somewhere, before quickly realising that their combined brainpower was just slightly more than twice what his was. I felt conflicted in that moment but reminded myself that we had a job to do, and opened the door.

We returned to being fully invisible again, and I poked my head through first. The hall on the other side was empty. I stepped through the door, only opening it as much as I had too to fit through, and closed it again, the soft clink of the latch returning to its position echoing through the silent marble halls. I made my way down the hall, in entirely new territory, having no idea what to expect from here, memories from my childhood of the supreme omniscience of diamonds starting to seep in, temporarily making me nervous.

I wondering if Jezebel knew that we were already here, coming for her. But I rid myself of those notions, the clear mind of Ender free of those superstitions. I pressed on. The wide hallway was quiet and dimly lit, my footsteps echoing off the marble walls. I hadn't gone very far down the hall when I started finding windows on either side of the hallway, the view out of which was breathtaking. I stopped and stared out of the south-side window, facing the city. We weren't all that high up, only just tall enough to see over the wall and down onto the tops of some buildings in the inner city. There were plenty of structures and spires in the centre of the city that reached much higher than we were. However, we were only on the ground floor of the cathedral. It was dark now, the aurora set against the waves of the night sky above the city, the most breathtaking view that either of us had ever seen, and I found myself thinking, 'I wonder if my child will ever get to see such a beautiful view,' but the thought confused me and the sound of footsteps snapped me back to the hallway. Part of me panicked, pressing myself into the wall, soon remembering that I was completely invisible and relaxed a little bit, my childhood church teachings leaving me wondering if diamonds could in fact see through our invisibility. I stood by the window, peering down the hallway. A faint, warm light gradually grew brighter at the end of the hallway around the corner. After a few moments, I shuffled further down hallway watching the flickering light intently. A figure emerged, holding a torch. I let out a sigh of relief—it was just a priestess lighting the sconces on the walls. I continued down the hallway, keeping my footsteps and breathing as quiet as possible. I stopped in my tracks, however, when I saw another figure emerge from the other direction at the end of the hallway, but continued after realising that she was just lighting the fires along the opposite wall. The priestesses didn't notice us as I snuck past them, their jewellery and robes indicating that they were both diamonds.

As I reached the end of the hall, I found myself with a choice. Both directions looked identical from this spot. Both curved hallways hid whatever was down them, but not enough to not show the first door down each. They must lead to the priestess rooms. I surmised that given the cathedrals penchant for symmetry, that the rooms of the High Priestess would likely be in the centre, meaning that we would find them where both hallways connected, and that it didn't really matter which direction we chose. I turned left at random, slowing down as I passed the first door, listening for signs of people inside, for voices, but anything I did hear as I passed the rooms was too muffled to understand. Starting to become disoriented, figuring that we were surely close to halfway around the tower now, I came across a door on the opposite side of the hallway, the addition of gold inlay indicating higher status. The High Priestess' rooms. This was it. This was where we would find Jezebel and finally put an end to the genocide.

My fear slowly turned to curiosity as I approached the door, wondering why there were no sounds coming from inside. The other priestesses mostly seemed to all be in their chambers, or strolling the grounds. Then again, she was far from a regular priestess and had no intentions of sitting back and enjoying cathedral life. Starting to think up some kind of way to ambush her when she returned to her room, I hesitantly pushed on the door, finding it locked. I rolled my eyes at myself. How did I forget about locks.

My mind started speeding up, starting to feel exposed standing here in the hall. I knew I was invisible, but I couldn't just stand here and wait until Jezebel came back. I wasn't sure I'd stay fused if left alone to my thoughts right now, and that was a feeling that both of us seemed to acknowledge.

I activated my epicode, looking first for sapphire, thinking that I could unlock the door that way, before remembering that I had used it to… well, forget that. I had to focus. I shook my head a little too violently, knowing that we'd un-fuse if I let my mind wander, especially in that direction. I felt half of me squirm, Nadira uncomfortable as I activated the epicode, although, for some reason I felt that that wasn't right. My stomach turned, the discomfort growing, like a knot forming in my stomach, distracting me enough to draw my attention, but I focused on the lock again, not wanting to tell him just yet. Wait what. Being fused was confusing.

I shook my head trying to focus, worried that we were falling apart, a sentiment that we shared, aligning our thoughts once more. I went to switch next to the black moonstone, remembering that that too was broken. I still had my garnet, just the one at least, but I didn't want to melt the lock completely and give away that we were here and waiting. I had the aquamarine too but no water… or hold on, maybe. I pulled out a pearl-water flask and switched to the aquamarine. It took some concentration for such a small amount of liquid, especially fighting the discomfort half of me had to foreign magic, but I managed to find the threads and pull on them, lifting droplets of water out of the flask briefly before they fell back into the flask, frozen. It was a long shot, but perhaps the healing magic in the water would help me here, even if that was just wishful thinking.

I held the opening of the flask up to the keyhole, tilting it just enough so that none of it spilled. I took a deep breath and pulled the thread of magic out of the little bottle, the water quickly hopping out of the bottle and flowing into the keyhole. I had to be quick before it froze, and found a headache start to form as I tried to feel the edges of the inside of the lock while subconsciously fighting the foreign magic, as well as a nauseousness that felt out of place. I nearly fainted at the effort, my face probably bright red if it was visible, but I heard the lock click as I pushed the slush into the right corners of the lock, freezing as they stretched themselves too thin. I took a moment to steady myself, surprised by my body's reaction to such a small bit of magic, even it did take a lot of control and concentration.

I turned my gaze to the small gap between the door and the wall, a sliver of the room beyond now visible. I slowly pushed the door, and snuck through, closing it behind me. Trying to cover my tracks, I went to turn back to the door to melt the ice, but stopped, suddenly feeling like that wouldn't be a problem as I saw what this room contained. The room was massive, taking up the entire centre of the tower, and yet, there only stood a single object in it, at the very centre of the room. A teleporter. I stood there, puzzled, but the pieces began to fall into place as I recalled various things I had

240

heard. The old parliamentarian saying, 'When equal powers find themselves at odds,' and the cathedral guard's response when I asked why a cathedral guard protected the entrance to parliament.

This teleporter would take us straight down to a room aboard the very same ship that housed parliament—the ship whose hangar hosted the parliamentary trial's game of proelium, the trial where... No. Jezebel. She was down there on that ship somewhere, hiding beneath the city, so far below the surface that the only way down seemed to be through teleportation. I abandoned the lock and strode towards the teleporter, standing in front of its doorway, the flicker of hazy firelight all that was visible through the doorway, like the sheer volume of rock between the two teleporters was distorting the signal. At least there didn't appear to be any sign of Jezebel yet. I took a deep breath and proceeded through the teleporter, making sure I was fully invisible before I did so.

Chapter 13

It was quiet on the other side, even quieter than the hushed voices of the priestess' in the cathedral. But then a voice rang out.

"But how many are you going to destroy? All of the lower gems...or even some of the uppers?"

I recognised that voice. I hadn't heard it in a while, but there was no mistaking it. Cybele. I heard a scoff in response and my blood froze.

"Don't be ridiculous. It'll take time before our society is one hundred percent diamond. I'm simply purging the unproductive and the criminal. Everyone else will come in time."

"Even myself?"

"Of course, but I imagine you'll be an old lady by then. However, I wouldn't go around having any kids if I were you."

And there was the villain herself, blatantly telling her minion how she planned to murder her in the future. How she convinced Cybele to create the thing that she would use to kill her was beyond me. I poked my head around the corner, leaving the main room—an opulently furnished lounge room, where firelight danced in the reflections of gold and silver accents. The voices in the next room immediately caught my attention, leaving me little time to worry about my exact location. I peered my head through the open doorway, into the remains of a room whose intended purpose had been all but stripped away and turned into a workshop not dissimilar to that of Cybele's. This room was larger, but it wasn't designed that way. The rough edges of the wall that used to divide the space were still visible. My eyes fixed on the two women standing on the far side of the room. The room hadn't originally been part of the priestess quarters, but part of the ship. Now, a large machine stood there, connected to the ancient technology of the ship. The machine looked cobbled together from various kinds of technology, like those scavenged from crashed spaceships from all different planets.

This was it. I had found them. I had found it. And now all I had to do was confront both of them and destroy that machine. I entered the room and crept closer, gaining clarity of the details of the scene—the satisfaction in Jezebel's eyes, and the tiredness in Cybele's. The closer I got to them, the more anxious I felt, like they would see right through me at any moment. Memories flashed through my mind, of Cybele's scalpel held up to my eye, of Jezebel's golden claws coming down across my face, of something Jezebel first said to me when I was a little girl when I went to the cathedral for the first time with my parents. It was all too much. We were afraid of different things, both terrified of the monsters before us, but for different reasons, from different experiences, my stomach turned and I let out an audible groan before splitting apart right there.

I was only Ender now, staring at Nadira from across the floor, my head throbbing and her clutching her stomach, revealing that it was her stomach problems I had been feeling. My eyes flicked up to Cybele and Jezebel, the pair of them staring at us in shock. Jezebel's face twisted into a cruel smile as Cybele dropped her head and took a step backwards, closer to the machine.

"I wasn't expecting visitors today, but I guess I shouldn't be surprised that it's you two that've found your way here. Alexandrites always were sneaky, annoyingly so. They can't be trusted. Maybe I should move them up on my list of gems to eradicate. But then again, if it's only you two, it'd be much quicker to kill you the old-fashioned way."

Her claw flinched, and lightning arced out of it, looping back into her palm. Her smug grin was infuriating. Nadira and I were on our feet at the same time, a shared anger towards Jezebel that I hadn't understood from her perspective until I saw Jezebel through Nadira's eyes just now.

"You can certainly try."

She spat at Jezebel. The two locked their gazes on one another, a frightening intensity between them. Seeing them like this, and preparing for a fight, I activated my epicode, the light sparkling off Jezebel's diamonds giving me an idea. I knew I had to be quick, but as I began tuning up from sapphire, Jezebel raised her arm and Nadira dove forwards, apparently attempting to tackle her. Nadiras shoulder connected with Jezebel's hip, Jezebel being knocked sideways, bringing her arm down too late as lightning arced out and hit the ground, her claws following through but missing Nadira as she rammed into her and spun away, twisting Jezebel and temporarily disorienting her, but not for long enough to stop her protecting herself from Nadiras next attack. Nadira pounced, and my heart leapt to my throat when I saw she was too slow. But she fooled both Jezebel and me by dodging her own attack. She kicked her foot out behind her, hooking the base of a nearby spear with her foot. She slid it down the wall it leaned on, bringing the base close enough for her to grab and rolled towards me, just as lightning struck where she had been. She leapt up from the ground next to me, flicking the spear tip up at Jezebel, panting.

My eyes were drawn to her hair as she stood in her fighting stance, spear raised. I remembered the moment seconds after it happened—the lightning had hit the tip of the spear as she rolled and dragged it with her. The leather bindings on the handle weren't thick enough to stop the electricity from travelling up the spear and out the other end. It struck her with enough energy to make her hair stand on end and leave her lungs weak. My epicode was out of hearing range now. Even if I found the resonant harmonic frequency of Jezebel's diamonds, I wouldn't know it. So much for that idea. Instead, I copied her in another way, switching to obsidian, and flexing my fingers as my nails flashed chrome. Jezebel was angry now,

"Cybele!" she barked, causing Cybele to step forward too quickly, like she already knew what was coming. The red beryl around her neck, as well as the smaller ones, grew brighter suddenly, their glow enveloping her in a red haze, the visible energy seeming to flow into Jezebel, her diamonds now giving off a weaker but similar red glow. I frowned, and Nadira looked terrified, afraid of what was coming. A wicked smile crossed Jezebel's face as she raised her claws. Nadira immediately tried to dodge, to run away, leaving me standing there stunned as sharp red lightning filled my vision, the horror on Nadiras face visible out of the corner of my eye as the red lightning hit me, a buzzing filling my ears, the energy running through my entire body, dissipating through my feet and into the metal floor, dispersing through the walls of the ship. I thought I would feel worse after that. Jezebel did too, an angry frown crossing her face. She tried again, but this time I had enough sense to dodge. However, it still wasn't enough.

The red lightning arced wider and flashed brighter than her usual lightning. The bolt hit my left arm as I dodged, sending energy through my shoulders and down my other arm. The electricity released from my fingertips and slammed into the wall behind Cybele. Holy shit. I grinned, realising the conductive benefits of having metal skin. I was ready this time. Jezebel lunged this time, filling her hand with red spikes as she brought her arm down screaming at me, I reached out with both my arms, one aligned with hers to catch the lightning, and the other pointed right at her. The electricity coursed through me zipping through my arms and launching itself back at Jezebel, her eyes wide as the bolt hit her square in the chest, stunning her, but not seeming to do much damage. I guess she was used to lightning running through her being a diamond and all, but how much of this enhanced energy could she take?

She tried again and I managed to do the same thing. In our battle, however, I failed to notice Nadira sneak around the other side of the room until it was too late. Jezebel was too focused on me as she shot more lightning towards me when Nadira lunged towards her

246

with her spear pointed into her back. The distraction was enough for me to lose focus, the lightning hitting me in the arm, but my fingers touched when it hit me, forming a feedback loop, causing the lightning to race around my arms, burning me, until it released itself and sent me flying. I spun through the air until the electricity dissipated and I hit the wall, crumpling to the floor, head spinning. I looked up, anxiously waiting for my vision to stabilise, searching for Nadira and finding her on the floor, the spear sitting beneath Jezebel with blood on the tip, and a long gash across her thigh. The blood pouring from it was camouflaged by the red scales of her outfit. I jumped up as soon as I could, running towards Nadira, planning to grab the spear while Jezebel was facing her, but as I reached for it, too many things happened at once for me to make sense of it all.

Cybele opened her eyes gasping, the red glow surrounding her and Jezebel dissipating, causing Jezebel to spin around angrily as I reached for the spear, seeing me before she locked her eyes on Cybele. My hand wrapped around the very end of the spear the same moment as Jezebel's scaly boot connected with my face, slamming my head into the ground, my head throbbing but my hand still wrapped around the spear. Jezebel had turned towards Cybele the moment I had hit the ground, shouting at her,

"Start it back up now or I'll kill you decades early."

Cybele was quiet as she responded, but the stillness beneath the world on an ancient, buried ship was quieter, making her defiance echo in the silence.

"No. I won't. I can't."

"And why's that?"

"Because…" she locked eyes with Nadira across the room as she propped herself up on one arm, wrapping the other around her stomach. Cybele seemed to draw energy from Nadiras strength, her face hardening as she spoke, "Because she's pregnant, and I won't help you harm a child before its even born."

She was what? I stared blankly at the scene in front of me, not sure whether I was more surprised at the pregnancy, the way it was announced, or that Cybele was actually defending us, and against Jezebel of all people. Apparently, I was the only one surprised by any of this, as Jezebel's anger twisted into a wicked smile. She strode over to Nadira.

Nadira avoided my gaze until the moment before Jezebel's gold claws closed around her neck. The panic in Nadira's eyes brought me to my feet, spear in hand, as Jezebel lifted Nadira to her knees, blood starting to dribble down her neck as the claws dug into her skin. Jezebel started to shout at Cybele, stopping me in my tracks with a glare as I took a step forward, her claws tightening around Nadira's neck. I stopped, frozen with fear, not for my own life, but for Nadiras, and our child. The brief thought of our possible child was starting to break me as I tried to focus on the fight, and not on the future that might soon be lost.

"I don't need *you* to kill her, to kill all three of them. In fact, now that I have your machine, I don't need you at all."

Her smile twisted as her claws snapped closed, Nadiras arms going limp and her head flopping forward. Blood started to pour down her throat. Jezebel didn't even look. She just threw her body down on the ground, sapping up the horror on Cybele's face with glee like it was food for the starving monster that she was. I didn't

248

have the energy to scream out, choking on my own tears as my knuckles went white wrapped around the spear. My eyes flicked from Nadira to Jezebel, my emotions doing a somersault, flipping immediately to pure rage as I ran at her, throwing caution aside. I drove the spear right at her, her lightning ricocheting of my metal skin as she threw bolts at me. As I reached Jezebel, Cybele's gem glowed an intense red, but I had no time to worry about what that meant. I plunged my spear through Jezebel with such force that I found my hands gripping the pole while lodged in her guts, as the spear tip poked out behind her. She stared at me wide-eyed, disbelief etched on her face, glancing at Cybele with a look of betrayal before flopping limp to the floor. I noticed for a moment that my chrome fingernails had a red sheen, brighter than the blood coating them. The skin around them was a strange grey, but it was slowly returning to normal now as the adrenaline died down.

I ran to Nadira, finding her on the floor, and practically tripped over myself, falling at her feet. I brought my hand up to her neck, my face so close to hers that I could feel her weak breath on my lips. My tears carved their way down the same tracks on her face where her own tears had fallen. Amazingly, she managed to force out a whisper as she slowly took my hand, hers trembling with the effort as she moved my hand to her stomach. She whispered, closing her eyes and scrunching her face with the effort,

"Take care of her." before drawing one final, deep breath and exhaling. Her skin began to glow a soft, twilight purple, reminiscent of her eyes at dusk. She seemed to almost dissolve into a fine purple mist, like floating sand with a will of its own. The ethereal cloud swirled and coalesced around the hand she had placed on her stomach. A small creature drew its first breath, almost as if it were a continuation of Nadira's last. I sat there stunned as the woman I loved died, returning to the dust of the universe, and a small child emerged from her formless body. My daughter, now curled up in my arms. My tears fell on her as I sat there and wept.

A hand landed on my shoulder, and I spun around defensively, pulling my newborn daughter closer as I sat there staring at Cybele, not knowing what to think, or feel, or do. What now? Cybele must have sensed my thoughts, as she had sensed the baby. She started explaining, without me having to ask,

"Soulmate pregnancies can be a little bit different than normal. I know you haven't been in this world as long as would usually be required, but having your soulmate near, it creates a kind of optimal hormonal level, speeding up the process a little bit."

She sighed as I continued to stare at her, knowing that that surely wasn't enough,

"I noticed that you came here fused as well. Soulmate fusion is rather powerful, and for pregnancies it means that two people are working together to make a baby, also speeding up the process. That combined with the gift of Nadira's last bit of lifeforce to your daughter, would've been enough for her to be born in such a short amount of time, and still be a strong, healthy child."

Cybele's smile was warm, an unusual expression on her, but somehow, I believed it.

"What now?"

I whispered, not sure if I was talking to Cybele or myself. I stood up, staring into the tiny face of the creature that was half of me, and half Nadira. I couldn't help but smile when she opened her eyes then, the motion catching me off guard causing me to laugh.

"You have her eyes."

I said to her as she stared up at me with her bright purple eyes. I wasn't sure what was next, but I would protect her with my life, no matter what was to come. I looked up at Cybele, who seemed to be at war with herself. She saw my questioning look and the baby in my arms, and sighed, explaining,

"I think I can get you home, back to Earth, if that is what you want."

I stared at her, disbelieving, "Even if that's true, why would you help us?"

"Because it's my fault that she's dead. It's my fault that everyone is dead. I threatened you once, telling you how destructive you were, how you were a danger to the city." She shook her head, looking at the ground, unable to meet my gaze anymore, "But I was the one who brought destruction, used your technology to bring genocide about for a psychopath. I know I can never apologise for what I've done, but I can at least help you and your daughter get back home."

She looked back up at me, offering a weak smile. All I said in response was, "How?"

Cybele turned and walked over to the machine, moving past it to the control panels and screens. Upon closer inspection, they seemed to be showing readings of the ship's systems. My eyes went wide as I found the screen displaying the condition of the ship's engine, which seemed to be active. Very active. Cybele saw my reaction and smiled sadly.

"Yes, this ship is at the very centre of our planet. It used to travel through the universe with its multiversal anti-matter engine. That very engine is still active today and replenishes itself by taking anti-matter from different universes and bringing it here. Of course, the anti-matter isn't the only thing that it takes, often catching people and ships as well, dragging them here. That's how the city grows, from the new materials and people that the engine brings along with the anti-matter."

My jaw fell open.

"That's what brought me here!? A big engine? And from a different universe? That must be why the whole planet vibrates too."

"Correct, on both accounts."

"How do we stop it."

"Well, stopping it would mean depriving the city of new resources, but…"

"Seriously? You're back to rationalising preventable catastrophes all over the multiverse, just for new metals for the city?"

"I didn't say I wouldn't help you."

She sighed and reached around to something on the wall, bringing it into the light, revealing the petrified chryacal tail known to be the staff of the High Priestess."

"That's the…"

"The key, to the ships systems. With it, we can stop the engine from drawing in new anti-matter, letting you use its energy to send you back the way you came."

"But my ship…"

"I… have a ship that I've put together, hoping to escape this planet, maybe this universe, one day. But it's yours now. You can use it to get back home."

Yes, home. I took a deep breath. This was a lot. A chance to make it home. A villain turned friend, a daughter, and finally some explanations. I exhaled slowly, "Okay, what do we need to do?"

Chapter 14

With my newborn daughter safely strapped to my chest, and Cybele leading the way with the petrified key, we made our way through the corridors of the ancient ship, towards the section controlled by parliament. Cybele had explained that the Fovan Church and parliament had been formed as the two equal powers of the city, each having access to half the systems necessary to change the planet, to make changes to the ship that essentially controlled the weather of the planet, crash landings and all. The High Priestess had the key, and parliament had the physical control room, the only place from which to access the engine and make changes. I found myself impressed by Cybele's knowledge as we made our way through the corridors and through teleporters, wondering if that pursuit of knowledge was the whole reason she had made it this far and why she let Jezebel exploit her. Was it really just so that she could find out the secrets of the church, and of the planet?

After one more teleporter, Cybele stopped, and to my surprise I found that I recognised this corridor, the portraits of parliamentarians hung up all along the wall. A voice rang out and the noise of a door opening echoed through the hallway. I immediately jumped back into the teleporter, not going anywhere without selecting a destination. Cybele did the same, the look on her face telling me that she didn't know how we were going to get past the door that led into the main hall of parliament, where I had been publicly shunned. Even with my dishevelled parliamentary robes, I would be recognised immediately, having made all of parliament mad recently as well as being the only one wearing this particular shade of green.

We remained still for a moment, uncertain how to proceed. Relief washed over us as we listened to the voices receding down the corridor. Looking down into my daughter's eyes as she lay against my chest, an idea sparked. I wondered just how invisible we would be if I used alexandrite magic. I tried to tap into the magic, remembering how it felt when I was fused with Nadira. There was really no way to tell when I wasn't using my epicode, but then I heard Cybele whisper, looking in my direction, but not into my eyes,

"That's impressive, but how am I supposed to get by?"

"Are we both invisible, or just me?"

"I can't see either of you."

As Cybele spoke, the child laid her head back, twisting it to peer over the bindings at Cybele,

"Whoa, that's kind of creepy when they just appear like that."

She must have meant her eyes. Just like her mother, they cut through her own magic. I couldn't help but smile, the reminder of Nadira quickly turning to pain as the memory of her throat being crushed overtook that of her eyes shining in the night, just like her daughter's were doing now. I sniffled, and Cybele frowned, not being able to see anything but the two purple orbs still staring at her.

I looked down at my robes again. They were pretty wrecked, and quite bloodstained, but they would have to do. Perhaps they would think Cybele had just come from the trials, fighting off a new recruit. Nevertheless, it was the only idea I had.

"Here, take these. Hopefully it'll be enough, just to get us down the hallway without being stopped."

I handed Cybele the bloodied green robes, her taking them gingerly and putting them on, trying as best she could to hide the blood in the folds and cover her regular clothes underneath. When she was done, she nodded, and led the way down the corridor, walking with purpose as I silently followed her, making sure I kept my daughters curious purple orbs from being seen. No one exited parliament as we walked past the door. We turned the corner before stopping in front of a secure looking door on the left side of the corridor. The door had no handle and didn't automatically open. We stood there staring at the door, neither of us sure how to open it. The voices from before started getting louder, returning from their stroll down the hall. Cybele started trying to move pieces on the door, none of them moving, the panic starting to set in, not sure what we were supposed to do. The voices were clearer now and it sounded like they could emerge around the next corner any second. I looked back to the door, searching for answers, wondering if the tail-key would help, or maybe something only a parliamentarian would have. That's when it clicked. I stepped forward and pressed my purple and blue wrist tattoo, used for teleporting to parliament, against the thin rectangle beside the door. A soft beep and a click sounded as the door slid open. We stepped through just as I saw the toes of the voices appearing around the corner. The door closed behind us, and I let out a long, steadying breath. Cybele continued towards the large cylindrical machine in the centre of the room, her eyes darting around taking it all in, clearly loving this but trying not to show it. She shuffled the robes off and left them in a pile on the floor, pulling the tail-key that she had secured to her back out and orienting it with the wide slot on the centre console. The handle stuck out awkwardly. I wondered why it was designed like that, and why the key was so big, and a tail.

As Cybele inserted the key, a large holographic display came to life above the large cylinder. Cybele tapped away at the little screen on the console, the large 3D holographic display eventually bringing up a more detailed analysis of the engine systems I had seen in the other room. Cybele pointed at something on the display, an icon, kind of resembling the recycling icon you see on recycled paper and bottles and such. I reached out and poked the holographic icon in front of me, bringing up a log. A list of insanely long coordinates popped up on the screen. I scrolled down the log, hoping that Cybele knew what she was doing, and that this was in fact the list of places where the ships and anti-matter had come from, including mine. I kept scrolling, knowing that my ship crashed months ago and had quite a number of logs to get through, trying to figure out the coordinate system as I made my way there. About two months backwards through the log, I figured out one of the sets of numbers; the time. It was perhaps the shortest section of the coordinates, but it was enough to figure out which one was me. After discovering this, I zipped back through the log much faster, finding the day that I had crashed, two entries on the screen. I was the crash earlier in the day, the second being the creature I had watched Jezebel murder right in front of us. The day I met Nadira. I wiped my eyes on my sleeve, turning my attention to Cybele,

"It's this one."

She nodded, and I tried my best to keep focused on the projection, following Cybele as she searched the console for a way to send me home, and stop the ships from drawing in more anti-matter, more doomed pilots like me. A warning flashed on the screen, and I almost smiled, seeing the message floating in the air, a warning asking, 'Are you sure you wish to deactivate engine self-regeneration?' Yes, we were.

I nodded to Cybele, and a new notification popped up saying 'Deactivated' and that was that. It was over. There were no more pilots to save. No more Jezebel threatening the city. No more Nadira, and no reason left for me to stay. This city once felt like home, but every part of it that once felt like home was now gone, and it was time to go back to my real home. I wondered how long it would take anyone to realise what we'd done. Would parliament undo it? Would the church be against us too? It was too risky, the concerned look Cybele gave me telling me she knew what I was thinking,

"Wait…" she whispered, but seemingly didn't have a reason to stop me. I walked over to the tail-key, resting my hand on it first,

"How do I get home?"

Cybele sighed, "I've programmed it into the engine. It will lock onto the energy signature of my ship and send you back home once it starts up. We… don't need the key anymore."

"Perfect."

I responded, pulling out the petrified chryacal tail and admiring it for a moment before I brought it down on the steel floor, the impact jarring my shoulder but successfully breaking the key into four pieces. The shattered key was now on the ground, incapable of making any changes to the ship, to its engine, stopping anyone from turning the regeneration back on and dooming pilots and destroying space stations in other universes, in my universe. Maybe now we would finally be able to leave our solar system.

I squatted, looking at the pieces of the key on the ground. Cybele looked conflicted, but I felt nothing but relief. The smallest piece was the very tip of the key, the point. It was a fossilised blade similar to the one that had left the scar across my scalp that now parted my hair awkwardly. I ran my fingers through my hair, feeling the mark, before picking up the point, the broken piece no larger than my hand. I slipped it in my pocket. I didn't know if the key could be fixed, but it definitely couldn't be if one of the pieces was in an entirely different universe.

"Alright, to your ship then."

Cybele's eyes lingered on the broken key, snapping out of it as I spoke.

"Yeah, um…this way."

Making sure the hall was clear, we emerged from the engine room, Cybele not bothering to put my robes back on, having left them on the floor. They would know it was me once they figured it out, my bloodied robes sitting there next to the broken key. But what did it matter anyway. Soon enough they wouldn't be able to do anything about it, and the multiverse would be all the better for it.

No one came in or out of parliament as we walked past, coming across the set of teleporters we had used to get here. Cybele brought up the map in the centre on the middle teleporter, zooming in on the museum, and performing some sort of encrypted scan. After a few moments, a new teleporter option popped up in the museum. She clicked it, and we both walked through, finding ourselves on the other side of a large bookcase, heading down towards her workshop beneath the museum.

"Wow, so that thing is a teleporter. I had always wondered."

"Yeah, once I figured out how to use and hack into the world ship's systems, it made my life a whole lot easier, teleporting from here to there instead of having to walk every time."

We continued in silence, eventually turning down an unfamiliar corridor, my skin prickling with familiar terror. I squeezed the child in my arms a little tighter.

We emerged into a large room with a tall ceiling, Cybele flicking the lights on to reveal a much larger ship than I was expecting. I figured it would be about the same size as my original ship, and all the other small fighters and escape pods that crashed here, but this was nothing like those at all.

"It's been a project of mine for many years now, adding bits and pieces as I found new and interesting technologies. Maybe now that I'll have to start over, I'll build something better. With what I've learned from building that machine, and hacking into the world ship, I'm sure version two will be much more advanced."

Oh shit, the machine.

"The machine… it's still active."

"Don't worry, not for long. As soon as you're gone, I'll be right back there dismantling it."

I wanted to trust her, and some part of me did after she had helped me this much. She was giving me her one and only working ship after all, but I couldn't help but worry. Or at least I thought I would. It turned out I didn't have any energy left for worry. I was drained physically and emotionally. I didn't have the energy to focus on what would happen to this planet after I left. I just wanted to get home, and Cybele seemed to want to do good, to fix her mistakes, and all I could really do was trust that.

"Okay then, where's the entry?"

Before long I was strapped into the ship, the larger cockpit letting me sit there comfortably with my daughter in my arms. Cybele had given me a brief rundown of the controls, just enough to activate the engine, and hopefully fly and dock well enough to make it back to Cronus. What would they say when they saw me? A mess of scars, strange clothes, and a baby. I surely was a sight to behold. I chuckled as I thought about this, my thoughts quickly moving to my family, my parents, my sister. What would they think of me now? How strange it would be for them for me to disappear for five months and then show up again unannounced and covered in scars, and with a baby with magically bright eyes.

The engine of the ship started, the edges of the exterior seemingly starting to glow gold, tendrils of light growing longer, like they were a moss growing on the outside of the ship. In a instant, they stiffened and doubled back, my vision going black as the light exploded.

My sight returned slowly, my hearing returning first, hearing the child in my arms crying out, wailing now as we jumped through universes, the process quite violent, even when done on purpose. It took much longer than I was prepared for, but eventually I calmed her, taking her out of the bindings and holding her in my arms, closer to my face trying to comfort her. She was probably starving too. I really hoped Cronus would have something akin to breastmilk, but it was a military ship after all.

Once everything was quiet, I looked out of the cockpit window, a smile spreading across my face. The big yellow ball was on my right, and a little grey dot lay in the distance ahead of me. I smiled. I was home. Almost. Soon, I would be close enough to contact the ship and come back aboard, and then… Well, I guess I would start a new life, whatever that looked like. I held my daughter up in front of me, a giggle escaping her, making the emptiness of space suddenly seem so full.

"What do you think Alira, where should we go next?"